## PASSION'S FOLLY

"Why have you completely changed your looks lately, Ellie?"

Her eyes dropped away from his guiltily. "I haven't...no more than you have, T.J."

"Whatever happened to those nice, understated dresses you used to wear?"

"What happened to those wild suits *you* used to wear?"

He ignored her question. "And your hair. Now what kind of style do you call that?"

"Stylish. And while we're on the subject, you're wearing yours ten times shorter than you used to."

His hand went up to smooth his shorn locks uneasily. "Don't you like it?"

"I liked it better the other way."

T.J. frowned. "You're confusing me, Ellie. The men you date seem so conservative and low-key, yet when I try to be like one of them you get all bent out of shape. I just don't know what your idea of Mr. Right is anymore."

## A LOVE OF OUR OWN

"Can you step on it a little?" Lee demanded. "A man could starve to death waiting for you to fix something to eat."

Abby eyed him in disbelief. Who did he think he was? "Sorry. One burrito coming up!" she shouted, hurling the beany concoction at him.

He ducked seconds before the tortilla hit his plate. "Now, that's disgusting," he said curtly.

"Want some hot sauce?" she asked, ignoring him.

Once more he was forced to duck as the jar flew by his head, splattering into tiny pieces when it hit the wall. "Good Lord! Have you gone berserk? All I wanted was a simple burrito—"

"How about something to drink?" she interrupted. "Sure! Got to have something to wash that burrito down with! And ice! We can't forget the ice!"

Cubes came raining down on the table as he cowered beneath it.

As her anger finally subsided, Abby paused and shot him a challenging look. "Anything else I can get you?"

# LORI COPELAND

## A LOVE OF OUR OWN

#### ❦

## PASSION'S FOLLY

LOVE SPELL ✦ NEW YORK CITY

LOVE SPELL®

June 1995

Published by

Dorchester Publishing Co., Inc.
276 Fifth Avenue
New York, NY 10001

The name "Love Spell" and its logo are trademarks of Dorchester Publishing Co., Inc.

Printed in the United States of America.

# A Love Of Our Own

*For JoAnn Ross and Carol Wagner—*
*thanks for always being there*
*when I need you.*

# CHAPTER ONE

"I'm not sure what to tell you to do this time, Lee, but if you really want my opinion, I think I'd probably tell her to go suck an egg."

Abby King crossed her arms behind the bright mop of red hair that covered her head in tight, kinky ringlets and leaned back against the trunk of the towering maple tree she was sitting under.

The relationship between Celena Fenton, Lee MacNair and Abby King was beginning to get downright juvenile, and it worried her.

For a brief moment she gazed up into the faultless blue of a Vermont October sky, mulling over the latest problem she had just been presented with. It wasn't a new problem. On the contrary, it was beginning to be a very old one, and she thought the time had arrived for her to be completely honest.

The man reclining next to her on the grass shifted restlessly, his handsome face puckering in a worried frown. "Celena would break my neck if I told her that!"

"Oh, for heaven's sake! Why do you let her bully you that way?" Abby propped up on her elbow and faced the man irritably, wondering for the hundredth time why he was suddenly becoming so fascinating to her.

11

For the last few months Lee MacNair had been dating her best friend, Celena Fenton, and at best, their relationship could only be termed *stormy*.

Abby and Celena had met Lee and a friend of his, Matt Avery, at a fund-raising dance for the local hospital where Abby's father was executive director and chief of surgery. Since Lee was associate administrator, and Matt, assistant administrator, it seemed only natural for the four of them to strike up a conversation.

Actually, it had been Lee who had caught Abby's eye instead of Matt, but Celena had latched on to the tall, handsome man, and Abby had suddenly found herself paired off with Matt.

Lee had not seemed to object to Celena's advances. That had come as no surprise to Abby, since her friend had been turning men's heads with her dark, sultry looks and provocative nature for as long as Abby could remember.

Matt and Abby had begun dating occasionally, but Celena had seemed more dedicated about trying to form a lasting relationship with Lee. Abby wasn't sure how Lee felt about the matter, but she had stood back and watched in dismay as the couple fought their way through the better part of six months, each one running to Abby for advice when the going got tougher than usual.

For the life of her she couldn't understand why the mismatched couple even bothered to continue their relationship, but they plodded relentlessly on, making everyone's life miserable.

"I don't let her *bully* me," Lee protested sheepishly. "It's just that Celena's so hotheaded at times I figure I have to be a little more diplomatic with her than I would with anyone else . . ." His voice trailed off meekly.

12

Abby's temper simmered quietly. Diplomatic? Although Celena could be the most loyal and closest of friends at times, Abby knew she could also be very difficult to get along with.

"Lee"—Abby sat up and absently brushed at the stray pieces of grass on her jeans—"I don't know why you keep asking me for advice about Celena. I really think you two have to work your problems out alone."

It was hard enough to sit back and watch Lee date her best friend, but continually trying to patch up their sizzling spats was more than Abby could stand—especially now, when he seemed to grow more attractive to her every day.

With his natural good looks Abby could see why any woman would be taken with Lee, but their particular personalities were exact opposites, so she had no idea why she felt so drawn to him lately. It wasn't that she wanted Lee MacNair for her own—they really had nothing in common. Abby loved bright lights, crowded cities, staying up all night, and hot fudge sundaes with mounds of whipped cream, whereas Lee was strictly low-key, preferred wide open spaces, and was early to bed, early to rise, and she'd *never* seen him put a piece of junk food in his mouth.

No, she was not attracted to Lee in a romantic sort of way—she hoped—yet there was something about him that seemed to linger in her mind more than it should recently. She had spent about as much time with him as Celena had over the past few weeks, probably more if the truth were known.

But it certainly hadn't been romantic! All they had ever talked about was "how to bring Celena to heel." Somehow, the whole situation was beginning to grate on her nerves.

"Look, I know I shouldn't be bothering you with my troubles, but you're the only one who understands Celena," Lee apologized. His serious blue eyes peered solemnly in Abby's direction, instantly melting whatever rebuke she had been prepared to make. "If it's upsetting you, I'll just go and let you finish your lunch in peace."

Abby sighed. She had been looking forward to a quiet, uneventful lunch.

Hoping to enjoy one of the last beautiful fall days before Old Man Winter descended upon this small town in Vermont, she had left the shop where she was a children's photographer and taken her sandwich to eat at the park across the street. Lee had found her there, as he did so often lately, and poured out the details of the latest pitfall in the ongoing saga of Celena Fenton and Lee MacNair.

Reaching for his hand, Abby relented compassionately. "I'm sorry, Lee." She sighed. "Now, tell me again what the fight was about this time."

"She takes me for granted," he began as Abby silently mouthed the all-too-familiar words along with him. "She thinks I should lie down in the middle of the floor and let her wipe her feet on me!"

"Which you do," Abby noted under her breath in disgust.

"Excuse me?"

"Nothing. Go on," Abby said halfheartedly and opened her brown-bag lunch.

"Take last night, for instance," Lee continued hotly, "I distinctly told her I would be by her apartment at seven o'clock to take her out for dinner. Was she there? Nooo, she sure wasn't! She was off wandering around some damn department store until nine o'clock, looking for a 'purple scarf to wear with my new plum pants,'" he mimicked in a fairly accurate imitation of Celena's nasal twang. "Then she comes sashaying back to find me sitting on her doorstep in a blinding downpour, and for some strange reason, she can't understand *why* I'm upset!" He let out an impatient snort. "That woman is going to give me an ulcer!"

"I don't know why that upset you," Abby reasoned, silently harboring the fact that they had both already given her an ulcer. "That wasn't the first time Celena's been late for a date, was it?"

"Of course not."

"Nor will it be the last," she reproached mildly. "So why don't you just take into account how unreliable she is and not even bother to show up for your next date until two hours after you're supposed to be there?" That sounded very reasonable to Abby as she broke off a piece of her sandwich and handed it to him.

Lee frowned as if to say he didn't find the situation quite so simple. "I don't want to live the rest of my life waiting around for some woman to learn to be punctual," he grunted as he bit into her offering. He paused and withdrew the sandwich from his mouth to examine it suspiciously. "Is this a cheese sandwich? I hate cheese sandwiches."

"Then give it back to me." Abby reached over and snatched the food out of his hand. She was too hungry to share her lunch with an ungrateful person, especially if he didn't appreciate her efforts.

Lee glanced at her sharply. "Now don't go getting all bent out of shape. I only said I didn't *like* cheese sandwiches. I didn't say I wouldn't eat

15

one." He retrieved his lunch hastily. "I really don't know how Matt puts up with your temper tantrums."

"Matt doesn't have to put up with my temper tantrums," she returned in a calm voice, reaching into her sack to rummage around for something else to eat. "He doesn't irritate me like you do. Besides, Matt and I only date on occasion . . . not that it's any of your business," she reminded him.

She withdrew a crumpled sack of potato chips and proceeded to eat the smashed crumbs contentedly while he watched her warily.

"It certainly doesn't appear to me that you date Matt 'occasionally.'"

When he failed to get a quick denial out of her, he leaned back against the tree and munched on his sandwich thoughtfully. Lee wasn't at all sure where his attraction was nowadays. It seemed to him that he was enjoying coming to Abby for advice more than he was enjoying being with Celena.

And he didn't have the slightest idea why. Abby King was the exact opposite of what he thought he wanted in a woman. She was constantly helping other people. If she wasn't involved in someone else's life, she was regularly running around town with some sort of new petition to sign, their contents ranging anywhere from banning the nuclear bomb to making the mayor pay a parking fee just like any other citizen of the town had to when they went to city hall. He cringed as he thought of her newest brainstorm. She had been hounding the public for the last two weeks, gathering volunteers to wash the pigeon droppings off the town's only statue every Saturday morning.

"Well, I can't help how it appears to you." Abby

picked up the conversation again. "Matt and I are only friends . . . you know, we *like* each other."

"Are you trying to say Celena and I *don't* like each other?" he challenged with a cool lift of his dark brow.

"Did I imply that?" she parried. "Well, please forgive me. I'm well aware that your relationship with Celena is a match made in heaven."

"Very funny. Now, are you going to help me or not?" Lee ignored her taunting and concentrated on trying to get the cheese sandwich down.

"I told you"—she shrugged—"I'd tell Celena to —pardon the French—go suck an egg."

"And she would tell me exactly where I could put that egg," he returned flatly. Lee could just imagine Celena's fiery reaction if he came up with a line like that one!

Abby tilted her head and looked at him thoughtfully. For one brief moment she debated the advisability of giving him her true opinion. As a rule she usually got into trouble when she was totally honest with a person, but after all, he had asked her opinion and she was always ready to give it.

Taking a deep breath, she plunged in headfirst. "No, she wouldn't. That's your problem, Lee. She has you buffaloed. A woman likes a man to be firm with her—not chauvinistic, mind you, but firm. Now, if I were you, I'd tell Celena how it's going to be and be firm about it. Take it from me, Celena doesn't like her men to be wishy-washy. Tell her that from now on there won't be any more of this showing up late for dates or taking you for granted. Lay down the law and make no bones about it!" She emphasized her words with a shake of her finger.

Lee cocked his head in acute skepticism. "And you think she'd listen?"

"Absolutely. She'll eat it up."

Still not convinced, Lee said, "I don't know, Abby . . . she can get pretty mean."

"Look"—Abby sprang to her feet and dusted the stray potato chip crumbs off her jeans—"you asked my opinion, and I gave it. Take it or leave it. I have to get back to the shop. I have a one thirty appointment, and then I have a new petition to work on. If you don't want to take my advice, then you'll have to learn to live with Celena's idiosyncrasies."

"Well, maybe you're right," he conceded as he rose to his feet and started to shuffle along behind her. "Maybe I'm not being firm enough with her."

"I know I've been wrong before, but trust me, Lee. I think I'm right on target this time."

"Thanks, Abby. I know Celena is a little demanding at times and a little annoying."

"And a little spoiled and willful," Abby continued.

"Yes, she's all those things," he noted perversely. "But she's worth it, don't you think?" He smiled at her expectantly.

"Oh, definitely." Abby could have had a sarcastic note in her voice now, but she wouldn't allow herself. Celena had been a wonderful friend to her over the years, and she really did care for her. Only this time Abby's heart wasn't completely dedicated to her friend's welfare.

*Darn!* she thought. Why did she have to notice what an unusual shade of blue Lee's eyes were today or how his dark, fawn-colored hair curled in soft waves and unruly wisps along the base of his neck? She wondered fleetingly how many times

18

Celena had run her fingers through that thick mass of hair, then grew extremely annoyed at the small spark of jealousy she felt surge through her. She didn't care *who* ran their fingers through Lee MacNair's hair!

Lee trailed along beside her as she started across the street, his face a controlled mask of congeniality.

"Well, that's what I'll do, then." He took her arm and solicitously dragged her back from the path of a speeding car. "I'll go over and lay down the law to Celena tonight. I'm sure that's all it will take. I can't understand why I didn't think of it myself," he conceded. "You and Matt have a date tonight?"

"He said something about going out for a pizza," she replied as the car whizzed by and they proceeded across the street.

"Well, why don't we make it a foursome?" Lee suggested in a friendly manner. "I don't eat pizza, but I can always have the salad bar . . . of course I hate all those preservatives they put on the greens to keep them crisp, but I'll manage."

"I don't know, Lee," Abby hedged, not at all sure she wanted to spend the evening in that manner.

"I'll set it up with Matt when I get back to the hospital," Lee offered. "I'll even buy. I need to do something to pay you back for all the advice you've been giving me lately."

"But not one ounce of it has worked," she pointed out.

He frowned. That was certainly true. In fact, most of her advice had been ridiculous. "I know, but I think tonight will be the turning point in our relationship," he predicted optimistically. "If it isn't, it sure won't be your fault. What about tonight? Are we on for pizza?"

Abby could see he wasn't going to let the subject drop. "All right. If Matt doesn't object, I don't see why not."

"Great. Why don't Celena and I pick you and Matt up at your apartment around seven?"

"Seven would be fine," Abby accepted hesitantly, not at all sure she wanted to spend the evening with a loving Lee and Celena. She was used to doubling with them and listening to them disagree all evening, but she guessed she could survive one more night.

Lee's face softened as he watched the play of indecision cross her sparsely freckled face. She was almost cute in a winsome sort of way. Not at all glamorous like Celena . . . but cute. . . . Her nose was slightly tilted, and her tousled hair was a rich, unusual shade of strawberry blond that he found very attractive.

He discreetly studied her from the corner of his eye. *Yes, it isn't hard to understand why Matt Avery's crazy about her,* he thought. "Anything wrong?" he inquired politely as he noted her lingering hesitation in accepting the dinner invitation.

"No, I'm afraid my mind was wandering," she replied lamely.

"Well, then, wish me luck." He made a round circle with his thumb and forefinger. "Be firm."

"Right."

"Celena will love it!"

Abby swallowed nervously. "Right!" Then to herself, *I hope.*

"Then I'll see you around seven tonight . . . and thanks, Abby. I really appreciate your help."

20

"You're welcome." Her smile was weak at best.

*Thanks, Abby! I really appreciate your help!* she mouthed snidely to herself as they parted and she entered the small photography shop in a gust of anger. When was she going to learn to mind her own business and stop trying to help Celena hold on to her men?

All afternoon she stewed about the forthcoming evening. Maybe, with a little luck, Matt would refuse Lee's invitation, and she would be off the hook. It was a small ray of light in a dark tunnel, but she could always hope.

What she really needed to concentrate her efforts on was finding a man of her own to worry about.

Abby was twenty-eight, certainly an age to be thinking about getting married and settling down. Her parents were continually reminding her they weren't getting any younger and they would love to enjoy their grandchildren before they were too feeble to play with them. But the years seemed to just slip away, and as yet, she hadn't met anyone with whom she would want to spend the rest of her life and raise a family.

Take Matt Avery. He was nice, handsome enough for any woman's taste, and had a good job at the hospital. He was dependable, trustworthy, all the traits a woman could hope for in a husband.

So why couldn't she encourage him more when he hinted at a permanent relationship? *Because I don't care for him that way,* she told herself stubbornly. She liked him as a good friend . . . but nothing more. The only reason she continued to date him was the fact that she didn't want to hurt his feelings. That and the small hope that somewhere in the future she might fall in love with him.

Since there was no one else in town she was interested in, she planned to continue dating Matt occasionally and pray that in the not-too-distant future he would meet someone who could return his feelings. Maybe then he would give up on her.

The slow afternoon finally passed, and she had just started to close the shop after her boss left when the phone rang. She hurried back in and breathlessly snatched up the receiver. "Children's World."

"Abby? Hi. I was afraid I wouldn't catch you," Matt Avery's pleasant voice greeted her.

"Oh, hi, Matt. You almost missed me. I was about to lock up for the day."

"I thought I'd better check with you about the plans for tonight," he explained. "Lee said something about all four of us going out for pizza?"

"Yes, I saw Lee at lunch today, and he suggested we eat together tonight. I told him to check with you."

"I told him it was all right with me." Matt's voice grew suspicious. "How did you two happen to be together today?"

"He stopped by the park while I was eating my lunch," she explained. "He and Celena are having trouble again."

"I thought we had decided it's best for you to stay out of Lee and Celena's troubles," Matt pointed out quietly.

"We did . . . but it's rather hard to do when they both seem intent on running to me every time something goes wrong."

"Sometimes I wonder just exactly which woman Lee *is* interested in," Matt grumbled.

"What's that supposed to mean?" She laid her keys down on the counter. She knew she shouldn't be involved in Celena's problems, but she was, and she didn't need him to keep reminding her how foolish it was becoming.

"Well, it seems pretty strange to me that Lee is spending about as much time with you as he does with Celena."

"The only reason Lee gives me the time of day is because he's crazy about Celena but can't get along with her for five minutes," Abby informed Matt in a controlled voice. "He only comes to me for advice."

"I'm beginning to seriously doubt that," Matt snapped. "I'm beginning to think he only uses that as an excuse to be with you."

Abby shook her head in disbelief. "You'd better not let Celena hear you accuse me of trifling with *her* property," she warned crossly.

"Look, I'm sorry if I've irritated you, but you know how I feel about you. Abby—"

"Please, Matt. Can't this wait until another time?" Abby interrupted. She had a blinding headache and still had to make it through the pizza fiasco this evening. She was painfully aware of how Matt felt about her, and she desperately wished she could return those feelings, but she just couldn't.

"Yeah, sure. We'll talk about it later. What time should I come by for you this evening?" he relented in a grumpy voice.

"Around seven. Lee and Celena are coming by for us. And, Matt, please be nice tonight. After all, Lee is your best friend.

"That remains to be seen," Matt returned softly. "I'll see you around seven."

23

When Abby replaced the receiver, she could have cheerfully strangled all three of them, Matt, Lee, and Celena alike.

After tonight, she *was* going to mind her own business. Lee would just have to pick someone else's shoulder to cry on.

Flipping out the shop lights, she slammed the door loudly and left for the peace and sanctity of her own little apartment.

# CHAPTER TWO

The impatient peal of the doorbell should have given Abby a clue that the evening was not going to go any smoother than her day had, but it didn't.

It was nearly dark by the time she had made her way home from work. Her head had still been pounding as she searched through the cabinets and found to her dismay that she was out of aspirin. She knew she would never survive the evening without some, so she had rushed back out to the corner drugstore and bought a bottle.

After reaching home the second time, she had raced through her shower and was just slipping her dress on when the doorbell rang.

Rushing through the small apartment, still trying to fasten the back of her gold-studded earring, she wondered if her clocks were wrong or if Matt was running early tonight. A fast glance at the clock assured her it was still twenty minutes before the appointed hour.

When the door swung open to reveal a very distraught Lee, she was caught momentarily off guard.

"You've ruined me."

"What?"

"I said, you've *ruined* me! She never wants to see my despicable face at her doorstep again." He slumped against the doorjamb and literally glared at her.

"Who doesn't want to see your despicable face at their doorstep again?" Abby asked meekly, fearing she already knew the answer.

"Want to guess?" he offered tartly.

"Celena?" she surmised brightly, forcing the quiver out of her voice.

"Celena," he verified curtly.

Abby's face turned gloomy. "I gather something went wrong?"

"Wrong?" Lee pushed his way past her and entered the apartment. He began to pace the carpet irritably. "Wrong? I think you might say that. She pitched me out on my ear!"

Closing the door hurriedly, Abby watched as Lee prowled the room, trying to walk off some of his anger. "I went over there just like you said and laid down the law to her. I was firm. I was authoritative"—he whirled and pointed an accusing finger at her—*"just like you said!"*

Abby cringed.

"I told her there would be no more excuses for missed dates and late appointments and that I was not going to put up with her taking me for granted any longer."

"You did? And what did she say?" Abby quizzed expectantly.

"Her exact words?" he challenged.

"Yes."

"Take a hike, turkey!"

"She didn't!"

"Afraid so, sweetheart."

Abby fell into stride with him, their steps becoming synchronized as they covered the small area of the front room in long, thoughtful paces.

"Maybe she was just in a bad mood," Abby offered optimistically.

"If she wasn't when I got there, I can guarantee you she was by the time I left." Lee paused and turned to face her. "What am I going to do, Abby? I think we've gone too far this time."

"Oh, she'll get over it," Abby consoled, patting him absently on the shoulder. "I'm sure it will all blow over by morning." *Darn that temperamental Celena! Why couldn't she have responded like she was supposed to?*

"You think I'm going to believe that? You were the one who told me Celena would 'love' a little authority and a man who would be 'firm' with her."

"Well, I thought she would," Abby defended herself. "Besides, I told you I thought you and Celena should work out your own problems and leave me out of it. From now on, I'm washing my hands of the whole mess!"

"Oh, come on, Abby. You can't leave me now," Lee demanded impatiently. "You got me into this. Now you're going to have to help me get out."

*Oh, brother! I've really done it this time,* she thought. She knew she should have kept out of this. Now Lee was mad at her, Celena was mad at him, and Matt would be furious when he found out about this newest outbreak of war, because he had warned her weeks ago to stop giving Lee advice about Celena.

Abby resumed her pacing. "I'm going to have to think about this."

"Well, think quick because, to tell you the truth, I've about had it with this whole situation."

"Don't say that," Abby protested. She felt bad

enough without his threatening to walk out at this stage.

She willed her eyes to avoid looking at him as she busied herself rearranging a stack of magazines lying on the coffee table.

As usual he looked great this evening. The wheat-colored slacks and bright-red polo shirt he was wearing accented his athletic build and sent her pulse racing. The faint, clean smell of him drifted pleasantly through the room, and Abby quickly decided Celena was a fool.

"Don't worry. I'll come up with something to get you back together," she promised sincerely.

He smiled evasively and breathed a silent sigh of relief. Actually, he didn't care if she did or didn't, as long as he still had an excuse to see Abby. If it wasn't for Matt . . .

The sound of the doorbell interrupted their conversation, and Abby hurried over to open the door.

Matt Avery's impressive physique filled the doorway this time, his boyish face breaking into a wide smile when he saw Abby standing before him.

"Hello, carrot top," he greeted her affectionately.

"Hi, Matt." Abby grinned at the use of his pet name for her. "Come on in."

Matt entered the apartment and dropped a friendly kiss on her mouth. When he glanced up, his face registered surprise at seeing Lee staring moodily out the large picture window that was filled with a multitude of lush hanging plants.

"Hey, Lee. How did you and Celena beat me here? I thought I was a few minutes early." His voice was cool but polite.

Abby closed the door and shot Matt a warning look. "Uh, Celena's been unavoidably detained, Matt."

Matt glanced at her and frowned. "Oh. Well—" he took a deep breath and grinned weakly—"I don't know about anyone else, but I'm starving."

"Me, too," Abby seconded quickly, casting a worried glance in Lee's direction.

"I gather they're at it again," Matt speculated quietly.

"Afraid so," Abby whispered back.

"Was that what he was talking to you about at lunch?"

"No, that was round nine hundred and thirty-five. This is round nine hundred and thirty-six," she confessed, hoping he wouldn't press her for the details.

"You two go on to dinner without me," Lee said from across the room. "I've suddenly lost my appetite."

Matt and Abby exchanged knowing glances before Abby walked over and took Lee's arm. "Come with us, Lee. We'll stop by Celena's house on the way to the restaurant, and I'll go in and talk to her."

"It wouldn't do any good," he insisted. "She told me in no uncertain terms that she didn't want to see me again."

"But she'll see me," Abby reasoned. "And when I explain what happened, she'll understand and everything will be fine again." Abby was urging him toward the doorway as she talked. "You'll see. She's probably sitting home, waiting for you to call her this very minute."

"I don't know, Abby—"

"If he doesn't want to go, Abby—" Matt interrupted.

"He wants to go, Matt!" She glared at him soundly.

Grabbing her purse, she ushered Matt and Lee out into the hallway. "Lee would just go home and be miserable if we left him. I know Celena will listen to me." She turned to face Lee and whispered, "I'll simply tell her it was my ridiculous idea for you to be firm with her, and we'll all have a big laugh about it while we're eating."

"Abby!" Matt paused and glowered at her sternly. "Have you been offering advice again?"

Abby blushed and hustled the two men down the hallway before Matt could find out just how badly her advice had backfired . . . again.

Thirty minutes later the three of them were driving down the highway in Matt's Honda Accord. Lee's face was as grim as it had been earlier as Abby tried to make light of the fact that Celena had been nowhere to be found when they had stopped by her apartment.

"She's probably at the market," she improvised in an upbeat tone, determined to bolster his sagging spirits.

"Celena never goes to the market, and you know it." Lee shot down that theory with alarming swiftness. "She's probably out with Gerald Metcalf."

"Gerald Metcalf? You're kidding! She wouldn't dream of going out with that cad." Abby laughed brightly. "My gosh, Lee. Give Celena credit for at least having some common sense. All you've had is a simple little spat that will be forgotten by tomorrow morning."

"Gerald Metcalf," Lee reiterated glumly. "That's who she's with. Mark my words."

Moments later they pulled into the parking lot of the local pizza parlor, and Abby's face nearly dropped to her lap. Celena was just getting out of a car with none other than Gerald Metcalf, town womanizer.

"Sitting home waiting for me to call, huh?"

Abby noted resentfully that Lee just had to get that in before they all tumbled out of the car and followed Celena and Gerald into the restaurant.

The pizza parlor was alive with evening diners as Lee, Matt, and Abby stood waiting for a table, trying their best to ignore the couple standing just to their left who were also waiting.

Finally, Abby couldn't stand it any longer, and she strolled casually over to Celena amid warning glares from Matt and Lee.

"Hi, Celena."

"Hi, Abby." Celena moved closer to Gerald and defiantly slipped her arm through his. "I believe you've met Gerald Metcalf?"

"I believe I have. Good evening, Gerald." Abby smiled politely. *What woman hadn't met him,* she was tempted to add but didn't. "I was wondering if I could speak to you for a moment, Celena," Abby inquired, trying to keep her voice pleasant when all she really wanted to do was strangle her friend.

"Now? Gerald and I were about to eat," Celena said, just as politely, but Abby knew by the tone of her voice that she wasn't interested in anything Abby had to say.

"Oh, I imagine we'll have a few minutes before any tables are available by the looks of the crowd," Abby assured her, reaching for her hand and ripping her away from Gerald's protective embrace. "You will excuse us, Gerald?"

"Yes, of course." Gerald flashed Abby one of his million-dollar smiles. "I'll be eagerly awaiting your return."

Abby's immediate reaction to his blatant flirting was one of irritation, but she kept the polite smile pasted on her face as she returned in a sweet voice, "We'll hurry."

Dragging her charge through the crowd like a recalcitrant child, Abby proceeded across the room, trying to ignore Lee's and Matt's frantic attempts to get her attention.

"Stop dragging me!" Celena hissed as they made their way through the crowd and headed toward the ladies' room.

"Then stand up and walk," Abby shot back. "We're making a scene!"

And indeed they were. Many patrons had paused with pizza raised halfway to their mouths and watched the two women argue their way across the room and slam loudly into the room marked "Hens."

When they were finally alone, Abby turned on her friend and demanded hotly, "Are you nuts?"

Celena marched over to the mirror and proceeded to rearrange her hair. "I don't know what you're talking about."

"I'm talking about what you're doing to that heck of a nice guy sitting out there mooning over you," Abby replied in a lower tone.

"I don't see where that's any of your business," Celena returned calmly. "Besides, this is *all* Lee's fault."

"You and Lee have made it my business," Abby reminded her. "For the last few weeks I've spent most of my time trying to appease first one, then the other of you, and I'm getting tired of it."

Softening, Celena turned and grasped her friend's hand. "Oh, Abby, I know you think this is silly, but I'm just trying to teach Lee a lesson."

"By going out with Gerald Metcalf?" Abby asked incredulously. "You would risk your relationship with Lee by flaunting that—that town gigolo in his face?"

"You don't understand," Celena protested. "Lee came by this evening—"

"I do understand," Abby cut in. "And I want you to know I'm responsible for Lee's actions this evening."

Celena looked stunned. "You are?"

Abby flushed. "Yes. I'm afraid I gave him some bad advice on how to handle you, and he took it."

"Well, I like that." Celena put her hands on her hips and glared at Abby. "You're some friend!"

"I was only trying to help, Celena. Lee's such a nice guy. How can you treat him the way you do? At times I think you don't care for him at all."

Celena turned back to the mirror and began to apply another coat of gloss to her already shiny lips. "Of course I care for him. He's just not going to push me around."

"I can't imagine Lee MacNair pushing anyone around," Abby returned with a defeated sigh.

It was obvious Celena had her own method of dealing with Lee, and nothing Abby said was going to change that.

Glancing up in the mirror, Celena's eyes narrowed. "Do I detect a note of personal interest in your voice?"

"For Lee?" Abby felt a blush flooding her cheeks.

33

"Yes, for Lee. Like you say, he's a very appealing man."

"I'm not interested in Lee," Abby retorted, feeling just a little guilty for the way her eyes had been literally riveted all evening to the snug way Lee's trousers hugged his masculine frame so enticingly, and she couldn't tell anyone what Matt was wearing if her life depended on it. "Besides, even if I were, he only has eyes for you, and I think it's a crying shame you treat him like you do."

"You let me worry about how I treat Lee," Celena tossed blithely over her shoulder as she freshened her blush and sprayed perfume lavishly around her. "But I suppose he is a little upset with me for showing up here with Gerald this evening."

"That was bad timing on your part."

"Bad timing? Don't be silly. Lee said we were supposed to come here tonight for pizza with you and Matt when he called earlier today, so I figured he would still come with you and Matt to eat. I consider it perfect timing." She smiled with smug satisfaction.

"That's rotten, Celena."

"I know, but Lee loves it." She tossed her makeup back in her purse and turned to face Abby. "Now, let's go back, and we'll all get a table together."

"You're not serious?"

"Of course, I'm serious. You don't think I'm going to spend the whole evening with 'hands Metcalf' without deriving *some* benefit from it, do you? I'll have Lee begging me for a reconciliation before the evening's over."

For the first time since Abby had known her, she was almost ashamed to claim Celena as a friend.

She was truly stunned when they rejoined the men and Celena suggested a table for five.

Lee looked a bit surprised at the request but quietly followed the group to a corner booth. Celena sat next to Gerald, while Matt slid in on the other side, followed by Abby, then Lee.

Conversation was stilted at best, and Abby wished a million times she had put her foot down and insisted on separate tables. The shadows of disgust that crossed Lee's face on numerous occasions throughout the evening as Celena and Gerald made light, flirtatious conversation was her punishment for not doing so.

By the end of the evening Abby felt drained and could discern no outward sign on Lee's part that Celena had him "begging for a reconciliation." On the contrary he now seemed very bored by the whole situation and directed most of his conversation toward Matt.

Abby didn't know why she felt so guilty about Lee and Celena's recent quarrel, but she did. So much so that she found herself frantically thinking of ways to make amends.

The conversation drifted around to the fact that Halloween would be upon them by the weekend, and a brilliant thought popped unexpectedly into Abby's head. *That's it!* she thought. *It's a perfect time to have a small party and reconcile the warring couple.* After all, she was responsible for the latest skirmish, and she couldn't live with her conscience until she had cleansed herself of that black stigma. Why Lee would even want Celena was beyond her, but if he did, he'd get her back or Abby would die trying!

"Anyone have plans for Saturday night?" Abby

asked impetuously as the conversation at the table trickled off.

"No," Gerald said quickly. "What's going on?"

Abby grimaced. *Oh, shoot! I forgot about him.* "I was thinking about having a small party . . . maybe a costume party. Don't you think that sounds like fun?"

Everyone at the table groaned at the prospect of having a costume party.

Gerald finally took the coward's way out. "Oh, hold it a minute. I do have plans for Saturday evening, now that I think about it." He grinned. "Sorry."

"Oh, what a shame. Maybe next time." She turned to Matt. "What about you?"

"Do we have to dress up?"

"Sure, that's the fun of it."

"Really, Abby, why not make it just an informal party?" Celena suggested.

Abby glared at her. She was planning this party for her benefit, and there she sat trying to discourage her plans. "It would be fun, Celena," she gritted under her breath. "Everyone but Gerald will be able to come." She motioned with her eyes in Lee's direction.

"Oh. Well, in that case I suppose a costume party would be fun." Celena had noticed that Lee was not exactly frothing at the mouth over her tonight, so she decided to let Abby handle it in her own way.

"Lee"—Abby turned to him—"you will be able to come, won't you?" she asked gently.

"Saturday night? I'm not sure. I'll have to let you know later."

If Lee didn't come, her plan would be ruined. With that thought in mind Abby kept after Lee the rest of the evening, mentioning the party numerous times until everyone at the table was sick of the subject.

When Matt dropped Lee and Abby by her apartment later that evening, Abby followed Lee to his car, still hoping for a commitment.

"You can come, can't you?" she asked for the tenth time as she hugged her sweater closer and shivered in the brisk night air.

"I don't know, Abby. I hate costume parties," Lee replied as he unlocked his Corvette and got in. "Maybe next time."

"No, it wouldn't be the same if you weren't there, Lee," she protested. "Celena will be there," she suggested in an afterthought.

"So?" he asked coolly.

"So, it would be a perfect time for you two to make up."

"I'm not at all sure I want to make up with Celena," he said absently as he started the car and pulled on the lights.

It nearly broke Abby's soft heart to think she had caused this pain for him. Her eyes tried to avoid his wheat slacks in the dim interior of the car but failed.

"I wish you'd come . . . for me." She was amazed to hear herself admit that, and she quickly caught her rash words as he glanced up at her in surprise. "I mean, I wish you would give me a chance to make this up to you," she corrected. "I feel responsible for tonight."

"You shouldn't. I think it was probably inevitable that we'd break up."

But Abby knew he wasn't convinced that was true. "Then at least come to the party for Matt's and my sake. I'll keep it small."

"But a costume party?" He groaned.

Abby nodded with a grin. "Come on, Lee, be a sport! It'll be fun. You'll see."

"I suppose I could come . . . but only because you're asking. There's nothing I hate worse than going to a costume party," he relented with a painful grimace.

She breathed a huge sigh of relief. "Oh, thanks, Lee. I really appreciate it. Come dressed in something real flashy," she encouraged brightly. "I want the party to be a big success."

"Flashy? Well, I'll see what I can dig up," he replied with a twinkle in his eye.

He looked and sounded so much like a little boy being forced to do something he hated that Abby laughed and leaned over, kissing him affectionately on the cheek. They both drew back in surprise and gazed at each other for a moment.

"What was that for?" he asked softly.

Abby felt herself coloring clear to her neckline, and she could have kicked herself for being so impulsive. Why in the world had she done that?

"I—I'm not sure. Probably because you look like you need a friend tonight," she improvised quickly.

Slowly he drew her head back down to his, and their lips met hesitantly. His kiss was soft and exploring and made her knees tremble.

It was she who drew back this time and gazed into the depths of his blue eyes.

"And what was that for?" she parried in a slightly breathless voice.

For a moment he looked as stunned as she felt. "I don't know," he admitted huskily. "It was just something I've been wanting to do for a long time."

38

Their lips touched briefly once more before they finally forced themselves to pull back.

"I'll see you Saturday night."

"Yes, I suppose you will if I can't think of any way to get out of it." Lee grinned and revved the car engine a couple of times. "Take care of yourself, turnip brain."

"Turnip brain?"

Lee gave her a rakish grin. "Isn't that what Matt called you when he walked into the apartment and planted that 'friendly' kiss on you tonight?"

Her heart fairly sang as she realized he *had* noticed the kiss. "Carrot top, Lee," she corrected curtly. Turnip brain? Good grief!

"Oh. Well, I was close." He slipped the car into gear and edged slowly out of the drive as she followed along beside him. "See you Saturday night."

To Abby it sounded as if his words were meant just for her, and she hugged them close to her heart as she stood in the cool night air and watched the red taillights of his car disappear down the street.

Turnip brain or carrot top, it didn't matter what he called her. What mattered was how pleased she was beginning to be that he noticed her at all.

Turning toward the front door of her apartment, she quickly tried to put Lee MacNair in his proper place. *Your job, King, is to put Humpty Dumpty together again, and nothing more,* she told herself. Still, the lingering effects of his kisses invaded her dreams that night.

# CHAPTER THREE

Planning a spur-of-the-moment Halloween party proved to be a lot harder than Abby had first anticipated.

After compiling a small guest list of those she wanted to attend, she tried to wedge in numerous phone calls to all of the intended guests Friday morning, along with her scheduled appointments.

By the end of the day she was wishing she had never heard of Halloween.

To begin with, most of the guests she invited were close friends and had no difficulty whatsoever in telling her they hated costume parties. No amount of pleading would bring them around, so by the end of the day Abby was bending to their will and telling them they didn't have to dress up if they didn't want to.

A fast check of the local costume shop informed her that the selection would be very limited at this late date, but they did have one pirate, one Richard Nixon, and one fairy princess costume available if she could be over there by the time they closed at five o'clock.

A quick glance at her watch told her she had exactly seven minutes to close the shop, drive fifteen miles, and choose between one of the three costumes. Thanking the clerk politely, she sighed and reconciled herself to the fact that she could be among the guests who would not be in costume at her own costume party.

Saturday proved to be every bit as harrowing as Friday had been.

Celena had called bright and early to bemoan the fact that she couldn't find a thing to wear that would do her justice. Abby wasn't quite sure what that meant, but she didn't have time to pursue the subject, so she merely assured her that a few of the guests had chosen not to come in costume, including herself, and if it made Celena happier, she could attend in ordinary street clothes.

She had barely hung up the phone when it rang again. This time it was Matt, who was having a terrible time trying to figure out what he would wear, so Abby patiently explained her problem to him but assured him if he couldn't find anything to wear, then he was to feel free to attend the party anyway.

"But at least try to come up with something, Matt," she urged. "I don't want the party to be a total flop."

"I'll try," he promised, but she noted that he didn't sound very enthusiastic. "I was a bit surprised when you mentioned having a party."

"I was a bit surprised myself," she admitted. "But I'm hoping to bring Celena and Lee back together . . . you know, I feel rather responsible for this new round of misunderstanding."

"If you would have listened to me and stayed out of it—"

"I know, I know. You don't have to remind me," she moaned. "After I get them back together this time, I swear I'll never interfere again."

"I'm not at all sure you're doing Lee a favor,"

41

Matt mused. "Somehow I can't ever picture Lee and Celena as anything permanent."

"Lee can."

"I don't understand why. They've fought the whole time they've gone together."

"Who knows why. All I want to do is get them back together and free myself of guilt, and then they can do anything they want." Abby dismissed the subject irritably. If Lee wanted to spend his life running after Celena, there was nothing she could do to stop it.

*And there really isn't,* she told herself over and over again as she cleaned the apartment and ran to the market for supplies for the party.

Lee was an intelligent thirty-one-year-old man who was certainly old enough to know what he was doing, even if he was slightly misguided. She could understand his fascination with Celena; she was a beautiful woman. Men were always fascinated with her. *And Celena's always been fascinated with men,* Abby thought dryly.

Abby, on the other hand, had never knocked men dead in the aisles, although at twenty-eight she had already received two marriage proposals. Granted, they had been from men she would never dream of marrying, but she contented herself with the fact that they had asked. In fact, she had never met a man who really caught her eye seriously . . . well, maybe one. But Lee MacNair didn't know she existed other than as someone who's shoulder he could cry on when things weren't going smoothly between him and Celena.

Late Saturday afternoon Abby was in the kitchen making sandwiches for the party when the thought occurred to her that she should ask her father to stop by the party tonight. Winston

42

King had been like a fish out of water the last week with Abby's mother in Europe on an art-buying expedition. Mara King was to be gone several more weeks, and Abby knew her father was lonesome.

Laying down her knife, Abby strolled over to the phone and quickly punched out her parent's number. After several rings a sleepy-sounding Winston picked up the phone.

"Dr. King."

"Dad? I was about to hang up," Abby scolded. "Were you outside?"

"Nope"—Abby heard her father give a big yawn —"I was sneaking a nap in."

Abby smiled. "With mom not there to keep you busy, you're getting lazy," she teased.

"Possibly," he conceded. "That coupled with the fact I had an emergency over at the hospital last night and didn't come home until six this morning."

Winston King was a busy heart surgeon in addition to being executive director of Bayfield General Hospital, and Abby knew the hospital occupied most of his time.

"Is your patient okay?"

"Don't know yet. It's still touch and go."

Abby noticed the weariness seeping through his voice now. Winston would soon be sixty-five, and both Mara and Abby had urged him to slow down, but to no avail. He still went about life with the attitude of a man half his age, and Abby seriously doubted he would ever change.

"Listen, I'm glad you called. I was going to call you today," he said.

"You were? Why?"

"Because I haven't seen you in the halls much

this week, and I wondered what you'd been up to." Abby did volunteer work at the hospital, and Winston was used to seeing her rushing down the corridors several times a week with either flowers or mail in her hand.

"Oh, I've been busy," she excused absently. "Dad, are you going to be tied up at the hospital tonight?"

"I'm going back over for a while, but if my patient's stable, I won't stay. Why?"

"Well, I'm having a little get-together this evening, and I thought you might like to drop by."

"Any wild women coming?" He quipped.

Abby had to laugh. Winston King was so crazy about his wife it was ludicrous to think of him ever looking at another woman. If there was ever anything Abby desired in life, it was to find a man she could love as madly and to settle into a marriage as filled with love and affection as the one Winston and Mara King shared.

"Maybe a few. Celena will be here."

"Well, you can't get much wilder than that." Winston laughed.

"And a few people from the hospital are coming. Lee and Matt and a couple of others."

"You still seeing Matt?"

"Some." Abby toyed with the small floral arrangement sitting next to the phone and braced herself for what she knew would follow.

"Nothing serious yet?"

"No, Dad. Nothing serious."

"Abby, honey, you need to find a good man and settle down," he chided. "You're not getting any younger."

"Thanks. I don't know what I'd do without your constant reminders," she said dryly.

He chuckled. "Your mother thinks you're not even trying real hard."

"I'm not taking want ads out in the paper, if that's what you mean, but I'm looking . . . sort of."

"You ever date Lee?"

Abby straightened abruptly and stiffened. "Lee MacNair?"

"Do you know any other Lee?"

"No, but why in the world would you think I'd date Lee MacNair? He goes with Celena."

"My grapevine tells me they see him with you more than her!"

"Oh, that. I'm his sounding board when he and Celena fight."

"Good man, Lee. I like his work at the hospital, and he has a bright future ahead of him," her father revealed, none too discreetly.

"That's nice," Abby returned patiently. "I'm sure Celena will be delighted to hear that. Why don't you tell her tonight when you come to my party?"

"I wasn't aware I had agreed to come, but I suppose I could stop by for a few minutes," he conceded with another chuckle.

"Oh, by the way, it's costume. I don't suppose you'd want to—"

"You supposed right," Winston broke in.

"Oh, well, it doesn't matter. I have a feeling a lot of the guests aren't going to be in costume tonight," Abby fretted. "But come anyway."

"What time does this gala affair take place? I probably won't be through over at the hospital until seven or so."

"Seven will be fine, Dad."

A short time after seven that evening, Abby's small apartment began to fill up. Each time she opened the door, she was dismayed to find no one had come in costume, but she managed to paste a welcoming smile on her face and cover her disappointment.

*After all,* she reasoned, *Celena and Lee can reconcile their differences as easily in or out of costume, so it doesn't really matter.*

The apartment was decorated with streamers of black and orange crepe paper, and assorted witches, spiders, and black cats hung suspended from the ceiling. A card table was set up in the corner, with a huge punch bowl, donuts, cider, sandwiches, and chips and dip threatening to overflow the small space.

The continual peal of the doorbell kept Abby busy for the next half hour, and the party began to take on a festive air.

Winston arrived and gave his daughter a peck on the cheek, then went directly to the food.

Abby called out to remind him of his diet, but he only grinned and waved away her warning with a handful of donuts.

Matt and Celena showed up at the same time, and Abby let them in with a frown when she saw they were not in costume either. "You couldn't find any costume to wear?"

Matt grinned sheepishly. "You said we didn't have to," he reminded her, "and you don't have one on."

"I know," she said, as she took their coats, "but so far not one person has come in costume."

"Well, I simply couldn't find anything that looked good on me," Celena complained. "Besides, I wanted to look nice for Lee tonight."

46

Matt wandered away to join the party as Celena followed Abby into the kitchen.

"Is Lee here yet?" Celena asked expectantly.

"No, not yet."

"He is coming, isn't he?"

"He said he was. I haven't talked to him since we all had pizza together."

Celena sighed and sat down on a bar stool to watch Abby spoon out coffee into the basket of the percolator. "I haven't either. He hasn't called."

"Did you really expect him to?" Abby asked patiently.

"He always has before," Celena complained. "And he might have. I really haven't been home much."

"Oh?"

"Yes, Gerald has dropped by a couple of times," she confided, carefully studying one of her nails.

Abby irritably replaced the lid on the coffeepot and plugged it into the wall socket. "Look, Celena, are you or are you not interested in Lee?"

Celena's dark brows shot up defensively. "Well, well. Aren't we snappish tonight!"

"Yes, we are! This whole party is being given to allow you and Lee to settle your differences, and you sit there and calmly tell me you've been seeing Gerald Metcalf. That *does* make me snappish!"

"Calm down, Abby," Celena soothed. "I'm only seeing Gerald to make Lee jealous. Of course I want to make up with Lee, but you just don't understand that a woman has to make herself a mystery for another man, or he won't be interested in her. That's all I'm doing." She smiled like the Cheshire cat. "I'm only making myself a mystery for Lee."

"I think it's low-down and completely under-

47

handed, and for the life of me, I can't understand your reasoning!" Abby said disgustedly.

Celena stood up and walked over to give Abby an affectionate squeeze. "That's because you're Abby and I'm Celena," she returned sweetly. "You've been my best friend since the sixth grade, and I've always known I can count on you when I'm in a tight spot. You just let me worry about my men. I know how to handle Lee, and it will be worth everything we've gone through when you see me walking down the aisle to become Mrs. Lee MacNair."

Abby's stomach rolled over. "You're really that serious about him?" she asked miserably.

"Well, naturally. He's not only handsome and eligible, he's also financially secure." She grinned again. "What more could a woman ask for?"

"Love?"

"Oh, he loves me." She dismissed that suggestion away with an airy toss of her hand. "And don't forget, I will definitely want you to be my maid of honor, and you'll wear that darling creation we saw last week. You know, the lavender-colored—"

"There's the doorbell again," Abby interrupted, thankful she could walk out on this conversation before she said something she would regret later.

The party was beginning to grow louder as Abby walked back through the living room and called out to a couple of friends standing next to the punch bowl.

Winston had decided his daughter had not heard the doorbell this time, so he rose from the sofa, where he had been having a discussion with Matt, and went to open the door.

Moments later Abby heard a loud gasp come

from her father as she glanced hurriedly over to the doorway.

Standing in the hall was Lee, dressed in socks, shoes, a flesh-colored bathing suit, a disreputable-looking trench coat, and a battered hat. When the door had opened, Lee had jerked the front of the coat wide open and slapped a lewd grin on his face as he came face-to-face with his superior.

Lee MacNair had dutifully come in costume as a flasher.

The smile slowly dripped off his face, and his hands sagged as he realized who had opened the door.

Abby nearly felt sick for a moment as it dawned on her that Lee would be the only person at the party in costume. Her eyes were drawn like a magnet to the width of his bare shoulders. His legs were sturdy and muscular, with the same dark covering of hair on them that spread in a thick mat across his broad chest. It took all her willpower to force her gaze back up his tall, masculine frame and light on his astounded face.

"Lee," she called weakly.

"Lee?" Winston's voice boomed out in surprise. "My Lord, boy, I didn't recognize you!"

*What an understatement!* Abby thought frantically. Who would have recognized nice, refined Lee MacNair standing in the doorway, flashing?

Rushing over to rescue him before he bolted and ran, Abby took his arm and ushered him into the apartment. He glanced around blankly at all the well-dressed people standing gaping at him, and she heard him mutter a low "Oh, hell."

"Look everyone, it's Lee!" Abby made her voice sound deliberately bright and gay as she dragged him farther into the room, then could have bitten

49

her tongue off as she realized what she was doing. The entire crowd fell silent now as they all turned to stare at Lee. He was nervously clutching the front of his coat together and trying to smile at the other guests as Abby kept up a flow of incessant chatter.

"Oh, I'm so glad to see you came in costume!" She applauded for the benefit of the gawking guests. "Isn't that nice? Lee came in costume!" she praised lavishly.

A few snickers broke out before Abby shot them a murderous glare, and they quickly fell silent.

"I hope this isn't your idea of a joke," Lee gritted through clenched teeth as she led him over to the sofa. "If it is, I'm not laughing."

"Uh—I probably should have called you," she apologized under her breath. "You see, there were so many objections to coming in costume that I finally just gave up and told everyone they could come any way they wanted to. Oh, Lee, I'm sorry." She bit her lower lip, feeling very guilty.

"You mean I'm the only person here dressed like this?" he asked weakly, his eyes traveling around the room in desperation.

Abby surveyed his clutched trench coat and bare, hairy legs dismally, then nodded her head hesitantly. "Now, don't get upset," she pleaded.

"Oh, hell!" he said again, with much more emphasis this time.

"I *said* I was sorry. I've been so busy trying to get this party together that I didn't even think of calling to warn you that there might be some people who wouldn't come in costume. I'm not Wonder Woman, you know!"

"If you'll remember, Ms. King, I didn't want to come in costume either, but *you* said, 'Oh, come on, Lee. Be a sport!' " His voice had risen to a high pitch now, and his blue eyes shot pure bolts of fire in her direction. "Now I'm standing in a room full of people who think I just got off the bus from the crazy farm—not to mention the sickening fact that I just flashed my boss—and you tell me not to get upset?"

"Don't yell at me!" Abby hissed in a loud whisper. "All this is your fault to begin with!"

"My fault?"

"Yes, your fault! If you and Celena could get along for five minutes, I wouldn't have to be constantly trying to find ways to bring you back together."

"I don't know why I keep listening to you," he moaned. "Between you and Celena, I'm going nuts."

"Me? After all I've tried to do for you?" She could understand how Celena would be driving him nuts, but certainly not her!

"Why don't you just leave my love life to me from now on?" he shot back irritably. "Maybe I don't want you trying to help me anymore."

Their heated conversation was interrupted when Celena shot out of the kitchen and crossed the room to loop her arm through his.

"Lee, darling!" She paused, her eyes distraughtly taking in his costume. "Oh . . . how quaint."

"Hello, Celena," he mumbled self-consciously.

"Why don't we all sit down?" Abby invited cordially, finally remembering this was supposed to be a party and she was the hostess. "Here, Lee, you and Celena sit here, and I'll just sit here next to Dad."

Abby patted the place she wanted Lee and

51

Celena to sit, then crossed over and took her place next to Winston, who was still staring at Lee's attire with a quizzical frown on his face.

"Now, isn't this nice?" Abby asked pleasantly as Lee sat down in the appointed spot and tried in vain to stretch the trench coat to cover his hairy legs. Abby had to admit he was quite a contrast to her dignified father, and she found herself desperately trying to smother a giggle.

"Well, Lee, how have you been?" Winston opened the conversation.

"Fine, sir. And you?"

"Fine. Just fine." Winston drummed his fingers on the arm of the sofa and tried to find something to look at other than Lee's hairy legs.

"Would you like me to take your hat?" Abby offered. She certainly didn't dare ask Lee for his coat!

"Oh, yeah . . . here." He reached up and snatched the battered hat off his head and handed it to Abby with relief.

The doorbell rang again, and Abby hurried to answer it. She was nearly floored to find Gerald Metcalf standing before her when the door swung open.

"Hi there! I decided I could make your party after all," Gerald greeted her in a sexy drawl.

*Oh, horsefeathers!* she thought fleetingly, then pasted her hostess smile back on her face. "Why, Gerald. How nice." She took his coat and introduced him to a few of her friends standing near the door, worrying all the while that he would throw a kink in her plans.

Sure enough, it wasn't long before he spotted Celena on the sofa with Lee and crossed the room to join her.

The look of disgust on Lee's face said it all when Abby joined them a few minutes later with a tray of refreshments and the five of them tried to make normal conversation. Winston was monopolizing Lee's attention, talking about a new project the hospital was about to undertake, and Abby noticed Celena was growing increasingly edgy. Lee had barely said two words to her since they had arrived, and it was evident she wanted more of his attention.

Gerald, however, took care of Celena by flirting outrageously with her, and Celena, her attention diverted, loved every minute of it. .

Finally, Abby could stand no more and decided to take the bull by the horns.

"Dad, I think Celena wants to show Lee my new patio furniture," Abby interrupted when there was a brief pause in the men's conversation.

"Your patio furniture?" Winston glanced up in surprise. "Haven't you stored it for the winter yet?"

"Yes, it's out in the garage, but they can go out there and see it."

*The garage should afford them enough privacy to make up,* she thought resentfully and was shocked when that strange feeling of jealousy assaulted her once more.

"I think that sounds lovely, don't you, Lee?" Celena sprang to her feet and reached for his hand. "Come on, darling, it's getting stuffy in here."

Lee rose slowly and cast a sour glance in Abby's direction. "All right, I could use some fresh air."

Gerald stood, too. "I wouldn't mind taking a look either," he said hurriedly.

"Oh, no, Gerald"—Abby stopped him quickly—"I have someone I wanted you to meet."

"Oh?"

"Yes, Diana's just been dying to meet you," she fibbed, hoping her friend would forgive her for what she was about to do.

Gerald straightened his tie. "Well, lead the way!"

"Just follow me."

After Abby completed the introductions between Diana and Gerald, she quietly excused herself and went back to the sofa. Matt strolled over and put his arm around Abby's waist as Lee and Celena started toward the garage door to look at the furniture.

"Hey, buddy, *love* your costume." Matt winked at Lee playfully. "Wish I'd thought of it."

"That makes two of us," Lee returned blandly, his eyes resting briefly on Matt's arm wrapped around Abby's waist.

For the next thirty minutes Abby and Matt mingled with the other guests. Abby tried her best to keep her mind off what was taking place in the garage but failed miserably. In a way, she hoped Celena and Lee reconciled their differences, and then she could disentangle herself from their lives. Still, hidden somewhere in the most secret part of her heart, she hoped Lee would realize that Celena was not the woman for him. Somewhere in this world there was bound to be a man that could match Celena's strong personality, but Abby seriously doubted if Lee ever could. She was afraid he would only end up getting hurt. *Either way, it's really none of my business,* she decided, and for what seemed like the hundredth time, promised herself she was going to stop worrying about it.

After tonight they would be back on their way to the altar, and her conscience would be eased.

When Lee and Celena came back in the house, Abby knew all was not well. Celena's cupid bow mouth wore a definite pout. Lee made his way back to Winston and talked to him for the rest of the evening, totally ignoring everything and everyone else. When the party started breaking up around midnight, Abby was mortified to see Celena leave with a smiling Gerald.

Standing alone in the rubble of the front room, she almost felt like crying after the last guest left.

All this for nothing.

Lee had left with barely a decent good night, and she could hardly blame him. She knew he must have been miserable all night dressed as he was, but he had certainly carried it off with more dignity than she could have mustered.

It took over an hour and a half for her to put the apartment back in order. By then the clock on the mantel had struck one thirty. For some crazy reason she wanted to call Lee and apologize once more for the disastrous evening.

Picking up the phone book, she found his number and dialed hesitantly.

The phone rang twice before he answered, and her heart began to flutter.

"Hello!" he barked.

"Lee?"

"Yes?" His tone altered, softening when he recognized her voice.

"Uh, this is Abby."

"Yeah, I know."

"You did?"

"Sure."

"Well, I hope I didn't wake you. I know it's late."

"I wasn't in bed yet."

"I—I really feel awful about tonight . . . you know . . . about no one else being in costume."

"I have to tell you I was ready to wring your neck there for a minute," he admitted with a soft chuckle.

"But you're not mad?"

"No. Did me good to be humbled like that. And believe me, that was the most humbling experience I've ever had."

"I want you to know I really appreciated your effort," she said sincerely.

"That's okay." His voice then took on a teasing note. "I hope I was 'flashy' enough for you."

"Oh . . . yes." She laughed. "You were marvelous. And if you're worried about Dad, I explained it all to him and he understood," she hastened to add.

"Now, that was a shock to my nervous system to see him open the door," Lee confessed.

"And I wanted to apologize for . . . Celena. Apparently you and she didn't get things worked out?"

Lee's voice turned gruff once more. "No, we didn't."

"I'm sorry. I'll talk to her—"

"Abby," Lee broke in, "don't bother."

Abby paused and held her breath. "Are you saying you don't care for Celena any longer?"

"I'm just saying I hate to keep bothering you with our problems," he hedged. "Why don't I handle things from now on, okay?"

"Well, sure," Abby replied, feeling a little hurt that she was being dismissed so abruptly. "I was only trying to help."

"I know you were and I appreciate it, but I can't keep imposing on your friendship."

"Oh, but you're not imposing," she assured him warmly. "I want to do this for you, Lee—and for Celena, too."

"I don't know, Abby . . ."

"Well, it's late and I know you must be tired," Abby said hurriedly before he could tell her he didn't want her help any longer. "I just wanted to tell you I was sorry things didn't work out."

"Matt stay around very long after the party broke up?" Lee suddenly asked.

"Matt? No, no he left about the same time you did. Why?"

"Oh, no reason. Just wondering."

"Well, I guess I'll be seeing you."

"Yeah, I imagine you will."

"Good night, Lee."

"Good night, turnip brain."

"Carrot top," she corrected.

"Whatever."

"Oh, by the way, have you signed my petition to clean the pigeon droppings off the town statue?"

"No, and I don't plan to."

"Oh. I've already asked you?"

"Four times."

"Well, I know you must be tired, so I'll say good night." Abby smiled as she slowly replaced the receiver. He was such a nice guy.

She yawned and started walking toward her bedroom, unbuttoning her blouse as she went. No matter what he said, she was going to have to try harder to get Celena back for him. *Well, I'd redouble my efforts, and by hook or by crook, I'll deliver*

*Celena Fenton right back into Lee MacNair's arms or my name isn't Abigail Teresa King!*

That thought should have made her much happier than it actually did.

# CHAPTER FOUR

The old adage, Where there's a will there's a way, kept popping into Abby's mind the next couple of days. As hard as she tried, she couldn't seem to come up with any reasonable way to patch up the differences between Lee and Celena.

And if she were totally honest, she was growing increasingly out of sorts with herself for even making the effort. Why she should keep racking her brain to bring those two extremely stubborn people together was beyond her, but for some reason she was hell-bent on trying.

Her mother had always said, "Abby, you're too good for your own sake," and Abby had to admit that at times she probably was. But what were friends for if they couldn't help each other out?

One thing she had to admit, though: Her heart was becoming less enthusiastic about the whole idea of catering to Celena's irritating whims when it came to men, and Abby was seriously beginning to toy with the idea of telling her it was high time she grew up.

So, it was with a heavy heart that Abby worked around the shop late Monday afternoon, her mind wandering back to the conversation she had had with Celena the day before.

It had certainly come as no surprise when the

phone rang bright and early, and Celena had proceeded to bombard her with questions before she could swallow the last bite of toast she had just taken.

"I'm dying to know! What did he say after I left?"

"Who?" Abby knew exactly "who," but she thought she would make her friend suffer a little for acting the way she did at the party last night.

"You know who! Did that louse cry on your shoulder after I left? If he did, I hope you told him he'll be extremely lucky if he ever sees me again! Why, the *nerve* of that guy," she fumed. "Do you know he was downright rude to me when we went out to the garage to see your patio furniture? He implied that I was deliberately flirting with Gerald just to make him angry, and he thought it would be best if we stopped seeing each other. Well! I told him that if he thought for one moment he was going to tell me what I could or couldn't do—"

"Wait a minute." Abby curtly interrupted Celena's tirade. "If the louse you're referring to is Lee, he didn't even mention your name before he left," she stated calmly. *There!* she thought. She was a horrible friend to feel such puckish delight in being able to tell Celena that and not even try to force the grin off her face while she was saying it.

"He didn't?" Celena's voice had suddenly lost all its former belligerence.

"Nope. Not a word."

"It isn't funny to tease me like this, Abby," she said irritably. "I've spent a very restless night worrying over this whole thing, and I don't find your flip replies at all amusing. Now tell me what Lee said," she demanded. "He was upset, wasn't he?"

"Not that I could tell." Abby refused to lighten her load. "He merely said, 'Goodnight, Abby. I'd like to say I had a great time . . . I sure would like to, but I can't,' " Abby repeated Lee's teasing exit words dutifully. Her smile widened from a tiny grin into a full-fledged beam when she thought of the way he had winked at her in that cute, sexy way he had about him, then tipped his hat in a mock salute and backed hurriedly out her doorway, clutching the front of his coat tightly.

"Nothing about me?" Celena gasped indignantly.

"Take my word for it, Celena. I'd consider myself real lucky he didn't say anything, if I were you."

"Aha! Then he *was* upset," she said gleefully.

"Wouldn't you be if the woman you were dating spent her entire evening flirting with the town's self-proclaimed womanizer right under your very nose?"

"Now you sound like Lee."

"Well, honestly!" Abby's temper snapped. "I don't know why you treat the guy the way you do. Personally, if Lee were interested in me, I think I'd show a little more respect toward him than you do."

"Oh, for heaven's sake. Spare me the sermon," Celena retorted. "You know, if I didn't know better, I'd swear you had a crush on Lee yourself!"

"Now, that *is* ridiculous," Abby grumbled, not at all sure it was.

"What's ridiculous about it?" she pressed. "You have to admit you're forever taking Lee's side when we have an argument."

"Only because he's usually right."

"Well, I like that. I thought you were on my side in this."

Abby sighed hopelessly. This was going to be one round she wasn't going to win. "You know I'm on your side, Celena. It's just that I get tired of being a referee between you and Lee, and I really think from now on I'm going to stay out of your love affairs."

If Lee MacNair wanted Celena back, he would have to do his own dirty work. After all, hadn't he as much as told her to stay out of it when they talked on the phone Saturday night?

"You can't do this to me," Celena pleaded. "You know that Lee and I both have quick tempers and say things we don't mean. You have to help me get him back, Abby. I rely on you to be our go-between—I know I'm not being very reasonable about this, but I think he's really mad at me this time!"

"I think he is, too," Abby agreed. "I also think he has every reason to be."

"I know." Celena sounded like a willful child suddenly brought to heel. "I did act pretty awful last night, but he wasn't any angel himself," she grumbled.

"Look, be honest with me Celena. Do you really care for Lee, or is he just another challenge?" Abby petitioned for what seemed like the hundredth time since this stormy relationship between Lee and Celena began.

Silently, she begged Celena to give up the whole idea of pursuing Lee. Maybe then Abby's life could return to normal.

"I don't know . . . but I'm really beginning to think he's that special someone, Abby. It's just that he makes me so darn mad sometimes." She paused thoughtfully. "Don't you think deep down that he really cares for me?"

Abby had to admit that, much to her growing dismay, she really did think that Lee cared for Celena despite their differences. Why else would he always be seeking advice and getting so upset when he and Celena fought?

"Yes . . . I think he probably does."

"Then I'm sure you want to see us get together, don't you? After all, it's my future happiness we're talking about here, not just an ordinary, run-of-the-mill liaison."

Abby wasn't so sure about that. "Well, I'm willing to *try* and help you, Celena—"

"Oh, I knew you would! Now, what do you think my next move ought to be?"

Abby frowned. *How about to Outer Mongolia?* she thought resentfully, then caught herself. "I don't know. He was pretty upset with you last night."

"Then he did say something about me before he left?"

"No," Abby replied, "but I don't have to be clairvoyant to realize he was upset with you."

"I guess it was pretty daring of me to leave with Gerald, but at least *he* was paying some attention to me," Celena defended herself.

"No, not 'daring.' It was 'irresponsible,' 'unpredictable,' and downright 'fickle,' maybe, but not 'daring,' Celena. Any fool could have run off with Gerald the way you did, but if you want my opinion, I can't see how your actions Saturday night could possibly further your cause with Lee in any way," Abby told her candidly.

Once again Celena's voice turned frosty. "As I

said earlier, I don't need a sermon, Abby. I need some good, sound advice."

"Well, I'm sure we're both aware of my less-than-outstanding track record in that area," Abby relented, "but if you want my advice, I'd call Lee and sincerely apologize for acting the way I did and just hope he's willing to start over."

"I can't do that," Celena promptly dismissed the idea. "I'm sure at this point he wouldn't listen to a word I said."

"Then I'm afraid I don't know what else to tell you," Abby returned impatiently. The topic of conversation was beginning to get on her nerves, and she wanted to see it end as soon as possible.

"Now, don't go losing your temper." Celena softened immediately. "I didn't say it wasn't a *good* idea; I simply meant it wasn't going to be that easy to get Lee in a position where he'll hear me out."

"I would think it almost impossible."

"Now, I think what we should do is sort of trick him into hearing me out," Celena plotted deviously.

"Trick him?"

"Yes . . . You know, maybe you could arrange for him to take me out tomorrow night without him being aware of who he was going to be with," she suggested brightly.

"Oh, now wait a minute," Abby protested. "I'm in enough hot water with Lee myself for letting him come to the party in costume when everyone else refused to. He'd break my neck if I set him up with a blind date, and it turned out to be you! Don't you think it's time we started acting our ages in this matter?"

"I thought you were willing to help?"

"I am, within reason, but this is ridiculous."

"Nonsense. It'll work, I tell you. You just let me figure out the details, and then I'll call you back tomorrow afternoon."

Abby was just about to tell her to save her energy when a sharp click on the other end of the line announced the end of the conversation.

That had been yesterday morning, and Abby had still not heard from Celena.

Maybe, with a minuscule piece of luck, she wouldn't. But that hope was dashed a few moments later as the bell over the shop door rang, and Celena came breezing in.

"Hi, I'm sorry I'm so late in getting back to you, but I've been busy trying to work this thing out," she apologized in a breathless rush.

"Haven't you been at work?" Abby asked in surprise.

"No, I called in and took the day off. I figured my problem was much more pressing than my job." She grinned pertly.

"You're lucky your father owns World Travels," Abby put in sourly. It seemed to Abby that Celena rarely worked the full three out of the five days a week she was committed for.

"I know. Daddy's a real pet for letting me off like he does," Celena agreed readily. "Now, I know you're dying to know what I've cooked up!"

"Yeah, dying." Abby nodded dismally. She wasn't quite sure when the tables had turned and Celena had taken charge of the plans to "get Lee MacNair back" and Abby had become a mere participant.

"It's brilliant. Positively brilliant," she gloated. "Sometimes I even amaze myself. You're going to love it!"

65

"I can hardly wait."

"Instead of a blind date, I've come up with something simply priceless. I thought the blind date might be going a bit far if you had to set it up, and chances are I'd only succeed in making Lee madder than he originally was. So, I've arranged for him to take *you* out tonight, and Matt is going to escort me." She looked at Abby and beamed. "Isn't that brilliant?"

Abby shook her head to clear her confused thoughts. Surely she had heard Celena wrong. "You mean, you've decided to swallow your pride and ask Lee to double with Matt and me tonight? Is that what you're saying?"

"No, no, no! I said, Lee is going to take you out, and Matt is going to take me out. That way, I'll still be with Lee, and sometime during the evening you and Matt can discreetly pair off and leave me alone with Lee. Naturally, I'll take it from there," she finished with a sly grin.

"Celena, I think you're two bricks shy of a load."

"For heaven's sakes, why?" Celena peered at her friend expectantly.

"In the first place Lee is too much of a gentleman to take me out when he's been dating you, and I really don't think Matt would agree to such a ridiculous—"

"Oh, he already has," Celena interrupted hurriedly.

"He has?" Abby glanced up in disbelief. Although she wasn't romantically interested in Matt, Abby still felt a little resentful that he would jump so readily at the chance to go out with Celena.

"Well, sure he did. After all, none of us are actually committed to one another—you know, not really. So, after I explained to Matt that you were only trying to help Lee and me get back together, he was nice enough to agree to my rather unusual suggestion."

"You told him this was all *my* idea?"

Celena looked at Abby suspiciously. "Are you upset? I thought you told me there was nothing serious going on between you and Matt."

"There isn't!"

"Then what's the problem?"

"He'll think I'm crazy coming up with an idea like this," she protested. "And what about Lee? I suppose you breezed over there and told him I wanted to go out with him?" she asked in a sick voice.

"Good heavens, no!" Celena laughed in disbelief. "Do you think I'm that stupid? He would never go along with anything like that coming from me. I had Matt ask him," she declared smugly.

Abby sank down on the stool behind the counter and stared at her in disgust. "You didn't. Please tell me you didn't."

"I did!"

Abby groaned and laid her head down on the counter. Matt and Lee would think she should be locked away in a padded cell after this!

"What in the world is the matter with you? Can't you see what a perfect opportunity this is for me?"

"Yeah, for you it may be perfect, but what about me?" Abby complained in a muffled voice. "I can't believe Matt would go along with such a ludicrous scheme." Matt was the very person who had been warning her to stay out of Lee and Celena's troubles.

"Well"—Celena's face grew decidedly sheepish

—"to be quite honest, it did take a bit more persuading than I had originally thought, but he finally saw my reasoning when I promised him that, after tonight, I wouldn't include you or him in any more of my problems."

Abby raised her head slowly to face an angelic-looking Celena. "And he believed you?"

"Don't you?" she asked in a slightly miffed tone.

"No, and even though Matt agreed to such a bizarre plan, I still can't picture Lee going along with it."

Celena shrugged indifferently. "I don't have any idea how Matt accomplished it, but he called me a few minutes ago and said everything was arranged. I'm certainly not going to look a gift horse in the mouth," she added blithely.

"And I'm not going to go along with any of this," Abby announced as she decided to snap out of her stupor and put her foot down once and for all. This plot was beginning to thicken to the point that even she couldn't wade through it.

"I knew you'd try to back out, so I arranged to have the guys pick us up here at the shop," Celena declared triumphantly.

"Well, you can just march yourself over to the telephone and unarrange it."

"It's much too late." Celena smiled as the bell over the door sounded.

Abby worriedly glanced up to see Matt and Lee entering. She hastily slid off the stool and came to her feet, her hand shooting up unconsciously to smooth her unruly hair as she mentally cursed Celena for not dropping her bombshell a few minutes earlier. At least then she would have had time to freshen her makeup. As it was, she knew she looked as if she had been caught in a hurricane.

"Hi, fellows!" Celena pasted on one of her brightest smiles and walked over to greet Matt and Lee.

Matt smiled weakly in Abby's direction and let Celena entwine her arm with his. "Hi, Celena, Abby."

Abby nodded mutely and tried to keep from looking in Lee's direction.

"Good evening, Lee." Celena turned her charm toward Lee, her smile increasing to a dazzling brilliance.

"Hi, Celena," he said cordially. Abby watched as Lee returned her friend's smile, then walked over to where Abby was standing. "Hi, Abby."

"Hi, Lee." She managed an apologetic smile in his direction, trying to force down the spreading blush she could feel engulfing her face.

, His very presence seemed to unnerve her as she hurriedly busied herself behind the counter.

As Celena chatted with Matt, Lee moved closer to Abby and smiled down at her. "Sorry to take you by surprise like this, but it was sort of one of those last-minute things," he explained lightly.

*I'll just bet it was!* "Yes, I was rather surprised myself," she returned hurriedly. "In fact, I didn't know anything about it until a minute before you walked through that door." She was immensely relieved that he seemed to understand the situation without being told, and her eyes gratefully told him so.

His eyes in return quietly said that it was perfectly all right. He did understand, and it didn't bother him in the least.

"So, where would you like to eat?" he asked.

Abby surveyed the jeans and sporty top she had worn to work and grimaced. "I'm afraid I'm not dressed for anything other than something very casual," she replied, casting an envious glance in Celena's direction. She was dressed in a perky, blue-and-green plaid skirt and blazer that only enhanced her stunning looks.

"Oh, I was hoping we could eat somewhere nice," Celena chimed in. She named an expensive restaurant in town and then looked at Abby pointedly. "You could always go home and change, then meet us there."

"Well . . . I suppose I can . . ."

"I don't think that's necessary," Lee said calmly. "There's a good Italian restaurant close to the hospital that Matt and I eat at once in awhile. I think the ladies would love Papa Tony's lasagna, don't you, Matt?"

"I'm sure they would." He had been standing quietly by, casting uneasy glances in Abby's direction as Celena hovered close to him. "Tony makes all his pasta and sauce from scratch."

"Whatever Celena wants," Abby conceded. After all, this was her party. "I'd be happy to run home and change."

"Oh, Celena wouldn't want to pass up Papa Tony's pasta and bread," Matt interposed, taking Celena's arm and ushering her toward the front door. "We'll wait for you outside."

"I'll just be a minute." Abby smiled at Lee self-consciously as she started counting the cash from the register and sticking it into a leather bank bag. "Jean went home early tonight, so I'll have to close the shop." She looked at him expectantly. "You can visit with Celena if you'd like while I finish up here."

"No, I'll just hang around in here with you," he

said absently, and her heart started thudding like a jackhammer. He was so darn good-looking!

Her chores were completed in record time as she scurried around the shop. Lee wandered around the studio, admiring the photographs on the wall as she worked.

"You do any of these?" he asked in admiration.

"Mmm. Almost all of them," she said proudly. "The owner of the shop, Jean, doesn't work much anymore. She takes care of the books and makes appointments, whereas I do most of the actual photographing."

Lee paused before an outdoor portrait of a child sitting under a tree, hugging a beautiful Irish setter. "This one's great," he commented, leaning in to peer more closely at the expression on the child's face. The photographer had managed to capture the child's unqualified love for the animal.

"Thanks. That's one of my personal favorites." She smiled warmly as she came to stand beside him and stare at the picture for a moment with pride written all over her face.

"You must like children," he mused thoughtfully.

"I do. I want to have a whole house full of them one of these days." She paused and glanced at him questionably. "How about you? Do you want children?" For some inexplicable reason she prayed his answer would be a firm yes.

Lee nearly choked at her family goal. His estimate for a family was considerably lower. "Yes, but only a couple."

Abby noted with satisfaction that it was a firm yes.

*Well, two children would be more in Celena's range,* Abby decided as she straightened up and

71

walked back over to pick up her purse and the bank bag.

"I'm ready if you are."

Casting one last admiring glance in the direction of the portrait, Lee escorted her out the front door and over to Matt's car.

After a quick trip to the bank's night depository, the two couples arrived at the restaurant well ahead of the usual dinner crowd.

Abby had felt extremely foolish riding in the backseat with Lee while Matt and Celena were up front, and she hoped it wouldn't be long before she could slip off somewhere with Matt. Not that she particularly wanted to. To her dismay, all during the meal she found herself enjoying Lee's company immensely. She found herself laughing at his corny jokes and teasing back with him in friendly camaraderie. In fact, she was having so much fun, she forgot her mission and just enjoyed the evening.

As the night wore on, she noticed uneasily that not only was she getting scathing glances from Celena now, but they were also coming with increasing regularity from Matt's direction.

"Let's dance!" Matt demanded as Abby's laughter spilled out again over another one of Lee's jokes.

She glanced up guiltily, her smile fading quickly when she observed Matt's imposing frame looming over her.

"Who? Me?"

"Yes, you!" Without waiting for an answer, he took her hand and nearly dragged her out to the small dance floor.

Lee stood up and started to protest, but Celena

pulled him back in his chair and smiled invitingly. "Let them go, Lee. I want to talk to you."

"I was under the mistaken impression you were supposed to end up with me tonight," Matt accused as he angrily whirled Abby around the deserted dance floor.

"I was—I was just getting ready to suggest something," Abby fabricated, glancing jealously over at Lee and Celena. Celena hadn't wasted a second in cornering him. She simmered down instantly when she realized she was being foolish again.

"I should never have listened to Celena's crazy idea in the first place," Matt grumbled under his breath, "but the pushy broad wouldn't take no for an answer."

"No, you shouldn't have," she agreed sourly. "And you're hurting me." She wiggled out of his tight embrace crossly.

His hold loosened immediately. "I'm sorry, Abby, but it burns me to sit there and watch you flirt with Lee."

Abby's mouth dropped open. "Flirt with Lee?"

"Yes, flirt!"

"Now listen here, Matt, I wasn't flirting with Lee, but even if I was, I can flirt with anyone I darn well please. I wasn't aware there was any commitment between us."

"There isn't," he admitted sheepishly, "but that's not my fault."

Abby sighed hopelessly. Matt would never be anything to her but a good friend, and somehow she was going to have to get the message through his thick skull.

"Oh, Matt"—she reached up and touched his cheek gently—"I don't want to hurt your feelings, but you and I have had this discussion a hundred times before. I don't care for you in that way—"

A deep voice interrupted her next words as Lee tapped Matt on the shoulder politely. "Pardon me," he said dryly. "But your 'date' wants to dance, and I think it's only polite that I ask mine to dance." He smiled patiently. "I'm sure you don't want to keep Celena waiting. She can be a real pain in the tootie when she wants to be."

Matt reluctantly released Abby to Lee's custody and shot his friend a look of pure disgust. "This isn't funny anymore, MacNair!"

"I didn't think it was to begin with, Avery." Lee pulled Abby close and waltzed her out to the middle of the floor.

By now, Abby was getting sick of both men. "What do you think you're doing?" she demanded hotly. "You're supposed to be over there taking advantage of Matt's and my absence!"

"Oh, so that's what this was all about," he mused thoughtfully. He drew her closer to his tall frame and wrapped his arms tighter around her waist.

Abby suddenly felt herself going light-headed at his touch. All resistance drained out of her, and she settled more comfortably in his arms.

"Now, that's much better," he murmured softly as she buried her face in his neck and sighed. She seemed to fit in his arms so perfectly, it disgusted her. Although he was a good eight inches taller than she, she was nestled securely against his athletic build, and she found herself loving every minute of it.

"You want to tell me what's going on?" he asked patiently as they moved in harmony to a slow love song that was playing on the jukebox.

At the moment Abby didn't want to do anything

other than burrow deeper against him and pray the song wasn't over for at least an hour.

"You honestly don't know?"

"I honestly don't."

"But you agreed to this silly date," Abby pointed out in a shaky voice.

"Silly date? I agreed to go out with you. What's silly about that?"

"But Celena is your . . . girl," she protested inanely.

"Wrong."

Abby's pulse raced at the sound of irritation in his voice.

"She thinks she is."

"That's her problem," he returned lightly. "She knows as well as I do we have no commitment between us."

"Well, this is sure a switch. I was under the strong impression you were interested in her."

"Times change."

Now what was that supposed to mean? Men and their vague answers drove her up a wall! Apparently, he was more upset with Celena than she realized.

They danced in silence for a few moments before Abby spoke up again. "Lee, why did you agree to our date this evening?"

"I didn't have anything better to do."

"Well, thanks a lot!"

He chuckled. "No insult intended."

"I'm just a little baffled as to why you would go along with something like this," Abby persisted.

"Oh, I don't know—let's just say the idea intrigued me. Now, if you had approached me with this plan—and by the way, I'm very surprised you didn't—I would have laughed in your face and told you no! I would have known in a minute what you and Celena were up to. But when Matt said he had arranged a double date for us tonight, I thought it might be interesting to see what happened. If he's upset about the outcome of the evening, he has no one but himself to blame."

Abby glanced over at Matt and Celena sitting at the table. "I don't think he's having a very good time."

"Good."

"You're terrible," she chided, but felt as gleeful about it as he did. "I'm sorry they roped you in on this mess," she apologized.

"What's to be sorry about? I'm having a good time. What about you?"

"As a matter of fact I am, too. But Celena—"

"Maybe we should do it again sometime." Lee ignored her reference to Celena.

"Oh, I don't think so."

"Why not?"

"Uh . . . I just don't think that would be wise. Now, don't you think you should ask Celena to dance?" She hurriedly changed the subject before she found herself pursuing the idea of going out with him again.

Lee grimaced. "Is this part of the plan?"

She smiled encouragingly. "Afraid so. The purpose of the whole evening is for you and Celena to get things straightened out."

"That isn't my purpose."

"Then I strongly suggest you make it your purpose. They're both ready to kill us," Abby warned.

He sighed in disgust. "This is getting to be ridiculous."

"Maybe so, but I don't want Celena mad at me!"

He laughed. "I can't blame you. She isn't nearly as cute when she's mad as you are."

"We're not talking about— I'm cute?" She cocked her head and looked at him suspiciously. "You really think so?" His words had tempered her loyalty momentarily.

"I'm afraid I'm beginning to," he confessed, nipping gently at the tip of her nose. Their eyes refused to leave one another's as they glided around the room, blotting out the couple anxiously watching them from the small table.

Abby knew she was playing with fire. The look in Lee's eyes assured her that at the moment he found her much more than just cute, but she was powerless to move away from his intoxicating warmth.

His tender gaze continued to tell her he found her a lovely and desirable woman as his hands moved in slow exploration over the small of her back, pulling her ever closer to his taut body.

"I'm serious, Abby. I'd like to see you again sometime . . . if you're not tied up with Matt."

Tingles of desire flared brightly in her as he continued his discreet but virile assault on her senses.

"Oh, Lee"—she didn't know what to say as her emotions warred with her good sense—"I don't think so."

"I suppose that's out of the question under the circumstances," he conceded, almost to himself.

"Yes, I think that would be impossible . . . under the circumstances."

His hold grew tighter as she laid her head on his chest and snuggled closer. "Well, if you and Matt ever decide to call it quits, I'll be around."

"Lee, Matt and I are only friends," Abby murmured. "But if anything ever happens between you and Celena—"

"It already has, Abby."

"Don't say that."

"Just shut up and dance." If it hadn't been for the light kiss he had given her on her ear, she would have thought he was mad at her.

When the dance was finally over and he escorted her back to the table, there was such a sexual awareness between them it was almost tangible.

Matt and Celena were not in the best of moods, so the four agreed to call it a night.

Lee insisted on seeing Abby back to her car as they pulled up in front of the shop.

"This wasn't necessary," she protested as he unlocked her car door and handed her the key.

"It was for me." She could see his face in the bright harvest moon, and she longed to reach up and touch him. But she didn't dare.

"Well, good night." Abby got into her car and started the engine.

"You go straight home," he warned her. "It's getting late, and I don't like the idea of your being out by yourself . . . Listen, why don't I follow you—"

"No!" Abby shot back.

Lee looked taken aback by her sharp refusal. "Oh, yeah. I forgot about Matt," he apologized.

"Matt?"

"Yeah, he probably wouldn't care for that idea too much. I think I've already upset him enough for one night as it is. I better not press my luck."

"Yes, I have a feeling Celena is spitting nails right about now, too."

"Well, you drive carefully." He looked at her

longingly for a moment, then suddenly gave her the sexiest wink she had ever received.

He turned and was gone before she could shamelessly return it.

# CHAPTER FIVE

As Abby feared she would, Celena called the next morning with both guns blazing.

"How could you do this to me?"

"Good morning, Celena." Abby yawned and looked at the clock with bleary eyes. *Gad. Six thirty!* She still had another thirty minutes to sleep before the alarm went off.

"Lee didn't look at me *once* last night," the voice on the other end of the line accused angrily.

"That's only your imagination." Abby yawned again. "He would have had to look at you. I personally saw the two of you talking while Matt and I were dancing."

"Do you call 'Abby's not a bad dancer, is she?' thrilling conversation coming from *my* boyfriend?"

"I don't see how you can blame me for that!" It seems to me it was you who said all I had to do was go along with your infallible plan and leave the rest up to you. Well, I did and your plan failed. Not me."

"You were deliberately flirting with Lee."

"I was not." Celena sounded like Matt now, and it irritated her. Could she help it if she happened to enjoy some of Lee's outrageous knock-knock jokes?

"Well, I want you to know you're barking up the wrong tree if you think Lee is interested in you in any way," Celena announced. "I called him when I got home last night, and we had a very long, very interesting discussion. We're going out tonight. Really, Abby, I find it hard to believe I'm going to have to start worrying about you in addition to all my other problems."

"Celena,"—Abby closed her eyes wearily—"the last person in the world you have to worry about is me. Do you think I would honestly try to vie for Lee's attentions when I know how you feel about him?"

"No, not really . . . but you do cause me to be a little suspicious. It seemed to me you and Lee were having a heck of a good time together last night."

"Well, I'm sorry if it appeared we were overly enjoying each other's company. I'm not about to deny I find Lee an attractive man, but we've been friends long enough for you to know I don't go around stealing other women's men."

"I know . . . and I'm sorry if I implied you would. It's just that I find myself so confused by all of this. And I suppose what worries me the most is that no matter how confident I talk, deep down I'm really not sure Lee cares that much about me. It's frightening, Abby."

"I'm sure it must be, but I just don't think this is something you can force. Did you say you were going out with him tonight?" Abby found her voice sounding more wistful than it should have.

"Yes, we're going dancing."

The memory of Lee's arms around her as they floated around the dance floor the night before dominated Abby's thoughts for a moment. She could almost smell his now-familiar scent and feel the warmth of his breath gently caress her cheek as he had hummed softly to her while they danced. Tonight it would be Celena who would be in his arms.

"I'm very happy for you," Abby said softly. "Lee's a heck of a nice guy, Celena. I wish you both a world of happiness."

"Oh, I think we'll be *very* happy if I can ever make him see that we were meant for each other. Well, I have to run. I just thought I'd let you know what was going on."

"Thank you. I appreciate that."

When Abby hung up the phone, she still felt a nagging sense of disappointment. Lee and Celena were going out together tonight.

In a way, that surprised her. Especially in view of Lee's mood last night. He certainly didn't seem as if he were interested in Celena's company then.

She sighed and rolled out of bed to face the new day. *Men! Who needs them?*

The next few weeks drifted by peacefully. Abby devoted more time than usual to her work. The holidays were fast approaching, and business was booming at the shop. Parents wanted to give portraits of their children as Christmas gifts, and for once, the customers were allowing enough time to do that successfully.

The hospital was filled to capacity with cases of flu and people wanting to get their surgery over with before the holidays, so she found herself devoting more evenings to her volunteer work.

Matt insisted on taking her to dinner a couple of times a week, even if it meant grabbing a quick sandwich in the hospital coffee shop, but their relationship had been strained ever since the night she'd been Lee's date.

Celena called occasionally to report that things were progressing slowly between Lee and her.

Abby couldn't help but feel sorry for her friend, even though she had to wonder if Celena really knew what she wanted. But since she was still seeing Lee, her disposition had improved considerably, even to the point of suggesting a shopping trip the following Saturday. Abby had begged off, using work as an excuse. Things just weren't the same between them. Abby was torn between being a friend and trying to keep her mind off Celena's property . . . namely one Lee MacNair. Neither one was working out with much satisfaction.

Abby tried to put Lee out of her mind but found she was thinking about him more every day. She had bumped into him at the hospital a few times, and they had exchanged polite small talk. One time on the elevator, when the car had stopped at her floor, he had held the door open while she pushed her flower cart out. For a brief moment their eyes had met, and she sensed he wanted to say more to her, but moments later the door swished closed and he was gone.

Another time she and Matt had stopped to grab a quick hamburger at a local drive-in, and Lee stopped by to pick up his dinner on the way home. The three exchanged a few pleasantries, and Abby found herself once again trying to avoid Lee's gaze as they carried on small talk. He had just come from work and was still wearing a tailored, three-piece suit with a blue shirt that exactly matched the color of his eyes . . . he looked great.

Occasionally, he managed to catch her eye

briefly, and he smiled before she would look away hurriedly.

"What's with you two?" Matt asked grumpily. Lee had left the table only moments before Matt jumped her.

"What?"

"I asked, what's between you and MacNair?"

"I don't know what you're talking about," she said stiffly. She was getting very tired of being accused of having more than friendly feelings for Lee. "He's a friend. Just like he's a friend to you. And if I'm beginning to sound like a broken record, it's because I'm tired of the question!"

"I see the way you two look at each other," Matt replied crossly. "And believe me, those are not just friendly looks."

"Lee MacNair is Celena's property at the moment," Abby said calmly, forcing herself to retain her composure. "There's nothing at all between us, nor could there ever be as long as she's interested in him."

"Aha! Then you admit you could be interested in him if the way was clear."

"Would you please get up and get me some more catsup before I stuff this bag of french fries down your throat?" she asked politely, hoping he would take the hint and drop this annoying conversation.

Matt hung his head and studied his napkin carefully. "I take it you're telling me to mind my own business?"

"I wouldn't put it quite so bluntly, but yes, I don't think I should have to keep explaining to you that Lee and I are just friends."

"Just a 'friendly' word of warning." Matt's expression grew even more serious now. "Celena does have him pegged as hers even if he doesn't seem too keen on the idea."

"I'm more than aware of that, and I hate to repeat myself, but Lee and I are just friends."

Matt shook his head tolerantly. "I really think you believe that."

"It's the truth!"

"Good. It would be a shame for several friendships to be broken up by all this chaos."

Abby looked at him sourly. "Several?"

"Well, after all, Lee and I have been friends for years. You have to realize that I wouldn't take kindly to him stepping into my place in your life . . . and I've told him so."

"Oh, Matt, he wouldn't be stepping into your place. I thought I had made it clear. I like you a lot, but I'm not in love with you. And even though I would hate to lose your friendship, you're going to force me to stop seeing you with this kind of talk," she said with dismay.

Lee undoubtedly thought he was dealing with a bunch of idiots if everyone was going around warning him not to get involved with her!

"Sure, drop me so you can run to MacNair! I know you're not in love with me at the moment, Abby, but that doesn't mean you won't be one of these days, and I want Lee to be absolutely clear on where I stand," he stated firmly. "A friend does not cut in on another friend. When the four of us first met, Lee wanted Celena. I want him to stick by his original choice and leave you alone."

"I really don't think it's necessary to warn Lee about me," she returned sharply. "He's a grown man, for heaven's sake, not some teenybopper!"

"Nevertheless, he's been warned." Matt's eyes suddenly lost their anger and turned hopelessly pleading. "Abby . . . we've had a lot of laughs together. Let's not spoil things. Let Lee and Celena go their own way."

Abby laid her half-eaten hamburger down on the table, her appetite completely gone. If she didn't have such a darn good time with Matt most of the time, she would call it quits right now.

"I think you better take me back to the hospital now."

They moved out of the booth, and Matt signaled for the check. "I'm sorry if I've upset you, Abby, but there's a code of honor among friends, and that's what all this amounts to."

And so the days drifted by, and before she knew it Thanksgiving was approaching. The air was brisk and invigorating as she rode her bike to work. Abby knew this would probably be one of the last days she could ride before the weather would force her to go back to driving her car, but for now there was nothing more beautiful than an early, fall morning in Vermont. There were dark clouds building in the north this morning as she pedaled toward the shop, a sharp reminder that the weatherman had predicted snow by evening.

"Telephone!" Jean called as Abby opened the door to the shop and stepped in.

"For me?" Abby peeled off her gloves with her teeth and stepped behind the counter. "Hello?"

"Oh, Abby! You have to help me!" Celena cried.

Abby sank down on the stool and grimaced disgustedly. "What now?"

"It's Lee!"

"You're fighting again?"

"Well, not exactly."

"Then 'exactly' what is it, Celena? I have my first appointment coming in, in five minutes."

"Well, as I said, it's Lee. I don't seem to be getting anywhere with him."

Abby felt instantly ashamed and elated at the same time at her friend's words. "Oh? What's wrong?"

"I'm really not sure," she confessed. "It isn't that we're fighting . . . at least not that much. It's just that he seems—well, so indifferent to me."

"I'm sorry to hear that, but what can I do?" *If you want me to take him off your hands, I'll be happy to,* she thought fleetingly, then mentally slapped her hands and focused her mind back on what Celena was saying.

"Oh, I knew I could count on you!" Celena seized her opportunity quickly. "I got to thinking last night about the situation, and I believe I've come up with an infallible solution this time!"

"Of course. And how do I fit into this masterpiece?" Abby asked blandly, dreading the answer before it was given.

"Do you suppose you could borrow your parents' motor home this weekend?"

Celena's question took her completely off guard. "Well, Mom is still on her buying trip, so I doubt Dad will be using it. I suppose I could—"

"Fantastic!"

"Why? Did you want us to go somewhere?" Abby asked in a puzzled tone.

"No, not us, silly. I want you to kidnap Lee."

Abby's mouth dropped open. "What?"

"Kidnap Lee! I just had this marvelous idea last night. I want you to borrow your parents' motor home, then go over to the hospital and kidnap Lee when he gets off work tonight. Then I want you to bring him by my house and pick me up. We'll drop you at the nearest bus stop, and you can go home while I take him out to some secluded spot for the weekend. Isn't that brilliant?"

"That's the most disgusting idea you've come up with yet!"

To which came Celena's standard reply. "It'll work, I tell you. It just can't fail!"

" 'It just can't fail!' " Abby mimicked. "But it always does, Celena, and I'm left holding the bag, looking like a complete idiot!"

"Not this time, you won't be," she assured soothingly. "This time it will work, and I promise this will be the last time you'll have to help me. After this weekend Lee MacNair will be mine, hook, line, and sinker or else I'm giving up on him forever!"

"No! Absolutely not!"

"Oh, *please*, Abby. You remember the time I went out of my way to get you a date with Phil Preston for the senior prom? You were absolutely dying to go with him, and who arranged it for you? And the time not so long ago you wanted a date with that junior executive over at the bank? May I remind you who was responsible for getting you that date?" she asked primly. "And may I also remind you of your exact words that day: 'Oh, Celena, if I can ever return the favor, all you have to do is ask.' Well, I'm asking!"

"But I've returned that favor a hundred times since you met Lee."

"Just one more time," Celena begged. "I know I can wrap it up this time."

Abby drummed her nails on the countertop, her mind quickly assessing the situation.

"Were you serious when you said you would give up on him if this plan fails?"

Celena sighed. "What other choice do I have? But it won't fail, Abby. I know it."

"All right. I'll help you one more time, Celena, and if it doesn't work this time, I'm giving you fair notice that I will *not* help you capture Lee MacNair again. You had better accomplish your mission this weekend, because I'm out of it after this," she warned ominously. *Then I'll go after him myself!* she added silently.

"Agreed. Now, go by the hospital before four thirty. Lee gets off work then, and he usually takes out of there as fast as he can."

"How in the world am I going to 'kidnap' him?" Abby asked crossly, beginning to realize what she had just consented to do.

"You'll think of something," Celena replied brightly. "I have to rush, sweetie. I have to go do some shopping for this weekend." She paused and giggled. "I want to get some very sexy 'work clothes.'"

Abby grimaced as the mental picture of Lee and Celena together in a cozy motor home all weekend rushed in on her. She had tried not to think about the possibility that the two of them were sleeping together, but it would be impossible to avoid that conclusion now.

Well, what did she expect? Lee MacNair was a virile man if she had ever seen one, and she was sure Celena would use that to her advantage. That thought hurt, but there was absolutely nothing she could do about it.

After a hurried phone call to her father to assure herself she could have the use of her parents' motor home, Abby brought her mind back to business. It had been difficult trying to explain why she wanted the motor home without letting the cat out of the bag, but she managed to pull it off successfully . . . or so she hoped.

By late afternoon the weather was deteriorating rapidly, and Abby was having several cancellations. The wind had begun to gust, and a heavy layer of dark clouds blanketed the city. By three o'clock the weatherman had issued a heavy snow warning of up to ten inches by morning.

"You might as well go on home early," Jean suggested as she crossed out the last appointment in the book. "It looks like the storm has scared everyone away for the day."

Abby eyed the ever-darkening sky warily. "Yes, I think I will, if you don't mind," she accepted gratefully. She still had to pick up the motor home, 'kidnap' Lee, pick up Celena, and take a bus home before the storm broke.

A few minutes later she was riding her bike the short distance to her parents' house, the stinging wind blurring her eyes. She pedaled up into her parents' drive and hurriedly unlocked the garage door.

The twenty-three-foot Heritage motor home was stored snugly in the bowels of the garage interior, its huge frame taking up most of the space.

Abby opened the door and flipped on the lights. The motor home was completely self-contained with a generator and water tanks and would only require a fast trip by the grocery store to make it ready for the weekend.

Winston and Mara King loved to travel when time permitted, and they had bought the home on wheels several years ago for their vacationing pleasure.

The sound of the howling wind outside made Abby shiver deeper into her fur-lined jacket as she checked to make sure everything was in order.

She had to admit that Lee and Celena would certainly have a cozy weekend for their tryst!

The inside of the motor home spoke of luxury and good taste. The two brown and beige captain's chairs served as driver and passenger seats. They sat before an impressive fiberglass dashboard hosting an array of optional equipment that made this particular motor home one of the finest money could buy.

The sofa and chairs were done in shades of brown and wood tones in the living area. Next came the kitchen, where there was a built-in microwave in addition to a conventional oven, a large refrigerator, a double sink, and a kitchen table that would seat four comfortably or serve as an additional bed. The master bedroom was in the back of the motor home, joined by a shower and lavatory.

Abby had always been impressed with how much room the manufacturer could maneuver into such a small area.

Twenty minutes later she was carefully backing the massive vehicle out of the driveway. She cringed as she ran over one of her mother's summer flowerbeds, completely pulverizing five bricks.

She shrugged. She didn't profess to be a motor home driver. She was a photographer.

After a quick stop at the local market for supplies, Abby was soon making her way through the afternoon traffic, desperately hoping the grocery cart she had hit on the way out hadn't put a dent in the front bumper.

She pulled into the drive of the hospital at exactly four ten and shut off the ignition. Because she didn't want to attempt to park the large vehicle between other cars, she was forced to leave it at the very end of the lot and walk the remaining distance to the entrance of the hospital. By the time she reached her destination, large puffy flakes of snow were beginning to fall from the sky, and it was four thirty on the dot.

Rushing to the elevator, she punched the button and waited impatiently for the car. On the drive over she had been rehearsing the story she would present to Lee. She had to admit it still had a lot of holes in it, but it was the best she could come up with.

*Darn that Celena, anyway!* she thought irritably. What would she do if Lee had left the hospital early to avoid the storm?

A bell chimed softly as the doors to the second elevator opened, and people began to walk out. Abby was just starting to step into the elevator when she caught sight of Lee emerging from the back of the first car with a briefcase in his hand. At the sight of his tall, handsome physique her stomach fluttered and she cursed herself a hundred times for helping Celena try to trap the poor guy!

Backing rapidly out of the elevator, she called hurriedly to his retreating form, "Uh . . . Lee!"

He stopped and turned around to search for the unexpected voice. His face brightened when he saw her, and he strode briskly to where she stood. "Hi, Abby. You looking for your father?"

"Uh—yes," she improvised quickly, "but I'm afraid I've just missed him."

"Oh?" Lee looked clearly puzzled. "I thought I

just passed him in the hall a few minutes before I came down."

"Really? Well that's strange. His secretary told me he's already gone home for the day . . . you know, because of the storm and all." She hated to fib to him.

"Yeah? Well," he shrugged, "I guess I was mistaken." His eyes discreetly surveyed the rosy flush of her cheeks and the tousled array of her strawberry-blond hair. "I guess it's getting cold out there."

"Yes, very," she agreed.

"Well, I think I'll try to beat the brunt of the storm home," he offered with a polite smile. "Good to see you again, Abby." They both looked at each other longingly.

"Yeah, good to see you again, Lee," she murmured, forgetting for the moment what she had come for.

He looked extraordinarily handsome this afternoon in his gray wool suit and salmon-colored shirt. His striped tie had the same salmon and gray colors, and it suddenly occurred to her that Lee had the best taste in clothing of any man she'd ever met. In fact, at that particular moment she was powerless to find one thing about Lee that didn't suit her tastes to a tee.

"Haven't seen you around much lately," he procrastinated.

"No, I've been pretty busy at the shop."

"I guess with the holidays approaching you're busier than usual?"

"Yes, it seems like everyone wants to bring their children in at the same time." She smiled.

"You still seeing Matt?" he asked casually, yet there was a note of expectancy in his voice.

"Occasionally." Her eyes devoured his hungrily. "Are you still seeing Celena?" she asked inanely. *Of course he's still seeing Celena, you idiot!* she thought.

"Occasionally," he returned without any sign of emotion.

They were standing in the lobby blocking the flow of traffic as each of them racked their brains to come up with something to prolong the conversation. Finally, Lee smiled and said in a resigned voice, "Well, I guess we'd better be moving along."

"Yes, I suppose we should. Oh!" Abby suddenly snapped out of her dreamy haze and remembered why she was there. "Oh . . . uh, Lee."

"Yes?" He glanced at her expectantly.

"I'm having a little bit of car trouble. Do you think you—"

"Sure. I'll be glad to help you."

He snatched the bait so eagerly it made Abby feel even worse about what she was going to do.

"You sure you don't mind? It's starting to snow." She wanted to give him every opportunity to back out on his offer of assistance. Then she could simply call Celena and tell her the plan had failed.

But Lee was only too eager to be of service. "I'll be glad to help you. Where are you parked?"

"On the hospital lot. You'd better get a heavier coat," she warned as they started toward the front entrance. "The temperature is dropping."

"Oh, I'm tough." He laughed. "Besides, I was in a rush this morning and forgot my coat."

She smiled again. "That's nice." Anything he did was nice in her opinion, and she was barely paying attention to what he was saying. Her eyes were too busy drinking in the sight of him.

He held the front door open for her, and they both walked out. A frigid blast of cold air assaulted them as Lee hurriedly turned his suit collar up around his neck and shouted above the wind. "Where did you say you were parked?"

"Follow me!"

They started across the parking lot, struggling against the howling wind. The snow was coming down in wet sheets now as they continued to fight their way across the slippery lot.

When they had walked five minutes, she heard Lee yell again. "Where the hell did you park? New Hampshire?"

Abby cringed as she noticed his hair was completely covered with snow and his face was beet red from the stinging wind.

"Just a little farther," she encouraged brightly.

By the time they staggered into the motor home another five minutes later, they were both nearly frozen.

"Good Lord!" Lee collapsed back against the door, feebly trying to slap some feeling back into his numb face. "Why in the world did you park out this far?"

"You should have worn a heavier coat," she snapped. The walk had not exactly been any picnic for her either!

Lee sat up and knocked the snow off his jacket. He paused and glanced around him. "What is this? A motor home?"

"Yes, it's my parents'," she muttered, trying to peel off her frozen gloves with her teeth. For the misery she was going through for Celena, she deserved a gold medal! And she still had to stand out on a corner and catch a stinking bus before the day was over.

"It's nice."

"Thanks. They like it."

"What kind of trouble are you having?"

"Trouble?" She looked at him blankly.

"Yes. You said you were having car trouble," he reminded her. He looked around him again. "I have to confess though, I thought you meant you were having trouble with that little car you drive. I don't know if I know a thing about one of these monsters."

"Oh, that's all right," she murmured guiltily. "I'm not really having car trouble."

It was his turn to look at her blankly. "You're not?"

"No, I only wanted to get you out here . . . alone."

"Well, all you had to do was ask me," he teased. "I imagine I would have come willingly."

"No, it wouldn't have been that easy."

"Wait a minute. Let me get this straight. You tricked me out to this motor home on the pretense of having car trouble, but now I find out you only wanted to get me out here . . . alone." Lee bantered with a teasing note. "Are we going camping?"

"No," she snapped crossly. Then, seeing his look of surprise at her harsh answer, she softened and added more meekly, "Just you."

## CHAPTER SIX

At any other time the pathetic look on Lee's face as he stared back at her would have made Abby laugh. But not this time.

"*I'm* going camping?" he asked incredulously.

"Uh, not just you. You—you and someone else," she grumbled. "And please don't say anything, Lee. Just let me do what I have to do and get this over with."

Abby crawled over his snowpacked form and got into the driver's seat. She hurriedly started the engine and turned on the windshield wipers before he was able to say a word. The steady slap-slap of the blades trying to keep up with the heavily falling snow was the only sound discernible as Lee sat in the middle of the floor and stared at her in disbelief.

"You want to tell me what the devil is going on around here?" he demanded.

"No. I have a strong hunch you're not going to like it," she replied as she determinedly gunned the motor and inched the motor home forward. The tires spun for a moment before they gained traction, then moved slowly out of the parking lot.

"I'm sure I won't, but don't you think I'm eventually going to find out anyway?" He cast an apprehensive glance at the worsening road conditions. "Do you know how to drive this thing?"

"Not very well," she confessed, tapping the brake with her foot several times as she approached an intersection. Even though the vehicle she was driving was very heavy, it still slid several feet before she was able to bring it to a complete halt.

"Then you better move over and let me drive," he said firmly.

He crawled over to the driver's seat and stood up as she pulled out into the line of traffic that was creeping along at a snail's pace in front of the hospital.

"No, I can't do that either," she told him sharply. She would love nothing better than to turn the responsibility of the driving over to his very capable hands, but that would be ludicrous. *I'm kidnapping the poor man, for Pete's sake!*

"Why not?" he shot back irritably.

Abby didn't reply—for a very good reason. Just as she felt his fingers digging into her shoulder blades, she looked up to see a bread truck sliding out of a side street, heading right for them! Abby slammed on her brakes, and they skidded another hair-raising twenty feet before they came to a shaky halt.

"Will you get out of that seat and let me drive before we both get killed?" he bellowed.

She bit her lower lip nervously. Lee was becoming angrier by the moment, and she was going to have to explain why she couldn't let him drive so he would shut up and sit down. He was making her a nervous wreck, hovering over the steering wheel and digging his fingers into her shoulders the way he was.

"Will you *please* just sit down? You can't drive, so you may as well forget it!"

"I demand to know what the hell is going on!" He crossed his arms belligerently and stood his ground.

"I'm kidnapping you, you dolt! Now sit!" Her eyes locked obstinately with his.

"You're what?"

"You heard me. I'm kidnapping you for the weekend! Now just go sit down and be quiet," she grumbled. That disgusting, telltale blush flooded her cheeks again, and she longed for a hole to crawl into and hide. This was most embarrassing, and she wouldn't blame Lee if he never spoke to her for the rest of her life.

His arms dropped back to his sides in mute resignation of the situation he found himself presented with. "Let me guess whose idea *this* was."

"I'm sure it won't be too hard," Abby said sheepishly.

Lee slumped down in the passenger seat and studied the road ahead of him pensively. At the moment they weren't going anywhere. There was a small car off in the ditch in front of them, and traffic was halted as two men tried to get the car back on the road.

"You know how ridiculous this is, don't you?" he asked quietly.

"I know . . . I thought the same thing, but it seems very important to Celena." She meticulously avoided his eyes as she switched off the engine to conserve fuel. But she could still feel the warmth of his gaze piercing straight through her when he spoke again.

"Why do you let Celena talk you into these disasters?"

99

"Because . . . we're friends."

"Would she do such asinine things for you?"

It hurt to hear him put Abby's exact thoughts into words. *But, yes, darn it!* she thought. *I know Celena would do the same for me if I asked her . . . which I wouldn't.* "I wouldn't ask her to," Abby murmured. "I want you to know I realize how adolescent this all seems, and I can assure you that after today I'm never going to become involved with Celena's hair-brain schemes again."

Lee sighed and ran his hands wearily through the thickness of his light-brown hair. "Where have I heard that before? Do you mind filling me in on what she's got up her sleeve this time?"

Abby knew that if he really wanted to, he could simply open the door and walk out on her. There would be nothing she could do to prevent him from leaving, especially in view of the fact that he was several feet taller and at least sixty pounds heavier than she.

Turning to face him, she sighed, too. "She only wants a chance for the two of you to be alone together this weekend," Abby coaxed gently. "She feels something very special for you, and she hopes to have a chance to persuade you to return those feelings. I know that what Celena and I are doing is devious and underhanded, but I'm asking you to understand why I'm in on it."

Lee studied her solemn face thoughtfully. "I'm supposed to spend the weekend in this motor home with Celena?"

"Yes."

A wicked, almost devilish smile began to grow at the corners of his mouth.

"What's so funny?" Abby snapped. That all-too-familiar feeling of jealousy when she thought of

100

Lee and Celena together reared its ugly head once more.

He wiped the smile off his face instantly. "Nothing."

"Don't try to kid me, Lee MacNair. It just suddenly dawned on you what's in store for you this weekend, you—you—knave!"

This time he did grin. A big, wide, knowing one. "You sound like you don't care much for the idea, Abby."

"Don't be silly. I helped give birth to it, didn't I?"

His smile was lazy as his eyes ran suggestively over her flustered face, pausing to linger for just a brief moment on the gloss shining on her trembling lower lip. "I don't know. Did you, Abby?"

Her breath caught at the intimate tone of his words, and she cursed herself a million times for letting him affect her this way. "Whether I did or didn't, the plans have already been made," she stated firmly.

"And I'm supposed to just relax and go along with them?"

"If I can keep you from bolting out the door, I think you'll have to." She looked at him apologetically. "I hope I'm not interrupting any personal plans you may have made for the weekend."

Lee sat back in his seat and crossed his arms behind his head nonchalantly. He seemed to be mulling the entire situation over at great length. Abby was beginning to wonder if he was ever going to speak again when he finally said, "No, I didn't have anything special to do this weekend. Thought I'd watch a couple of football games and catch up on some paperwork. Nothing that can't be postponed."

"Oh, it's nice of you to be so understanding." Abby smiled with relief. "Then you'll do it?"

"Spend a stormy weekend in this camper with a sexy woman?" He grinned knowledgeably. "Do I look like some sort of a fool who would pass up a golden opportunity like that? Of course I will."

She frowned irritably. "Not that it makes any difference to me, but I think you should be ashamed of yourself for having such low morals," she snapped. "You certainly didn't spend much time protesting." She hadn't wanted any trouble from him, but it burned her to a crisp to see how little resistance he had actually come up with!

"You do understand that Celena wants you to stay in this motor home . . . all weekend . . . by yourselves," she reiterated, hoping he had misunderstood what his part was to be in the whole scheme.

"Yeah, I know that's what she wants, but that's always been one of my downfalls. Crummy morals."

*The dirty rat understands perfectly!*

"Listen, now that I know I'm being kidnapped, why don't you let me drive? I'm sure you'll want me to be in condition to enjoy my—uh—fate when I get there." He grinned solicitously.

"Oh, well, we certainly wouldn't want you not to enjoy your fate, now would we?" She shot him a scathing glare and proceeded to switch seats with him.

Their bodies brushed intimately as she tried to push her way past him. Since she had a bulky jacket on and he was fully clothed in his suit, there wasn't much to be felt, but there was enough to send shivers racing up and down her spine as they both paused for a moment. Lee's arms came

102

around her waist to steady her as he gazed down into her eyes warmly.

"Ms. King, I know I've just confessed to being a man of low morals, but I really must save all my strength for this weekend," he said with a straight face.

He pulled her closer, and she could feel the power of his large frame pressed against her. She found it hard to be stern with him.

"Very funny, Mr. MacNair."

"Say, have I ever mentioned how cute you are when you're mad?" he asked abruptly.

Abby could scarcely breathe now as he held her tightly. "Um, I . . . believe you did. But only once." Her heart was pounding, and she was sure he would be able to hear it.

"I have? Well, I just wanted to be sure." He paused thoughtfully, his blue eyes drinking in her loveliness. "Did I also mention I like the color of your hair?"

"No, you've never said a thing about my hair," she replied in a voice that was beginning to grow shaky. "Although I can't imagine why you would like it. It always looks like birds have roosted in it."

He carefully studied the wind-tossed curls framing her oval face. "I don't think it looks like birds have roosted in it. I think it's about the prettiest red hair I've ever seen," he assured her softly, his fingers reaching up to hesitantly touch her hair.

If Abby could have stopped time, she would have done it at that moment.

His face was so close she could have easily pulled his warm, inviting mouth down to meet hers . . . but she didn't. She longed to throw friendship to the wind and wrap her arms around his neck and bury her face in his clean, crisp scent . . . but she didn't.

Instead, she found her voice and said what a true friend should: "Thank you. I think Celena's hair is beautiful, too. Don't you?"

He held her for another brief moment before he chuckled in disbelief and let her continue her passage to the other seat.

Sliding in behind the wheel, Lee slipped on a pair of smoke-tinted sunglasses before he restarted the engine. "I'm going to pull over on the shoulder and get around some of this traffic. Hold on."

Abby was immensely relieved that he was behind the wheel this time. She hadn't realized how tense she was until now. She leaned back and felt the tautness slowly drain out of her as Lee masterfully pulled the motor home around a line of stalled vehicles and got under way again.

"It's really getting bad," he observed a few moments later as they pulled out on the freeway. "Traffic's going to be paralyzed in another few hours."

"I hope I make it home before the public transportation is affected," Abby fretted. She was trying her best to ignore how sexy he looked in those darn sunglasses.

Lee shot her a puzzled look. "What's that got to do with the situation?"

"You and Celena are supposed to drop me off at the first bus stop," Abby explained. "Then you can continue your trip, and I'll go home."

He swore angrily under his breath. "A bus? She asked you to take a bus home?"

"I don't mind."

"You may not, but I certainly do." They continued in silence for a few minutes, then he asked, "Have you planned on what I'm going to do about a change of clothes and a toothbrush this weekend?"

"I figure you and Dad are about the same size," she told him. "Some of his clothes are stored in the closet. I bought you a new toothbrush at the store when I did the grocery shopping, and the camper is well equipped with anything else you'll need." *Of course, he won't have any of that marvelously sexy aftershave he's fond of wearing,* she thought with a touch of resentment, but providing him with that sort of ammunition was where she absolutely drew the line for Celena!

Abby noticed a tense muscle working in Lee's jaw as he signaled to make a left exit off the freeway. "Sounds like you have me fixed up like a sitting duck. It should be an interesting weekend."

"Undoubtedly," she returned dryly.

"I don't suppose your dad knows what you're up to?"

"Not exactly," she grimaced. "I just told him I wanted to borrow the motor home to get away by myself for the weekend."

"And he bought that?"

"I've got the motor home, haven't I? Besides, it isn't all that unusual. He's loaned it to me several times for the same purpose."

They picked up speed now as traffic thinned beyond the town limits.

"You're going to love the menu this weekend," she said brightly, trying to forget that in a few minutes he would be in Celena's clutches.

"I'll bet. What are we having, nachos and bean dip?"

"I bought nachos *and* potato chips," she assured

him. "There are hot dogs in the refrigerator, pizza in the freezer, and frozen burritos. Doesn't that sound yummy?"

Lee cast her a look of distaste. "Is that supposed to be the menu or a torture session?"

"The menu. Why? Did I forget something?"

"Not one thing," he replied. "It sounds like a complete gastric nightmare. Where's the fudge and peanut brittle?"

"Oh, darn. I did forget that." She had walked right by the candy section!

"Thank God."

Abby frowned at his flagging enthusiasm. "Oh, gosh, Lee, I forgot you don't eat junk food." Junk food was Abby's main staple, so when she was shopping she selected what she would normally buy herself. "Anyway, I seriously doubt if you'll be all that concerned about what you eat this weekend," she accused with a touch of sarcasm.

"I may be comatose after meals like those and pass out in a corner somewhere," he couldn't resist teasing.

"Lee, you've turned the wrong way," Abby said a few minutes later as he turned off the highway. Celena's turnoff was at least five more miles down the road.

"I know that," he stated calmly.

"I think there's a side road up ahead where we can turn around."

"I know where I am," he returned casually, reaching up to adjust the rearview mirror.

Moments later the side road came into view.

"Slow down, the road is right . . . Lee, you missed it again," she scolded impatiently.

The snow was falling heavier by the minute, and it was growing increasingly hard to make out any of the landmarks. This storm was undoubtedly going to turn out to be a full-blown late fall blizzard.

"No, I didn't. I had no intention of turning there."

Abby glanced at him apprehensively. "Celena is probably standing at her door waiting for us this very minute," she pointed out uneasily.

"That's too bad. From now on you ladies better check with me before you make plans for *my* weekend," he announced in a frosty tone.

"But you said you were going along with this," Abby reminded him hastily.

"I said I was willing to spend a weekend in a camper with a sexy woman."

The camper slid around another corner and headed for the small lake that lay about three miles to the south of the city.

"Just what do you mean by that?" Abby demanded.

"It means that I intend to choose the woman I'm spending the weekend with, Ms. King, and I choose you."

"Me?" Abby nearly jumped out of her seat. "You can't choose me! Celena will strangle us."

"The last person in the world I'm afraid of is Celena," he replied defiantly. "And Matt isn't going to be too crazy about this either, but that's their problem. I have enough of my own right now!"

"You can't do this!" she protested indignantly. "My father will have the police out looking for me."

"Why? He'll think you're off somewhere by yourself in this storm for the weekend."

"Then Celena will tell him differently!"

"Now, I really can't picture Celena telling your

father the true story of what you two had hatched up for this weekend," Lee chided. "No, when we don't show up and she can't reach me on the phone, she's smart enough to figure out that you and I are together somewhere stranded in the storm. She won't say anything to your father."

"Lee MacNair, I hope you realize this is kidnapping in the first degree!"

His grin was defiantly wicked now. "Yeah. Clever of me, huh? I'm kidnapping you now."

"You'll never get away with it," she warned. *The nerve of this guy!*

"Why not? You were more than willing to do it to me."

"But that was different. Celena wanted you—"

"That's the problem," he interrupted sharply. "Celena wanted. Not me." His blue eyes turned tender as he glanced over at her. "I'd like to get it through your thick skull that I would like to be the caretaker of my own fate. Especially where my future happiness is concerned, Abby."

"I think for both our sakes you better just turn this vehicle around and head back to town. I'll call Celena and tell her I couldn't trick you into coming with me, and we'll both forget this ever happened." If Abby was forced to spend an entire weekend with Lee MacNair, she was afraid her friendship and loyalty to Celena would fly right out the window.

"You worry too much about what other people want. What do you want?" he snapped.

Abby was beginning to suspect she wanted to spend a lifetime with him—but not under these uncertain conditions. Not when Celena still loomed bleakly on the horizon.

"Abby thinks it's better to go home," she stated again firmly.

"And Lee doesn't want to." He suddenly gunned the motor and deliberately steered the motor home for the nearest ditch. Seconds later, the vehicle tipped and came to a sudden halt.

"Oh, my," Lee groaned in mock dismay, "I'm afraid we're stuck . . . probably for the whole weekend."

Abby's mouth dropped open in disbelief. "You deliberately put us in this ditch!"

"I did not!" he lied blatantly. "Can I help it if it's so slick out that I can't drive this thing?"

"You were doing a perfectly good job until a few seconds ago," she said angrily.

"So," he dismissed with an indifferent shrug of his broad shoulders, "I'm not perfect." He glanced around at the plush, homey interior of the motor home. "I can think of worse ways to be stranded, other than alone . . . with all the comforts of home . . . with each other." His eyes drifted suggestively back to hers. "Can't you?"

"Surely you're aware that this road isn't traveled much this time of year, and with the weather the way it is, it may be days before anyone finds us?"

He grinned smugly. "I've thought of that. But we have everything we need for a couple of days. Isn't that what you told me earlier?"

"You have everything you and *Celena* needed. I'm supposed to be on a bus on my way home!"

"Then I'm sure you and I have everything we need."

Abby slumped back in her chair and groaned.

"Just look at it this way," he argued. "Sitting here in this warm camper sure beats standing out there in the storm, freezing your tush off . . . waiting for a bus as your good friend Celena wanted you to do." His voice told her he didn't really think Celena was a good friend.

She turned a skeptical eye in his direction. "She is my good friend. She wouldn't have objected to me taking a cab home. I *wanted* to take the bus. I *want* to see the two of you together so I can get on with my life!"

"You are a real turnip brain," he noted with a tolerant shake of his head. He took off his sunglasses and laid them on the dashboard. "All the king's horsemen and all the king's men, can't put Lee and Celena together again. Face it, Abby, this plan failed just like all the others. For the last time, I am no longer interested in Celena Fenton."

"But she wants—"

"But I don't," he interrupted her. "Now, if you don't mind, I'm going to get comfortable."

"I don't mind, but I don't see how you're going to get comfortable," she chided. And for the first time she started to believe he was telling her the truth concerning his feelings. "In case you haven't noticed, we're tilted."

They both looked around the interior of the camper, their hearts sinking when they realized that although they had luxurious surroundings, they were going to be living on a twenty-degree angle all weekend.

"I'm sure we'll make do," Lee said. "How about fixing one of those 'yummy' meals you've planned? I missed lunch today and I'm starving."

"Now, just a minute. I have no intention of being your cook all weekend," she announced coolly.

"Oh, but you have to, because you're the kidnappee now." He winked and tweaked her nose. "Besides, I'm sure I couldn't do justice to a frozen burrito, no matter how hard I tried."

Abby sighed hopelessly and made her way toward the kitchen. Trying to live in a tilted camper and avoid his company all weekend was not exactly going to be her idea of fun.

Lee loosened his tie and stretched out on the sofa as she noisily rummaged around in the kitchen.

"Haven't you got any canned soup?" he asked with a tired yawn.

"There might be." She opened the storage cabinet and peered in at its contents.

"Yes, there's tomato, vegetable, and split pea."

He paused for a moment. "I don't like any of those."

*So, he's going to be difficult,* Abby fumed. *Well, let him. I can be just as difficult as he can any day of the week.* "This is not a hotel, and I'm not room service. It's either tomato, vegetable, or split pea soup *or* the frozen burrito. Take your pick."

"Is there any potato soup?"

"No. Tomato, vegetable, or split pea."

"I really don't like any of those—"

"Lee!"

"Vegetable!"

Abby could tell this was going to be a long weekend.

Dinner was ready in fifteen minutes, and they sat at the table and tried to eat their soup.

"Just look at this," she said disgustedly. Her bowl was so tilted some of the soup was spilling over the side.

"You have to pick up the bowl and hold it in your hands," he said sensibly. "Like this." He picked up

111

his bowl and made a big production of expertly spooning the soup into his mouth.

"Big deal. So you can stick soup in your mouth."

"Now you're getting cranky."

"Why shouldn't I? I'm tired and I want to go home. I don't want to sit here with Celena's boyfriend and have him teach me how to eat soup in a tilted camper."

"Just dry up and eat your soup."

"You eat the soup. I'm going to fix myself a burrito," she snapped.

Five minutes later she sat alone on the sofa, totally ignoring him while he ate the soup and she ate her burrito.

Shoving away his empty bowl a few minutes later, Lee eyed her dinner hungrily. "I've changed my mind. The soup isn't going to fill me up. Fix me one of those burritos," he ordered.

"Fix it yourself."

"Come on, Abby. I don't know the first thing about fixing one of those things," he grumbled. "Don't give me any more hassle. Just fix the burrito."

Shooting him a scathing glare, she slid off the sofa and marched to the refrigerator, retrieved the burrito, and shoved it in the microwave.

He sat like a king on his throne waiting to be served as she went back to the sofa to finish her dinner. Moments later, when the timer signaled that the burrito was done, he glanced over at her and snapped, "It's finished."

"Can't you reach over and take it out? That should be within your realm of abilities."

"You're closer," he returned absently.

Laying down her half-eaten dinner, she rose, walked to the microwave, and opened the door.

"Can you step on it a little?" he groused, thumbing through the magazine he had picked up earlier. "A man could starve to death waiting for you to fix something to eat."

She eyed him in disbelief. Who does he think he is? "Sorry. One burrito coming up!" she shouted, going into action.

Lee glanced up and his eyes widened as he saw her pull her arm back and hurl the beany concoction in his direction. He ducked seconds before the corn tortilla flew across the room and landed in the middle of his plate.

"Now, that's disgusting," he said curtly.

"Want some hot sauce?" she asked, ignoring his censorship. "Yes, sir! Hot sauce coming right up!" Once more he was forced to duck as a jar of sauce careened by his head and splattered into tiny pieces when it hit the wall.

"Good Lord! Have you gone berserk?" he asked incredulously as he tried to mop up the sticky mess with a napkin. "All I wanted was a simple burrito—"

"How about something to drink?" she interrupted. "Sure! Got to have something to wash that burrito down with!"

This time he hit the floor in a panic as a couple of cans of soda came barreling in his direction.

"Ice? Sure! We've got plenty. Help yourself!"

Cubes came raining down on the table as Lee cowered beneath it, wondering if she had completely jumped the track.

As her anger finally subsided, Abby paused and shot him a challenging look. "Anything else I can get you?"

"No . . . thanks. This will do just fine." He grinned lamely.

Picking up her cold burrito, she marched back to the bedroom to continue eating in peace.

*From now on I'll fix my own meals,* Lee decided as he proceeded to absently dip his burrito into some of the stray hot sauce that had splashed on the table. *Eating with her can be dangerous.*

Hours later they were watching the small twelve-inch television in silence, keeping their ears tuned to the mounting wind. Inside the camper it was cozy and warm, and Abby felt no fear—at least not from the storm.

Around ten, Lee walked over and opened the camper door to peer out at the storm. Huge drifts had already nearly buried the motor home as the snow continued to mount steadily.

"This is one of the worst storms I've ever seen," he commented as he shut the door. "They might not find us for weeks." He shot her a tormenting grin, which she promptly ignored.

"The weatherman has updated the storm to a blizzard now," she mumbled sleepily. "I think I'll take a shower and go to bed."

"That sounds good to me. Where do we sleep?"

Her eyes flew open. "We?"

"Well, unless I miscounted, there's just you and me in here."

"The table folds out into a bed," she returned sweetly. "You sleep there."

He smiled as she sailed regally by him, heading for the bathroom.

"I can't. It has beans and hot sauce all over it."

"Tough. I guess you'll have to get off your can and clean it up . . . because *I'm* certainly not."

"Yell when you're through in there," he called

as she shut the door in his face. "And don't use all the hot water!"

Thirty minutes later she emerged, her sweet floral scent floating through the camper. "You can have the bathroom now."

"Thanks. I thought you had retired in there." Lee's eyes dismally surveyed the thick terrycloth robe she was wearing. "Where did you come up with that thing?"

"I always keep this robe in the camper." She looked down to see what he was so upset about. "Were you perhaps expecting Loni Anderson to emerge?"

"No. Nor was I expecting Phyllis Diller. Couldn't we hit a happy medium?"

The robe *was* pretty disreputable-looking, but it was warm and comfortable. She smothered a smile when she thought of the sexy gowns Celena had undoubtedly packed for this weekend.

"You should have let the plans go through as scheduled," she taunted with a snooty look. "Celena shopped one whole afternoon for lingerie for the weekend. I'm sure you would have loved her wardrobe."

"I'm sure I would, but I'll try to make do with yours." He scowled playfully at her and disappeared into the small bathroom.

She was already cuddled in her bed when he came out fifteen minutes later.

"Good night, turnip brain," he grumbled as he passed her bed.

"Good night, Humpty Dumpty," she replied.

A few minutes later she heard him groan in disgust.

"Where the hell is my blank—"

A blanket, pillow, and sheet came sailing out of

the bedroom and hit him in the face before he finished his sentence.

Chuckling softly to herself, she heard him make up his bed and climb in.

Just imagine! She was spending the night . . . however innocently . . . with Lee MacNair!

A tiny, satisfied smile hovered at the corners of Abby's mouth. She had to admit she liked that thought.

*Well, he may sleep,* she noted irritably thirty minutes later as she lay and listened to his loud snores, *but it's obvious I'm not going to.*

# CHAPTER SEVEN

Something cold was trickling down the side of her neck. Abby unconsciously brushed away the frosty moisture and burrowed deeper into the warm blankets.

Again something frigid touched her skin, only it oozed slowly down the back of her neck this time. Wiping irritably at the spot, she murmured a cross rebuke at whatever was disturbing her peaceful sleep. She could hear the wind still howling, and she didn't want to get up yet.

An amused male chuckle made one eye fly open to encounter a mischievously smiling Lee with a huge, dripping snowball in his hand.

"Good morning."

"Oh . . . Lee," she muttered drowsily.

*Gads!* He was sitting on the bed next to her, cleanly shaven and dressed in one of her dad's red-and-black plaid wool shirts, reeking of soap and a different, but equally stimulating, aftershave, looking at *her.*

Her hand flew self-consciously up to the tangled mass of strawberry curls, and she groaned adamantly. "Lee!"

His hand came back up to playfully let the snowball plop big, fat, cold drops of water down the

117

front of the terrycloth robe she had slept in last night.

Hurriedly jerking the blankets over her head, Abby tunneled her way to the middle of the bed, away from his teasing antics.

One large, very cold hand swiftly followed her under the blankets and proceeded to tickle her.

"Lee, stop it!" she gasped a few minutes later when his assault failed to let up. She slapped out at his hands and came in contact with a mushy puddle of cold water.

They wrestled around on the bed for a few moments, their laughter contagiously building.

"If you don't get out of that bed, I'm going to pick you up and toss you out in a snowbank," he threatened as she scooted to the very foot of the bed and hovered there.

"I don't *want* to get up," came the muffled reply.

"We've had a good eight hours of sleep," he said. "Time to rise and shine! We're burning daylight, woman."

"You've had a good eight hours of sleep," she corrected him in a cross tone. "I haven't been asleep but a couple of hours!"

She crawled back to the top of the bed and threw the covers off. Her hair was standing straight up now, and she knew one of her cheeks still had the slight indentation of the chenille bedspread imprinted in it. She knew that because it always did when she slept in the motor home.

Lee made an exaggerated pretense of jumping back as he surveyed her rumpled, grumpy appearance. "My, you look stunning this morning, Ms. King."

"I can do without your comments this early in

the day," she grimaced. She really should make an effort to do something about her disreputable appearance, but at the moment it seemed like too much trouble.

"Think a cup of coffee would improve your less-than-sunny disposition?" Lee asked as he stood up and went over to the kitchen cabinet to retrieve a cup for her.

"How did you manage to dress and make coffee without me hearing you?" She propped herself up on her pillows and waited as he poured the steaming liquid into the cup and brought it over to her. Abby took a cautious sip as he settled himself back down beside her and reclaimed his own cup.

"I walk like a cat," he finally replied. "Besides, you were sleeping like a log. I don't think an atom bomb could have disturbed you."

"Like a cat, my foot," she scoffed. "It was because of you I didn't get to sleep until nearly daylight this morning."

"Me?"

"Yes, you! You snore."

"I do not! In fact, I don't think I slept but a couple of hours last night, myself," he protested.

"Don't try to feed me that," she taunted. "I can personally swear you slept your full eight hours without the slightest interruption."

He grinned and reached over to ruffle her already uncivilized hair. "I'm sorry if I disturbed you." Two large dimples appeared enticingly in his cheeks as he smiled back at her.

"I'm exaggerating a little," she confessed, "but I really didn't sleep very well."

"Oh? Why not?"

Abby noticed how strong and masculine his hands were as she watched him bring the cup to his lips and take another sip of coffee. They didn't look like the hands of a man who sat behind a desk all day but more like one who worked outdoors most of the time.

"I think it was the sound of the wind," she mused. "It was almost eerie the way it rattled the camper all night."

"Yeah, I noticed that, too." He lifted the curtain beside her bed, and they both peered out into the blinding whiteness. "It seems to be tapering off a bit," he noted a few minutes later. The curtain dropped back in place, and a strained silence seemed to suddenly fill the small room.

"Well, if you'll turn your head, I want to make a fast trip to the bathroom to brush my teeth and see if I can do anything with this mop of hair," she said as she handed him her cup.

He turned his head dutifully as she scurried out of bed and disappeared behind the folding door.

"I don't see why it was necessary to turn my head," he complained. "That robe you're wearing nearly swallows you. I can't see a thing."

"Have you been trying to see things?" she bantered lightly through a mouthful of toothpaste.

"You bet your life I have. Every chance I get. But you've been real successful in hiding all those sexy curves I know are lurking under there."

Moments later she came out of the bathroom and climbed back on the bed. She began to absently pull a brush through her tangled hair as he leaned back against the wall and watched her.

"Lee?"

"Yes?"

"Why?"

"Why what?"

"Why did you . ." She paused and took a deep

breath, then started again. "Why did you choose me to spend the weekend with?"

That thought had skipped in and out of her mind as she had lain awake last night and listened to the storm. Even though he denied he was seriously interested in Celena, why, when he could have had her very "willing" company this weekend, did he choose to spend his time with plain, not-so-very-interesting Abby? It puzzled her.

The blue of his eyes darkened with tenderness as he smiled and said softly, "Why does that surprise you?"

"Because you could have had . . . someone so much more interesting."

He moved off the bed to place his cup on the kitchen counter, then turned to look out the window.

"I think the time has come for us to have a little talk, Abby." His tone was so solemn now it worried her. Lee still had his back to her as he gazed unseeingly out the camper window. "I thought we should spend this weekend together to get a few things straight."

Abby hung her head shamefully. "I'm sorry I've caused you so much trouble, Lee. I'm certainly old enough to know better, but . . ." Her voice trailed off meekly.

"But you're too gullible. And too good a friend," he finished for her. "Maybe we both are. But the time has come for us to face what we're up against and get it out in the open."

"I told you I have no intentions of helping Celena again after this—"

"I'm not talking about you helping Celena," he interrupted. He slowly turned from the window to face her. "I'm talking about us."

121

Their eyes met for one heart-stopping moment. Abby didn't have the fortitude to play coy and ask him what he meant by "us"—she knew.

"Oh, Lee, I've tried very hard to fight my attraction to you," she murmured painfully. She was dismayed to find tears welling up in her eyes. She feared he would think she was a basket case before this conversation ended, because it was a subject too close to her heart.

"And I've tried to fight mine for you. For the last few weeks I've kept telling myself I would not allow myself to do anything concerning you and jeopardize Matt's friendship." He quickly retraced his steps to the bed and sat down. Reaching out, he tenderly tipped her face. "Abby, you have to be completely honest with me. No more games. What exactly do you feel for Matt?"

"Nothing but friendship," she returned without a moment's hesitation. "I've always enjoyed Matt's company . . . until lately. We've always laughed and had fun together, but that's as far as it goes. I've tried and tried to tell him there can never be anything more, but he refuses to believe me. He feels that, with enough time, he can make me fall in love with him."

Lee's smile was one of sheer relief. "That's what I was hoping you'd say, but it only compounds the problem."

"The problem?"

Lee reached for her hand and brought it up to meet his lips, his eyes locking with hers affectionately. "I'm in love with you, Abby King, and I'm getting damn tired of fighting it."

"Oh, Lee . . ." Her words caught with unexpected emotion.

"And don't try to tell me you don't feel the same

thing I'm feeling, because you're not a very good liar."

Hot tears began to slip down her cheeks as she gazed into the blue eyes she had seen so often in her dreams. She didn't know what to say. She was tired of fighting it, too. But what other choice was there? "I had no idea you felt the same way," she returned in a shaky whisper.

"Oh, Abby, honey. You want to know something ironic? From the first time I met you at that hospital dance, you struck a chord somewhere in my heart. Oh, I know at first I was attracted to Celena, but that attraction didn't take long to wear off. And when it did, Matt was already claiming you as his property." His eyes pleaded with her for understanding. "What was I supposed to do?"

Abby shook her head mutely, the tears coming faster and running down her cheeks.

"This isn't easy for me to admit, and it certainly doesn't make me out to be a very nice person, but all these weeks I've continued to see Celena . . . well it's all been an excuse to see you."

"Oh, Lee." Abby was growing more miserable by the moment. It was both exhilarating and depressing to hear him admit his feelings for her. "I can't help it. I feel exactly the same way about you."

"You don't know how relieved I am to hear you say that," he confessed in a husky voice.

"I've been afraid I've been too obvious."

"I wish you had been *more* obvious." He groaned and reached to take her in his arms.

All the barriers they had both so carefully constructed began to crumble, and Abby suddenly found herself about to do something she had only dreamed about from the first day she had set eyes

123

on Lee MacNair. She reached over and pulled his mouth slowly toward hers, their eyes meeting in silent surrender.

"I hope you don't mind me going a little bit crazy, but I've wanted to do this for so long . . ." she whispered just moments before their lips touched.

Her mouth touched his, sending tiny tingles of fire racing through her body.

"Not at all," he replied with a soft moan.

This time he took the initiative and his kiss was bold, hungry, and so very welcome. They both lay back in the soft folds of the blankets, and Abby wrapped her arms more tightly around his neck.

When their lips parted many long minutes later, Lee continued to shower kisses over her face, glorying in the fact that she was at long last in his arms.

"Do you have any idea how many times I've wanted to do what I'm doing right now?" he murmured, hungrily kissing her again before she could answer.

Burying her fingers in the thickness of his hair, she moaned softly as his kiss deepened and his tongue searched intimately for hers. She could feel his growing need for her through the thin blanket that separated them, powerful and intense, and she knew they were both playing with fire. They were too secluded, too cozy, and much too prone to forget reality.

Lee's hands were making exploring forages under the blanket now, sending shivers of rippling delight through her as she softly murmured his name and broke away from his ardent kiss.

"Lee . . . this is still wrong." Her heart wasn't

in her plea, and he heard the wistfulness in her voice.

"No, not for us, it isn't. Right now there's just you and me, Abby . . . no one else . . . don't spoil it, please." His mouth captured hers again in another long, searing kiss, blotting out all coherent reasoning.

But a few minutes later, when his breathing had grown labored and his kisses more insistent, she knew she had to put a stop to this madness while there was still time.

"Lee"—she pushed him gently away once more —"I don't want it to be like this. Not with Celena and Matt hovering over our heads."

Lee moaned and pulled her closer to him, burying his face in her hair. "I'm tired of worrying about two people we don't love, Abby! This is crazy. Am I expected to ignore my feelings for you simply because another guy thinks he has some sort of claim on you?"

"I know it sounds ridiculous."

"It's more than ridiculous. It's downright irritating."

"We do have a problem, don't we?" Abby sighed and relaxed in his arms as he gradually regained his control.

"Yes, I'm afraid so."

They lay in each other's arms, drowsy and content for a few moments, each one lost in their own thoughts.

Finally, Abby broke the silence. "Have you and Matt known each other long?"

"We were roommates for four years in college . . . yeah, Matt's been a good friend for a long time."

"I know," she commiserated. "Celena and I have the same sort of friendship."

Rolling over with her in his arms, he positioned her on top of him and nuzzled the tip of her nose. "This is one of the hardest things I've ever done . . . I want you to know that. If it were up to me, I'm afraid my friendship with Matt would have gone straight down the tubes about ten minutes ago."

He kissed her possessively for a moment before he continued. "But in respect for your friendship with Celena, I'll let you decide which way it would be best to handle this. But only because of you, Abby. I want you and I'm tired of being patient. You have to know that." He moved against her to prove his point, and she had to admit she was tired of being patient, too.

"I don't know what the answer is, Lee, but there has to be one."

"I think the only way to handle this is with complete honesty. I'm for laying our cards flat on the table with Matt and Celena. Granted, they aren't going to like it, but that can't be helped. We didn't deliberately set out to fall in love. The longer this thing goes on, the harder it will be for everyone concerned."

"I'm a coward, Lee. Even though she irritates me at times, I don't want to lose Celena's friendship. We've been through too many good times together to let this one madness she's experiencing get in the way."

"I know, honey. But you're too good for your own sake. I don't want to lose Matt's friendship either, but if they're really the friends we value them to be, they'll understand."

"When Celena and Matt find out we've been

marooned together for an entire weekend, the problem may solve itself," she sighed, stealing another long kiss from him.

"I'm in favor of giving them more ammunition for the kill," he whispered in her ear. "And I can personally assure you I will if you don't stop kissing me that way."

Another round of necking was touched off, and it was twenty minutes before they could force themselves to regain control of their spiraling emotions.

"I want you to know I've never controlled myself with such admiration," Lee breathed in a voice ragged with wanting when his patience had reached its limit. "And if we don't get off this bed and get our minds on something else, I'm not going to be held responsible for my actions."

"I want you every bit as badly, but I think we'll like ourselves so much more if we clear the air with Matt and Celena before we make love."

"Make love to you?" He sighed and kissed her tenderly. "The mere thought makes me go weak."

"I just want it to be right," she explained softly.

"Then you better be out of this bed by the time I count to three," he warned. "One."

Abby grinned at him impishly.

"Two."

Her confidence began to waver as he started methodically unbuttoning his shirt.

"Three."

She was on her feet, scurrying for the bathroom.

Lee cooked bacon and eggs for breakfast as Abby got dressed. They lingered over coffee, their eyes hungrily devouring each other. Often, they found themselves stealing short kisses one from the other across the table and wishing for more.

After the dishes were washed, they watched more television but soon grew tired of children's cartoons and weather bulletins. There were several puzzles in the motor home, and they worked companionably on one large one the rest of the morning.

After lunch they lay down on the sofa and kissed until they both dropped off to sleep, wrapped in each other's arms. When they awoke a couple of hours later, they were both beginning to come down with cabin fever.

Around three they could stand it no longer and decided to go for a walk around the lake.

After rummaging through the closets, Abby came up with enough warm clothing to allow them to go outside.

The snow was still falling lightly as they stepped out of the camper, pausing briefly to get their bearings.

"I think we need snowshoes and sled dogs," Lee grumbled as they trudged through the huge drifts.

"It's marvelous, isn't it?" Abby threw her arms out and took a deep breath of the crisp, invigorating air.

A snowball came whizzing over and hit her squarely in the face. Moments later the air was alive with flying missiles as they both tried to bombard each other into submission.

Their laughter could be heard ringing out over the stark white countryside as they tumbled about in the snow like two children at play.

Abby had just started to roll the beginnings of a snowman when Lee lunged at her, and they both rolled down a small ravine. They tumbled over and over before they came to a halt, both of them packed with snow over every square inch of their clothing.

Before she could speak, Lee was on top of her, his mouth claiming hers.

"I could stay here and kiss you the rest of my life," he told her with a contented sigh when their lips finally parted. "By the way, Ms. King, did I happen to mention this morning that I'm very much in love with you?"

Her smile was loving as she tenderly traced the outline of his face. "Only about sixteen times."

"Only sixteen? Well, that isn't nearly enough. I love you, Abby King. Multiply that by a thousand and stick it in your pocket."

She couldn't help but laugh when she thought of the times when she knew she had irritated him. "Have you forgotten you've always accused me of being a little bit nutsy?" she reminded him with a laugh. "And don't forget, I love junk food and working on committees and being a pest to the nth degree when it comes to something that's important to me."

"Well, I hate screwballs and junk food, I readily admit I detest any sort of committees, and I avoid pests like the plague"—their mouths touched lightly—"but I'm willing to work on making you a tolerable human being."

She picked up a wad of snow and stuffed it down his collar.

A massive snow fight followed, and when they had finally exhausted themselves they rolled over and lay on their backs and gazed up into the gray, overcast sky. Puffy flakes of snow coated their eyelashes as they blinked and laughed at one another.

"I haven't enjoyed a day like this since I was a

kid," he confessed when their laughter finally died. "You're good for me."

She rolled over and touched his cold lips with the tip of her finger. "Thanks, I want to be . . . for the rest of my life."

The look that came into his eyes was intoxicating to Abby. Then he pulled her closer, and they sealed their confessions with a deep kiss.

"I don't care if they don't find us until spring," Lee declared zealously, rolling to his side and propping himself up on his elbow to stare at her.

"I wish there was a telephone nearby," Abby fretted.

"For heaven's sake, why? That's the last thing in the world I would wish for," Lee said incredulously.

Abby smiled. She had forgotten that his life at the hospital was filled with ringing telephones and mountains of paperwork.

"I'd like to let Dad know I'm all right."

"And if I know you, you're worrying about Celena, too."

"Yes, I know she must be nearly frantic, and Matt has probably been ringing my phone off the hook wondering where I am."

"I'm sure Gerald Metcalf will pacify Celena. She's dropped the hint she's been dating him occasionally," Lee observed sourly.

Abby giggled. "She's only dating him to make you jealous. Are you?"

"Only when he turns his greedy eyes in your direction," Lee returned curtly.

"He doesn't know I'm alive," Abby protested with a disbelieving laugh.

"The heck he doesn't! I saw the way he was sizing you up that night at the pizza parlor."

130

"He was? I didn't notice . . . but then I was too busy sizing you up," she confessed with a sly grin.

"Yeah?" He turned over and took her in his arms once again. "I thought I caught you leering at me a couple of times."

"Leering?" She pulled away. "I was *not* leering at you," she denied indignantly as he grabbed her again and rolled over in the snow once more. "Okay! Maybe I was . . . just a little."

When they came to a halt, they were kissing again. "We'd better take that walk around the lake while we're still able to," he said huskily as their passion flared brightly again.

"I think you're right."

Arm in arm they wandered toward the shore of the frozen lake, pausing occasionally to admire various wildlife foraging for their daily food.

As they made their way slowly around the perimeter of the small lake, they found themselves talking about their childhoods. They discussed at length their beliefs, what their dreams were, where they both hoped to be in the next twenty years; and once again they talked about how many children they would like to have someday. The conversation gradually switched to more general themes such as favorite songs and movies.

At one point they found themselves spending the better part of a half hour arguing if Burt Reynolds was really talented or just darn good-looking.

Abby began to grow tired, so Lee found a fallen log and they both sat down to rest. He sat behind her and pulled her flush to the length of his body as she sighed and snuggled back against him in complete contentment.

"I never want this day to end," she said sadly.

"I don't either." He nuzzled her neck as they

131

watched a couple of wild ducks swim on a small part of the lake that was not frozen solid. The snow had trickled off to an occasional spurt now and then, and the temperature was dropping fast.

"We should be getting back to the motor home," he chided as he felt her body begin to tremble even through the heavy layer of clothing she had on. "Our clothes are wet, and I'm afraid you'll catch a cold." He pulled her fur-lined hat down closer to her flushed cheeks in a protective, loving gesture.

"Just a few more minutes," she pleaded, catching his hand and bringing it to her cheek.

Together they watched the shadows lengthen, and then dusk began to fade into darkness. The cold finally forced them to make their way back to the warmth of the camper.

Abby felt a sense of desolation as they left the beauty of the snow-covered lake. The storm was over now. With any luck she would have one more day with Lee before they would return to the real world.

It was strange. It seemed they had been together so much longer than the one brief day they had spent together. In such a short time she had come to know Lee MacNair better than any man she had ever met in her life. She didn't want this time with him to end. When they returned home, she knew without a doubt she would look back on this time as a very special one in her life, because she was quite certain that neither Matt nor Celena would gracefully accept what had happened.

"You can have the shower first," Lee offered as they stomped the snow off their boots and entered the warmth of the motor home. "I'll get one of those awful pizzas in the oven for our dinner."

Abby gratefully accepted his offer and made her way to the back of the camper. By the time she was finished, he had their dinner baking in the oven and a hot pot of coffee perking on the stove before he went to take his shower.

When he emerged ten minutes later, her breath caught and she almost dropped the towel she was drying her hair with.

Lee had not put his shirt on yet. He was still wiping the moisture lingering in the mat of dark hair that spread in a thick carpet across his broad chest.

Sensing her eyes riveted on him, he glanced and paused momentarily. Then, to her dismay, he smiled one of those knee-watering sexy smiles that he was such an expert at and asked softly, "See anything you like?"

"I'm afraid I like everything I see," she whispered dismally.

Laying his towel down on the kitchen counter, he held out his arms to her, and she went willingly into them.

"You didn't really think we'd make it through this weekend without making love, did you?" he murmured, noting the way her body was trembling next to his.

"No, but I still think it's wrong . . ." Her words faltered as he reached up and switched off the light. Catching her up in his arms, he carried her over to the bed.

"And I say that's a matter of opinion." He casually removed his pants, then slipped into bed with her. His hands gently removed the robe she was wearing and tossed it on the floor before his mouth came down to meet hers.

"Well, if this is fate . . . you haven't even given

133

me time to enjoy it," she teased with a shaky laugh. But her hands were busy discovering all the things about Lee they had always wanted to know.

"This isn't a one-shot, never-to-be-experienced-again sort of thing," he whispered, kissing her with tender possession. "This is only our beginning, my love, and I admit I'm overeager, but I've waited a long time for you, Abby King."

They kissed again, slowly letting down all reserves and inhibitions. It seemed to Abby that someone higher up had made one special man named Lee MacNair, then kindly given him to her.

And then, that special man made love to her. Powerfully, masterfully, and in a way she had never before experienced.

Maybe it was right . . . maybe it was wrong; only time would tell. But for now she could only cling to him as he took them to the very realm of pleasures and made her totally and completely his.

Later they lay in each other's arms, basking in the warm afterglow of what had just taken place.

Lee sighed and rolled over to face her in the darkness. "Hi."

"Hi."

"I love you."

"I love you, too."

For the next few moments they allowed themselves the luxury of just kissing.

"I think the pizza's burning." Lee sat up and sniffed the air.

"Oh, gosh. It is!"

Abby bounded out of bed and turned off the oven. "How about some nachos and cheese dip?"

"No, thanks. I'm not real crazy about the way you serve dinner," he chided, referring to her tan-

134

trum of the night before. "Besides, I'm not even hungry now." He yawned and pulled her close when she rejoined him on the bed. "This is better than eating any day."

"About last night . . . I'm sorry. You made me mad."

"I· gathered as much."

She smiled and snuggled down closer to him. "I'm not hungry either. I'll probably sleep like a log tonight," Abby added in a sleepy voice. "All this fresh air and very little sleep . . . Oh, Lee, I hope we haven't made a big mistake." Reality was beginning to replace the earlier glow, and she felt miserable. "I feel guilty . . . don't you?"

The sounds of his relaxed snoring reached her ears, and she shook her head in disbelief; obviously not.

# CHAPTER EIGHT

By late Sunday afternoon Lee and Abby could hear the distant sound of a snowplow working its way in their direction.

Earlier that morning a farmer with a four-wheel drive pickup had been out checking his stock when he came upon the marooned motor home. He had promptly offered to take the stranded couple back into town, but they had quickly refused his offer. Abby and Lee wanted these last few hours together, and the farmer had left, promising to send a snowplow and wrecker in their direction by evening.

The day had flown swiftly by as the contented couple once again played in the snow and walked the shores of the lake one final time.

Now, they were trying unsuccessfully to ignore the sounds of approaching help.

"I wish that snowplow would run out of gas before it got here." Lee wadded his napkin and pitched it in the direction of the wastebasket, missing it completely as he had all weekend.

"Lee, I'm trying to clean up," Abby scolded. Her nerves were on edge from the prospect of going back home and facing Matt and Celena. She reached over and secured the discarded paper and placed it where it belonged.

"Sorry." He patted his lap invitingly. "Come over here for a minute."

"No. You run the sweeper like you promised."

"I will . . . but not until you come over here," he wheedled.

"If I come over there, neither one of us will get any work done."

"Abby, that snowplow is going to reach us in another hour." He looked like a small boy pleading for one last cookie as he held out his hand coaxingly.

Abby had to admit she was a pretty soft touch when it came to Lee MacNair, so she wasn't a bit surprised to find herself nestled on his lap a few moments later.

"Mmm. Isn't this nicer than cleaning the sink?"

"I suppose you could make it that way," she teased suggestively.

And he did, kissing her deeply.

"I want to thank you for asking me to share your weekend," she whispered when they broke apart a few minutes later.

"I want to thank you for sharing it with me," he returned softly, stealing another long kiss from her.

Moments later they found themselves back over on the bed, their clothes melting away one by one.

"Lee . . . the snowplow will be here soon," Abby reminded him as his hands grew more exploring and bold.

"Not for a while."

"We should be ashamed of ourselves. Last night was spontaneous, but today is—"

"Ours," Lee finished, kissing her temple as he laid her back and proceeded to make love to her once more.

"You make me lose all power of reasoning." She shivered as he teased along her earlobe with the tip of his tongue.

"Good. I plan on keeping it that way."

"Oh, Lee, we have so many things to talk about. We should be using this time to try and decide what we're going to do about us."

"I know what we're going to do," he whispered.

"That isn't what I—" Her words were cut short as he took complete control and silenced her with his kisses.

They became lost in the pleasure of being together. This time, Lee took his time making love to her, teaching her the ways of pleasing and being pleased, and she realized once more how very much she had grown to love this man.

"You're something else," he murmured much later as he held her tightly in his arms. They had both experienced a powerful and explosive end to their lovemaking, and it had left them feeling drained and lazy. "Now, admit it. Aren't you glad I 'kidnapped' you this weekend?"

She smiled. "I hate to tell you this, but I haven't felt like a prisoner once. You're much too nice. I'm afraid you'd be a complete failure as a gangster."

"I hate to tell you this, too, but I thought you weren't so hot as a gang moll yourself."

"I wasn't?"

"No, I'm afraid not."

"I didn't do that bad," she protested. "After all, I got you to come with me, didn't I?"

"Only because I wanted to."

"Why, Lee MacNair, are you saying you saw through my plan to abduct you all along?"

"I'll have to admit you were pretty sly on that

one," he conceded, "but when I saw the motor home I knew something was fishy."

"And you have to admit I was wily enough to trick you all the other times Celena and I hatched up a new plan," she coaxed.

Lee grinned wickedly.

"Well, don't you have to admit that?" she demanded.

"No. You surely didn't think I was that naive, did you?"

Abby's eyes narrowed in suspicion. "I know you took my advice on how to deal with Celena on several occasions," she challenged. He would *have* to admit that. He wouldn't have had nearly the amount of fights with Celena that he had if he hadn't taken Abby's advice some!

"Are you serious?" He looked at her in total disbelief. "I never took your advice!"

"You told her to go suck an egg!" she reminded him heatedly.

He shook his head incredulously. "I certainly did not! She would have had my head on a platter, and you know it."

"Then why wasn't she with you when we went for pizza that night?" she asked smugly.

"Because she wasn't home when I went by for her. She had left a note tacked on the door saying she was off on another one of her shopping trips and for me to wait for her. I wasn't in the mood to wait for her, so I left," he said calmly.

"You mean I've been worrying my head off that I'd been the one causing most of the trouble between you and Celena and you're the responsible party?"

"Look, you and Celena are the ones who started

all this, not me." His grin was bordering on an outright smirk by now.

"Well, you might find all this very amusing, but I don't think either one of us will be laughing when we get back to town."

"I fail to see what all the hassle is about. We'll simply tell Matt and Celena how it is between us, and they'll have to adjust to it."

"It won't be that easy."

"It will if you'll just 'stick to your guns and stand up for what you want," he admonished.

Their conversation was interrupted briefly by another series of long kisses.

"Oh, Lee, what *are* we going to do?" she asked again, laying her head on his broad shoulder a few minutes later.

"We're probably going to end up losing two very close friends."

Abby sighed. "I don't want that. Isn't there any way we can avoid telling them? Maybe, with enough time—"

"Not a chance, Abby. Now that I've found you, I'm keeping you." His eyes grew tender as he absently stroked her abundant mass of fiery curls. "We could go on denying ourselves the pleasure of each other's company until Matt and Celena grew tired of the wait, but that wouldn't be fair to us, or them. And who knows how long that would take? You know how persistent they both can be."

Abby nodded dismally. She did know.

"Then what other choice do we have but to tell them?"

"None," she agreed, showing little enthusiasm.

He chuckled softly. "I couldn't believe my luck when you showed up at the hospital Friday evening and announced you were kidnapping me.

For once I didn't have to come up with some lame excuse to see you again."

Abby kissed him on the lips invitingly. "So that's why you came along so willingly. And I thought I was being so clever."

"I confess," he chuckled between snatches of kisses that were beginning to grow more heated.

The snowplow was getting close to the motor home, and Abby regretfully gave him one last kiss and slid out of bed.

"Well, we might as well get ready to face the music. Maybe the next time we're stranded for a weekend I won't feel so darn guilty."

Lee reached out and pulled her back to him, his face growing solemn. "Abby, I want you to promise me that when we get back to town, you won't forget what we've talked about."

Abby met his gaze shyly. "I won't forget . . ."

"I mean it," he warned. "Loyalty for both Matt and Celena is going to have to take a backseat from now on. You're going to begin thinking about Abby for a change."

"I know . . . and I will."

"And Matt?"

"I'll tell him when the time is right. I just can't see hurting either one of them if we can avoid it."

"We'll confess together." He kissed her once more and patted her bottom affectionately. "Now, you better get dressed before I go crazy again."

The sharp rap on the side of the camper a few minutes later broke them apart. Lee hugged her tightly one last time before he slowly released her and got out of bed.

"That'll be the man with the snowplow."

Abby nodded miserably, then hurriedly went into the bathroom to dress.

141

The weekend was over, and the time had come to pay the piper.

It was nearly dark by the time they pulled into the driveway of Abby's parents. A wrecker had been required to pull the motor home out of the ditch, so it was very late when they had finally gotten started. The roads were still nearly impassable in places, and the drive had taken much longer than usual.

"You want me to pull it into the garage?" Lee asked.

"If you don't mind. I'll open the door for you." Abby jumped out of the passenger seat and started to unlock the garage door.

Winston King came hurrying out of the back entrance of the house just as the motor home's taillights disappeared into the darkness of the garage.

"Abby! Goodness I'm glad to see you." Her father swept her off her feet and gave her a big bear hug.

"Hi, Dad. I know you must have been nearly frantic, but I haven't been near a telephone in the last forty-eight hours," she said lamely.

"I was worried, but when I found out Lee was with you I relaxed a little. Have you two been stranded somewhere?"

Abby looked at him in surprise. "How did you know Lee and I were together?"

Lee came out of the garage and paused when he saw his boss standing there. He glanced at Abby worriedly. "Hello, Dr. King."

"Hello, Lee." Winston extended his hand and shook Lee's in a warm welcome. "I was just telling

Abby that I was sure relieved when I found out you were with her this weekend."

Lee smiled meekly. "You were?"

Abby looked at her father warily. He certainly seemed to be taking it well that his daughter had just been marooned an entire weekend with a man!

"How did you know we were together?" she repeated.

"Come on in the house where it's warm, and we can talk," he said as he steered them toward the back door.

The warmth of the house was sheer heaven as Lee and Abby took off their wraps and huddled around the fire Winston had blazing in the fireplace.

"How about some coffee or hot chocolate?"

"That sounds great, Dad. But let me make it." Abby disappeared into the kitchen, leaving the two men alone. She could hear them making idle conversation as she fixed steaming mugs of hot chocolate and slipped some of her mother's banana nut bread she had taken from the freezer in the microwave to heat.

As she carried the tray back into the living room, she heard Lee say in a concerned voice, "Are they hurt?"

"Is who hurt?" Abby set the tray on the long coffee table and glanced at the two men in anticipation.

"You better sit down," Lee cautioned softly.

"What's the matter?" She looked at her father worriedly. "Is there something wrong with Mother?"

"No, dear, your mother is doing fine, and she sends her love," Winston quickly assured her.

"Then who were you talking about?"

"Matt and Celena." Lee's voice sounded ominous in the quiet room as she sank down on the chair next to him.

"What about them?"

"They were involved in a car accident yesterday," her father explained.

"A car accident?" Abby looked at the two men blankly.

"Yes. It seems that when we didn't come by Celena's house Friday evening, she called Matt," Lee began. "Matt called the hospital, and one of the nurses verified she had seen us leave together just before the storm hit. When we still hadn't shown up by the next morning, they decided to get in the car and go looking for us. On the way a car slid through a stop sign and broadsided them."

Abby's face turned pale. "How bad are their injuries?"

"Matt was hurt the worst. He has a broken leg, among other injuries," Winston supplied. "Celena just had a few cuts and abrasions. She was treated and released from the hospital yesterday, but Matt will have to stay for a while."

An overwhelming sense of guilt assailed Abby as she buried her face in her hands and sighed. "Oh, Lee, this is all our fault." If they hadn't betrayed their friends and carelessly spent the weekend in each other's arms instead of trying to get home, this would never have happened.

"I know you're upset, Abby, but I don't see how we're responsible for any of this," Lee replied. "If you'll remember, we were stranded in a ditch all weekend ourselves. There was no way we could have done anything differently."

"But we didn't even try to do anything," she

lamented, trying to avoid her father's attentive gaze. "While we were off having a good time, our friends were trying to find us, and now they've ended up in the hospital."

"Abby, you're letting your emotions overrule your common sense," Lee warned quietly. "We didn't ask Matt and Celena to come looking for us, and you know as well as I do why they were so hell-bent on finding us."

"I still say it wouldn't have happened if we hadn't been so caught up in . . . each other." She was so overcome by guilt she was nearing the point of tears.

"Now look, you two," Winston interrupted, "let's just simmer down and drink our hot chocolate. Matt and Celena are doing fine, so there's no need for either one of you to be upset."

Abby took the cup of chocolate Winston handed her and bit back her tears in silence.

"Thank you, sir." Lee accepted his cup and looked at the contents bleakly.

"I thought perhaps you two would want to go by the hospital for a short visit before you go home this evening," Winston was saying as he offered the tray of banana nut bread to Abby.

She refused with a curt nod of her head and went back to morosely studying the flames of the fire.

How could life have been so perfect for her just one short hour ago? Now Matt was lying up in the hospital with a broken leg, no doubt wondering where in the world she was, and Celena would be going out of her mind with worry over Lee.

Casting a quick glance over in his direction, she felt the tears spring to her eyes once more. She loved him so much. But how could she betray Matt

145

and Celena at a time like this? She just couldn't. Not with Matt lying in the hospital.

Lee's eyes found hers, and she glanced quickly away. Moments later her eyes unwillingly went back to his. A look of hopelessness passed between them as Lee set his untouched cup down on the table and stood up.

"If it wouldn't be too much trouble, I'd appreciate that ride to the hospital, Dr. King. My car is still parked there."

"Call me Winston, son." Winston placed a consoling hand on his shoulder. "And I'd be more than happy to drive you over."

Abby rose from the chair she was sitting in and reached for her coat and gloves. "I'm coming, too. I want to check on Matt."

A look of pain crossed Lee's face as he quietly helped her into her jacket. "Haven't you got a heavier coat? It's getting awfully cold out there," he admonished softly.

"Thank you, but this one will be fine." She couldn't meet his eyes because she knew what she would find there. A silent pleading that she could not deal with right now. His hands felt warm and very familiar to her as he gently squeezed her shoulders, then released her.

"I think we're ready, Winston."

The short drive to the hospital was made in almost total silence. Winston was concentrating on the hazardous roads while Lee and Abby were lost in their own thoughts.

The blue Cadillac pulled up to the front entrance of the hospital and eased to a halt.

"You want me to wait and drive you home?" Winston looked at Abby expectantly.

"No, sir. I'll take her home . . . if she doesn't mind," Lee broke in sharply.

Abby noted the tired circles under her father's eyes as she leaned over and kissed him on the cheek. "You go on home and get some rest. Lee will take me home."

"You're sure?"

"I'm sure. And Dad, thanks for not asking any questions." Abby knew her father was puzzled by the unusual events of the past couple of days, but he had discreetly refrained from prying into her personal affairs.

"Well, I won't say I'm not wondering what's going on," he confessed, "but it isn't too hard for me to remember when I was falling in love with your mother. I'm sure you'll fill me in on the gory details in due time. Meanwhile, I'll try to remember you're a grown woman now and should be able to handle your own life." He patted her shoulder lovingly. "Lee's a fine man, Abby."

"I know, but it's not that simple." She caught herself as her voice broke off in a ragged plea.

He arched his brow in surprise, then patted her shoulder again.

She smiled as she shut the car door and joined Lee, who was patiently waiting for her at the front entrance.

Hospital visiting hours were just coming to an end as Lee stepped over to the information desk and spoke with a pretty blond nurse who seemed to know him quite well. Abby could hear him ask for Matt's room number and assure the nurse that they would only visit with Matt a few minutes.

"That was easy enough," Abby said coolly as they got into the empty elevator and let it whisk them to the fourth floor. "Do you know her well?"

147

He shrugged his shoulders indifferently. "We've worked together on occasion."

"How nice." Abby bit her lip pensively. "She's pretty."

"Is she? I hadn't noticed," he commented absently.

"I'll bet. I had the strong impression if you had asked her if you could perform brain surgery, she would have consented!" Her jealousy was running rampant, and she was powerless to stop it.

"Brain surgery?" He grinned at her in disbelief. "Maybe a simple appendectomy or possibly a minor lobotomy—but never brain surgery," he denied innocently.

She shot him a scathing glare as the doors slid open and they left the elevator. "Very funny."

The door to Matt's room was pulled closed as they approached. Lee paused and rapped softly.

"Come in."

Abby froze as she recognized Celena's voice.

"Celena's here," she whispered frantically.

"Good." Lee looked at her sternly. "I know what you were thinking earlier. You don't want to tell them until Matt is back on his feet, but I think we should both go in there and get it over with."

"No!" she refused sharply. "I couldn't do that to a stranger, let alone Matt while he's flat on his back! We'll just . . . have to wait . . ."

"But you can do it to me? What about your promise a few hours ago? That you would think of what you wanted for a change?"

Their eyes locked stubbornly. "That isn't fair. I didn't plan on this situation arising."

"But now that it's come down to the nitty-gritty, you're still going to choose Matt over me," he said stonily.

148

Her stubbornness superceded his. "Obviously, that's how you're going to perceive it."

"Then perhaps you should join your friend," he stated curtly as he pushed the door open and followed her into the room.

"Lee!" Celena glanced up from her place beside Matt's bed and watched Lee and Abby enter the room. "Thank goodness you're finally here!"

Abby turned her head as Celena rushed over and threw her arms around his neck. Moments later she was kissing him so ardently, Abby thought she was going to be sick. Lee was trying to pull out of her strong embrace, but it seemed to Abby he wasn't trying hard enough.

"Where have you two been?"

Matt's angry question caught her off guard, and she looked at him guiltily.

"Hi, Matt. How are you—"

"I asked where you and Lee have been all weekend!" His normally pleasant face had dark bruises on both cheeks, and his disposition was bordering on nasty.

"We—we were stuck in a snowdrift."

"Where?" he barked.

Matt's surly words made Celena break her death lock on Lee's neck and pause to listen attentively.

Abby knew if she said out by the lake he would know something fishy had been going on. They would have had no purpose whatsoever being out in that direction when they were supposed to have been on their way to pick up Celena.

"Does it matter where, Matt?" Lee's voice sliced through the tense air. "We were stuck in a ditch for the last forty-eight hours. Let's leave it at that."

149

"I'll just bet you'd be more than happy to leave it at that!" Matt glared at him disgustedly. "Pretty convenient, MacNair! Stuck the whole weekend in a motor home with Abby."

"Matt, I realize you've been worried, but let's not get surly about this," Abby broke in. "This weekend was not Lee's idea."

"Well, it seems to me you could have had the common courtesy to walk to a telephone and let someone know where you were," Celena noted petulantly. "We've been worried sick about you."

Abby shot her a scathing glare. "We were stuck in a ditch," she repeated. "There isn't a phone booth on every corner, Celena. I'm sorry we caused you and Matt undue concern, and I'm terribly sorry you were involved in an accident looking for us, but I don't think we deserve this kind of treatment."

Matt finally relented as he reached for her hand and pulled her down on the bed beside him. "Dammit, Abby, I've been out of my mind worrying about you," he agonized. "When Celena told me what she had involved you in this weekend, I could have wrung her neck!"

He looked so pitiful lying there with his head swathed in bandages and one leg suspended in the air in a heavy cast that Abby found herself softening. "I'm sorry, Matt . . . I didn't mean to worry you."

It was Lee who had to turn his head away this time as Matt roughly pulled her down and claimed a kiss from her.

"Are you all right?" she asked moments later as she managed to discreetly wiggle out of his tight embrace.

"Thanks to you and Lee, I'm going to be laid up for a while," he grumbled, "but I'll live."

"We're just lucky that we both didn't have to spend the holidays in the hospital." Celena stared at Abby pointedly. "I was nearly killed myself!"

"Dad says you're fine."

"Maybe so, but it was still harrowing." She looped her arm through Lee's possessively. "You know, if you weren't my best friend, Abby, I could be very upset about this incident, too. What *did* the two of you do all weekend alone?"

Abby started to explain as best she could when Lee stopped her.

"I don't think we have to give a detailed account of our weekend," he said calmly. "Not one of us is wearing an engagement ring that I can see. Abby and I don't owe you or Matt an explanation, and we're not going to give one."

The occupants in the room fell silent as they waited for someone to dispute Lee's statement.

Lee's face was stern as he turned to confront Matt. "I think we'd all better let this subject cool down for a few days and continue the conversation when you're feeling better. I promised the nurse we would only stay a minute."

"If I find out there was any monkey business going on, Lee—"

Abby took Lee's arm and pulled him away from the bed. "I think Lee's right, Matt. We'd better leave."

Celena hurried over to reclaim Lee's attention as Abby leaned over and placed a perfunctory kiss on Matt's forehead. "Can I do anything to make you more comfortable?"

"No, and you don't have to run off yet. I've already got permission for you to stay . . . if you ever made it up here," he said petulantly.

"Tonight?" Abby was about ready to drop from exhaustion. Two nights with very little sleep was beginning to take its toll on her. "I don't know, Matt. Lee was going to drop me off at my apartment . . ."

"Please, Abby. It would mean so much to me." His eyes pleaded for just a small grain of her undivided attention.

"Can't you see she's exhausted, Matt?" Lee pointed out curtly.

"You stay out of this, Lee. Abby is able to make up her own mind," Matt stubbornly ignored Lee's warning. "How about it, Abby? Stay with me a couple of hours, then you can take a cab home."

Abby felt trapped. She longed to be alone with Lee and let him hold her in his arms for one more brief time before they were forced to separate. She glanced at his solemn face, looking for help, but she found none. His eyes told her it was a decision only she could make.

"Oh, Lee, I'm so glad you have your car here!" Celena smiled up at Lee invitingly. "I've been a little nervous about driving since the accident, so I had Gerald drop me off at the hospital tonight. Would you drive me home?"

Abby tensed to see what Lee's answer would be.

"Sure, Celena. My car's still parked out on the lot. I'll be glad to take you home." He stared at Abby in defiance.

*So, he's going to take that attitude!* "All right, Matt. If Lee is going to see that Celena gets home safely, then I'll stay with you awhile." Abby walked around a glowering Lee and pulled up a

152

chair beside the hospital bed. *If Lee wants a fight, he's got one!*

"Oh, marvelous!" Celena was all bubbles as she bid Matt a hasty good night. Abby noticed that Lee and Matt managed to ignore each other completely as Celena gathered her purse and coat. She also noticed Lee did a fine job of ignoring her.

*Well, if Lee MacNair wants to be that pig-headed, then I will be, too.*

But her confidence was nil a few minutes later as Lee walked out the door with Celena and left her sitting alone in the quiet hospital room.

She smiled a timid smile at Matt as the door closed and tried to keep herself from bursting into tears.

# CHAPTER NINE

The wind was a biting cold as Abby emerged from the hospital an hour later. Matt had wanted her to stay longer, but she had begged off. It had been all she could do to keep her eyes open the last half hour, and Matt had dozed most of the time anyway.

Pulling her collar up closer to her chin, she wished fleetingly that she had taken Lee's advice and worn a heavier coat.

*Lee.* What in the world was she going to do about him? There was no doubt she had hurt his feelings by staying with Matt. Abby knew Lee was as concerned for Matt's health as she was, but she also was aware that, now that he had expressed his feelings for her, he felt she owed him a certain amount of loyalty, too.

But how loyal was he being to her right now? Celena had been at her most possessive tonight, hovering around Lee like a mother hen. And Abby had not failed to miss the waspish looks her friend had sent in her direction.

Why was she being torn in two by some of the people she loved most in the world?

Another frigid gust of wind rocked her slender frame as she walked down the steps of the hospital entrance. As a rule there were always several cabs waiting to pick up passengers, but tonight there didn't seem to be one within ten miles.

Abby huddled down deeper in her coat, and it was all she could do to keep from shedding those despicable tears that had threatened all evening. She was bone-cold, tired, and hungry, and nothing, absolutely nothing, had gone right since she and Lee had gotten back.

From the corner of her eye she saw the headlights of a car switch on and heard an engine roar to life. Seconds later a black sports car braked to a halt in front of her, and a man leaned over and opened the door.

"Get in."

Abby peered through the darkness into the dimly lit interior of the car, her cares instantly growing lighter as she recognized the driver.

"Lee," she scolded affectionately, "you should be home getting some rest."

"Get in before you freeze to death," he growled.

Abby gratefully slid in the passenger seat and shut the door. The warmth of the heater stung her face as she shivered and took off her gloves. "I never expected to see you here."

"You didn't honestly think I'd let you take a cab home, did you?" He circled the hospital drive slowly and started to pull out on the main road.

"The last time I saw you, you didn't seem overly concerned about how I would get home," she noted crossly.

"And you didn't seem overly concerned about seeing me again tonight," he shot back.

They rode in silence for a few moments as Lee concentrated on the slippery roads and Abby concentrated on controlling her jealousy. It was such a relief to have him beside her again instead of worrying if he had decided to throw reason to the wind and spend the night with Celena.

Sharp gusts of wind rocked the small car periodically as it crept steadily through the sleepy town.

"I suppose you and Matt had a nice visit?" Lee's voice sounded as jealous as Abby felt.

"Not particularly," she admitted. "I'm surprised to see Celena let you go so early."

Ignoring her goading, he kept his eyes on the road. "You didn't stay as long with Matt as I thought you would either," he commented.

"No, I would have left much earlier, but it seemed important to Matt that I stay as long as I did." She reached over and placed her hand on his arm. "That's the only reason I stayed, Lee."

"Oh?" He turned to glance at her in the passing light of the streetlamps. "Weren't you enjoying the company?"

"No, not at all," she replied softly. "I would much rather have been with you."

Lee swore quietly under his breath, then seconds later he reached over and pulled her into his bucket seat.

"Lee, there isn't room for two in this seat!" Abby protested with a laugh but made no effort to change the seating arrangement.

"I wish that once, *just* once, I could stay mad at you," he grumbled, leaning over to steal a brief kiss from her.

Her laughter faded as she reached up and brought his mouth back down to meet hers in a more lingering one.

Lee groaned softly as he pulled the car over to the side of the road and let the motor idle as they kissed hungrily for a few minutes.

156

"I was afraid you were angry with me," she confessed a few moments later.

"I was . . . for about five minutes."

"Why so long?" she protested.

"Why not? You chose to spend your time with Matt instead of me. You can't understand why that should upset me?"

"You know perfectly well why I made that decision."

Lee sighed and reluctantly set the car back into motion. "I know why, but it doesn't make it any easier."

"It wasn't exactly a picnic for me when you left with Celena's arms draped around you," she reminded him.

Lee had the good sense to keep quiet as they drove the short distance to Abby's apartment and pulled into the drive.

He cut the engine and turned to devote his full attention to the woman snuggled contentedly against his chest.

"Let's not spend the time we have together arguing," he coaxed, pulling her closer to his warmth.

"Mmm," she returned drowsily. "I agree."

They kissed a long, leisurely kiss, reacquainting themselves with the taste of each other.

"Why don't you invite me to stay the night?"

"Why?"

"Why?" He growled suggestively. "I'll give you one guess."

She laughed and snuggled closer to his broad frame. "I don't think that's a very good idea."

"But I need to be with you tonight," he whispered. His hands slipped under her jacket and gently caressed her nubile curves. "I need to assure myself that this weekend really did happen."

"Don't make it any harder on me than it already is," she pleaded.

"Have you already forgotten the talks we had, Abby?" Lee's voice suddenly turned very solemn. "Remember? You agreed we are going to start thinking about us for a change."

"I know . . . but surely you can see we can't up and announce our love right now. Be reasonable, Lee. Let's at least give Matt a chance to get back on his feet before we hit him with the news."

"Matt." He sighed. "How long are you going to make *me* wait?"

"Just until he gets better," she said softly.

"There it is again. Matt. It seems like he's the only one you're worrying about."

Abby sat up and removed his searching hands from beneath her jacket so she could think straight.

"That's not true."

"Then tell me how long it's going to be before we can openly be together."

"I can't give you an exact date, Lee! Matt will be in the hospital for at least another week, and I can't just lower the boom on him the minute he gets out."

"This is crazy, Abby. You don't owe the guy anything! You act as if you were engaged to the man instead of just good friends."

Abby didn't understand her own feelings at this point. She didn't have any particular obligation to Matt other than one of friendship, but she couldn't stand the thought of hurting him with the knowledge she had fallen in love with his best friend—especially when she had denied it so vehemently when he had accused her of doing just that. Maybe it was a matter of pride or guilt . . . or loyalty. She just wasn't sure at the moment.

And of course there was always Celena to contend with.

"In a few weeks we'll sit both of them down and talk to—"

"Weeks? No way. I put my foot down at that, Abby. I'm not hanging around for weeks and living a lie." Lee straightened up and purposely sat her in her own seat. "If that's the way it's going to be, count me out until you decide what you want."

Abby felt bereft as she left the comfort of Lee's broad chest.

"If you insist on carrying on as if this weekend never happened, then you'll have to do it by yourself."

"Lee!"

"No, Abby," he stated firmly, "I'm not some teen-age kid who has a crush on you. I'm a man who loves you." His face was grim as he continued to lay down the law. "When—if—you ever decide which is more important to you, friendship to Matt and Celena or having me, you let me know."

"That isn't fair."

"I'm sorry. Maybe it isn't, but it's the only way I can handle this." His eyes grew pleading. "I can't just stand by and watch Matt claim you as his, Abby . . . especially now." His voice was soft. "I'm sorry. I'm just not able to handle that. I can't think of any man who would."

"Lee, I love you. Don't spoil it by laying down demands—"

"That's how it is, Abby," he cut in.

"You're being pigheaded, unreasonable, and downright mulish!" He may not think he was a teen-age kid with a crush, but he sure was acting like one. *Men!*

"Maybe I am. But when you decide to be honest with the man whom you supposedly consider nothing more than a friend, you look me up." His voice left little doubt that he was starting to doubt her alleged feelings toward Matt. "You're not going to string both of us along, Abby. You might as well realize that right now."

"String you along?" Now he had gone too far. "Well, maybe it is for the best this all happened the way it did." She reached for the door handle and shoved the car door open. "We'll both have time to reevaluate this weekend."

"Don't take too long, Abby. My patience has a limit."

"Then maybe you better think more seriously about Celena! Apparently she's willing to overlook your bullheadedness!"

"Let's not get ridiculous."

She was outside the car now, her temper barely in check. "Don't bother to see me to the door."

"I wasn't planning on it."

Slamming the door loudly, she watched as he angrily backed out of the drive and disappeared into the snowy darkness.

Abby couldn't make herself believe that Lee would seriously put them through this sort of punishment. No, by tomorrow he would realize how foolish he was being and call to apologize. In time they would both find a way to break the news to Matt and Celena and let them down easy, but until then, he would just have to be patient!

Her heart was heavy as she stepped wearily into her apartment and closed the door, but she still had hope. Yes, Lee MacNair would just have to calm down. If he persisted in being stubborn about this, it wouldn't take him long to find out that Abby King had invented the word *stubborn!*

But Lee didn't calm down the next day or the day after or even the day after that.

Two agonizingly long weeks dragged by, and she didn't hear a word from him. Thanksgiving came and went with little fanfare in the King household. Because of Mara King's absence, Winston and Abby decided to eat their holiday dinner out. They both agreed it was a poor substitute for the fun-filled day they usually enjoyed.

"I worry about you, Abby. You're just not yourself lately," Winston fretted as he brought her back to her apartment Thanksgiving afternoon.

"I'm fine, Dad. Really." She leaned over and kissed him good-bye.

She hadn't been herself since the night Lee dumped her at her door and drove off. He had meant every word he said about not seeing her, and she was so lonely without him.

"Your mother should be home in another week or so . . . Maybe you need to sit down and have a long talk with her."

"We'll see," she replied evasively.

What was there to talk about? The man she loved and adored refused to see her. Celena had been distant with her ever since Abby and Lee's weekend. Matt hadn't actually accused her again of any foul play that weekend, but he had an unnerving way of bringing up the subject unexpectedly and then watching her like a hawk for any sign of guilt.

What could she possibly have to speak to her

mother about? Everything was close to perfect in Abby King's life!

By the third week of Lee's indifference, Abby was ready to resign from the human race. Not only was she tired and cranky from the holiday rush at the shop, but she was working on a new petition that occupied most of her free time, not that she had all that much free time to spare.

Matt's injuries had been more acute than first believed, and his stay in the hospital had been longer than anticipated. At his almost petty insistence, she had dutifully stopped in his room every night she did volunteer work and visited him.

As she rushed in the hospital after work one evening, she noted what a welcome relief it would be tomorrow to drive up to the lodge that her parents rented every Christmas. She desperately needed some time alone to mull over her problem. It seemed as if Lee was having a tug of war on stubbornness with her, and neither one was winning. Something was going to have to be done. She loved Lee and didn't want to lose him. Hadn't he said his patience did have a limit? How much longer could she push this dilemma until he gave up on her completely? She could only pray he would hold on just a little longer. Matt was improving slowly, and it wouldn't be long now before she could disentangle herself from this sticky web.

It was strange. For the first time since she had met him, she was beginning to see what a really selfish person Matt Avery could be at times. Daily she could feel her resentment grow at his dominating attitude in their shaky relationship.

The darkening sky looked as if another snowstorm was imminent when she stepped through the hospital entrance and walked over to the elevators. When the doors slid open quietly, she stepped in and punched the fourth-floor button.

The car paused on the second floor, and once again opened its doors to admit new passengers. Abby's heart nearly stopped as she came face-to-face with Lee.

He glanced up and saw her standing alone in the elevator, and the blue of his eyes darkened. For a moment he didn't move, then he seemed to remember his purpose as he stepped into the car with her and punched the button for the floor that housed the administration offices.

The doors slid smoothly shut, and the car began its upward climb once more before he finally spoke.

"Hello, Abby."

The deep sound of his familiar voice sent shivers racing up her spine as she quickly averted her eyes and tried to block out his overpowering presence.

"Hi, Lee."

It was no use. She could smell that wonderful aftershave he wore, and the small car seemed to lock them in a private world of their own.

"How's Matt doing today?" he asked politely.

"He's fine . . . I think he may go home Sunday."

"Oh? Well, that's good to hear."

Abby was aware that Lee had not visited Matt since the first night they saw him together. Although it hadn't seemed to bother Matt in the least, it had broken her heart. She was desperately trying to save a friendship that apparently neither Lee nor Matt was any longer interested in.

"Looks like it could snow again," Lee commented.

"Yes, it sure does."

She felt as if she would scream if the car didn't reach her floor soon. It was much too painful to stand next to Lee and make idle conversation when she was dying to throw herself into his arms and plead for him to come to his senses.

In a last-minute attempt to make things normal, she shuffled nervously through the stack of folders she was carrying and withdrew a sheet of paper with three signatures attached to it.

"I know you'll want to sign my newest petition." She shoved a ballpoint pen in his direction.

He stepped back a fraction and peered at the document skeptically. "What am I signing?"

"You know the Park, over on Maple Street?"

"Yes."

"I'm trying to get enough volunteers to move it over on Morley Drive." She gave him a wavering grin. "There's a lot more traffic congestion on Maple Street than there is on Morley Drive, and I figure it will be safer for our children if the park is moved—I mean the town's children," she corrected hurriedly.

Lee raised his brows in disbelief. "You're trying to get the whole darn park moved?" he asked incredulously.

"Yes! Don't you think that's a great idea?" She beamed.

The pen and paper were placed firmly back in her hand. "No, thanks. That sounds like more work than I want to get involved in."

She frowned irritably. There was no more enthusiasm for this petition than there had been for cleaning the town's statue every Saturday morning.

The car bumped to a halt, and once more the doors opened to the fourth floor. She started to hurriedly exit the car when she heard his voice softly call her name. She turned slowly to face him once again.

"Yes?"

"I . . ." He paused and his eyes drank in the familiar sight of her. "Tell Matt I said 'hi,' " he finished lamely.

"I will. I'm sure he'll be glad to hear from you." The words wanted to stick in her throat, but somehow she forced them out.

When the elevator doors closed, she stared blindly at the place where he had been only seconds earlier.

Suddenly she found herself frantically banging on the closed doors. "Lee! Lee! Open this door!"

The doors slid back open, and Lee stared at her expectantly. "Yes?"

She took a deep breath and smiled weakly. "You *are* being pigheaded and completely unreasonable . . . but I still love you," she sniffed.

"Have you talked to Matt about us yet?"

"No, but—"

"Then it isn't me who's being pigheaded and completely unreasonable." He reached over to punch the button for the doors to close once more. Moments later he was whisked away and she was alone again.

*Damn! Double Damn!* she thought miserably as she angrily wiped at the tears in her eyes. Why did she have to see him today on top of everything else?

Her mood wasn't the best as she entered Matt's

room and threw her purse and folders loudly down on the table next to his bed.

"Wow. What's got your dander up?" Matt laid down the magazine he was reading and looked at her.

"The world!"

Matt chuckled. "That's all-encompassing. Want to narrow it down some?"

She sauntered over to the window and peered down at the parking lot below. Assorted hospital personnel were making their way against the gusty wind to get into their cars and go home for the day.

"I couldn't, Matt. I'm afraid I'm out of sorts with mankind in general today," she said irritably.

"Well, maybe I can cheer you up." He sat up on the side of his bed and watched as she continued to stare out the window pensively. "The doctor says I'm well enough to go home tomorrow."

"That's nice." Abby tried to sound enthusiastic, but she failed. At one time his news would have elated her, but now she felt nothing as she became engrossed in her own tortured thoughts.

If Lee MacNair had really loved her, he would have stuck by her during Matt's recuperation, but he had chosen to take the coward's way out instead of seeing this thing through together. She was also about to decide that their special weekend had been nothing but a game to him. Lee couldn't be in love with her. A man couldn't stand by and watch someone he loved die a little more each day, as she had been doing the last three weeks, and do nothing to help them.

There had been days lately when she hated Lee and Matt and Celena with a passion that was totally foreign to her. And at the end of those days she hated herself even more.

"You don't sound very happy about it," Matt complained.

"Sorry. I guess my mind's elsewhere."

And it was. It was still back in that elevator with Lee.

"Seen Lee lately?"

Suddenly, the room was filled with an expectant tension as Abby felt herself stiffen in silent resentment. No matter what the subject, Matt always managed to bring it back around to Lee.

"Yes, it so happens I have," she said curtly.

"Oh?" That one word was fraught with unspoken accusations.

"That's right. We rode up in the same elevator a few minutes ago. He said to tell you 'hi,'" she related indifferently.

"Oh, did he? Did he happen to mention why he works in the same building I've been living in for the last three weeks and has failed to stop in and give his warm regards in person?" he asked, letting the sarcasm seep through his voice.

"No, he didn't."

"But I suppose you had far more important subjects to discuss than the state of my health," he pursued in a silky tone.

"No, only the possibility that it might snow," she returned through clenched teeth.

"That's a little hard to believe." Matt rose from the bed and reached for his robe. "Most women find blue-eyed, brown-haired Lee MacNair almost irresistible," he taunted. "Don't you?"

Abby closed her eyes and sucked in a deep breath.

Her once lovable, kind Matt was slowly but

surely turning into a spiteful cynic. And all because she refused to be truthful with him.

Unexpectedly, the errant thought occurred to Abby. How much more painful could it be for Matt to know the simple truth, than for him to suffer over what he only imagined in his tortured mind?

Yes, he was in love with Abby, but she had not been doing him a favor by letting that love grow. On the contrary, in the end she had only added to his misery. It wasn't his fault he had fallen in love with her . . . but then neither was it hers. She had told him from the start that she didn't return that love, but he had refused to accept that fact. Instead, he had kept her trapped in a relationship she didn't want, and she had foolishly stood by and let it happen—all in the name of friendship.

"Yes, I can certainly understand that. I find him irresistible, too." She finally found the courage she had been searching for, for weeks.

"What?" Matt's head shot up, and he looked at her in disbelief.

Slowly, she turned from the window and faced him. "I said I find Lee irresistible, too. Isn't that what you wanted me to say?" she asked coolly.

Matt gave a nervous laugh. "Come on, Abby. Stop teasing."

"I'm not teasing you, Matt. I'm very much in love with Lee."

Matt's eyes narrowed. "You're serious, aren't you?"

"Very serious." Her eyes met his directly. "I'm sorry, Matt. I should have been honest with you a long time ago."

"Somehow that doesn't surprise me in the least. I suppose all this started that weekend you two were marooned together."

Abby could hear the pain and recrimination in Matt's voice, and it broke her heart.

"No, Matt. I was attracted to Lee long before that."

"I knew it!" Matt slammed his hand down on his pillow heatedly. "I knew he would try to move in on me."

"How could he move in where you have never been?" she asked gently. The words hung thickly in the air between them.

"Don't say that, Abby. You know how I've felt about you all along. We've had a lot of laughs together." Matt's face was a tortured mask.

"I know we have, Matt. But it's suddenly occurred to me that half the time I didn't know what we were laughing about. You have failed to accept that I don't return your feelings . . . and I never will. You're a very special person to me, but our relationship will never be anything but what it is. Friends . . . nothing more."

"How can you say that? I know you don't return my love right now, but I was hoping someday—"

"No, Matt!" Abby broke in sharply. "I want you to stop trying to make something happen that's never going to take place! I don't love you." Her voice grew more tender now. "Please listen and accept what I'm saying, for your own sake, Matt. You're a wonderful man, and someday someone will come along to return your love a thousand-fold, but it isn't going to be me."

Matt hung his head in mute acceptance, realizing at last that she spoke the truth. "Lee has brought all this on."

"If Lee didn't exist, I'd still feel the same way, Matt."

"Does he love you?"

"I don't know."

Matt sighed and rose from the bed to take his vigil at the window. "What does Celena think about all this?"

"She doesn't know."

"She isn't going to like it."

"I don't expect her to."

"I really don't see how you can do this to her," he snapped. "After all, she's your best friend. I can see Lee stabbing me in the back, but I can't see you doing this to Celena."

"Is she?" Abby asked sadly. "Sometimes I have to wonder." There were days when she was beginning to seriously question Celena's so-called friendship.

"If you can't trust your friends, then who can you trust?" Matt parried.

"Then again, there comes a time when you have to stop and ask yourself how much you owe a friend? Should a person be forced to set aside his own personal happiness in favor of someone else's? I know that's the admirable way to do things, but how many of us are really that strong?" she coaxed. "Tell me, Matt, where does a person draw the line on friendship?"

"Well, the only thing I can tell you for sure is that I'll think twice before I give my friendship to another person," Matt stated solemnly. "I would have never dreamed that Lee MacNair would have moved in on me the way he did."

"Oh, Matt." Abby picked up her purse and folders and started toward the doorway. "You'll never know what a good friend Lee *has* been to you."

"I'll bet."

"You do that. It's a sure win."

It was as if a heavy burden had been lifted from

Abby's shoulders as she stepped out in the hall and made her way to the elevators. The break had been painful, but she had expected it to be. Now she could only hope that someday Matt would see the wisdom of her words and all of their friendships could be restored.

*One obstacle out of the way, one to go,* she thought.

On the ride down in the elevator, Abby mulled over ways to confront Celena. She had to admit she wasn't looking forward to that one bit.

The doors opened on the ground floor, and Abby glanced up in surprise. Lee and Celena were standing in front of her, about to enter the car.

"Abby!" Celena rushed in and pulled Abby out of the empty car and threw her arms around her neck exuberantly. "Lee and I were just coming up to see you and Matt," she exclaimed.

"Oh? That's nice." This was the first time she had actually seen Celena in almost three weeks. They had had a couple of conversations over the phone, but Abby had sensed a change in Celena. She seemed preoccupied and not like herself at all.

Abby cast a nervous glance in Lee's direction.

"Lee thought you would be the first to want to know!" She thrust her hand out in front of Abby and displayed a sparkling diamond twinkling on the third finger of her left hand. "Look!"

Abby's mouth dropped open as she mutely surveyed the glittering stone Celena was waving in front of her face, then back to Lee.

*The rat! He's been lying all along, and I've been a gullible fool—I believed him.*

"Isn't it marvelous?" Celena demanded happily.

Tears sprang to Abby's eyes as she shot Lee a look of pure disbelief and shoved her way past the couple. "Congratulations. I hope you'll both be very happy."

# CHAPTER TEN

" 'I'm engaged! Lee wanted you to be the first to know!' Can you believe that, Mother? She actually had the nerve to flash that—that rock in front of my face and gloat about it!" Abby paced the floor in front of her mother, mad enough to spit nails.

"Now, Abby, let's be reasonable. Surely she isn't engaged to Lee. It must be someone else."

"At this point I couldn't care less if she was engaged to Lee," Abby ranted. "I'm totally fed up with the whole situation."

"Calm down, dear." Mara King studied the array of brushes positioned next to the easel she was seated in front of. "I'm sure there's a perfectly logical explanation for Lee's actions, and if you hadn't run off half-cocked, he probably would have given you one."

"I don't want one—from him or Celena. I'm washing my hands of the lot of them."

"I don't know, dear, but if what you've told me is true, I'm sure you're getting upset over nothing. A man doesn't tell one woman he loves her and then rush off and get himself engaged to another," she reasoned patiently, "especially if he's told you he doesn't care a thing about Celena."

"Mother"—Abby eyed her impatiently—"some men *do* those sorts of things."

"Well, I'm sure yours doesn't." Mara King had the cool elegance Abby had always envied. Her sophisticated and genteel manner made her daughter long many times for more of the same qualities in her own disposition.

"Three weeks. Three crummy weeks and he hasn't bothered to try and see me. Does that sound like a man who's in love with me?"

Before her mother could answer, Abby supplied the heated answer. "No, it does not!"

Abby's voice began to crack as Mara glanced up worriedly from behind the pastel watercolor scene she was working on. "Abby . . ."

Abby shook her head of tousled strawberry curls in mute grief. Mara laid aside her brushes and rose from the tall stool she had been perched on.

"Just let it all out, dear." She enclosed her daughter in the comforting haven of her arms, and the dam that Abby had been holding back for such a long time finally burst.

For the next fifteen minutes Abby sobbed out the events of the past few weeks, ending with the heartbroken confession that she was head over heels in love with Lee MacNair and didn't have the slightest idea what to do about it.

"But he told you he returns that love," Mara comforted softly.

"He said he did, but it was all a lie," she sobbed. "He couldn't have loved me and treated me the way he has for the past few weeks." Abby sat up and blew her nose loudly on the tissue her mother had handed her.

"You're not being rational, Abby. You said he told you he wouldn't be seeing you again until this situation between you and Matt was cleared up."

174

"Yes, he said that, but I didn't think he was serious!"

"Dear, I hate to be the one to add to your problems, but it seems to me you should never have let Matt take up so much of your time if you were not seriously interested in him. That wasn't fair to him or you. If you were in love with Lee, you should have let Matt know right from the beginning," Mara scolded gently. "This has been a no-win situation for everyone concerned."

"Mother, you just don't understand. Matt and Celena are close friends to both Lee and me. Celena is crazy about Lee, and Matt thinks he's in love with me. How would it have looked if Lee and I suddenly announced that we had decided *we* were in love with each other?"

Mara was clearly confused. "But if you didn't love Matt, and Lee didn't love Celena, but you both loved each other, what other choice did you have but to tell them?"

"We were going to," she agonized. "But when we returned from our weekend together, we found out Matt and Celena had been involved in a car accident while they were out searching for us. I couldn't tell Matt that I had fallen in love with his best friend when he was flat on his back in a hospital bed."

"Abby"—her mother turned her around to meet her searching gaze—"just how serious was this weekend you and Lee shared?"

Abby's verdant eyes met her mother's directly, then dropped away in guilt. "You don't want to know."

"Oh, dear." Mara sighed. "What about Celena? Have you spoken with her about your feelings yet?"

175

"Not yet. Besides, it apparently doesn't matter anymore. She's engaged."

"Maybe so, but I'll bet my last dollar it isn't to Lee."

"Lee and Gerald Metcalf are the only two men she's been dating lately. Surely she didn't go out and pick a stranger off the streets to become engaged to."

"Gerald Metcalf." Mara frowned. "Why would she have been dating that man?"

Abby shrugged and blew her nose once more. "She thought she was making Lee jealous."

"Mercy. This is all very confusing. I think I'm going to make us a nice cup of hot tea."

"I suppose we both could use a cup of tea. Want me to help?"

'No, you just sit here and get yourself under control," she insisted gently. "I won't be long."

While her mother was gone, Abby wandered over to gaze out the massive glass windows that encompassed the entire south wall of the log cabin.

The King family had been coming to this rustic resort for Christmas as long as Abby could remember. As an only child, she had missed the companionship of other children during the holidays, so Winston and Mara had brought their daughter here on a regular basis to be with friends her own age.

It was snowing again. Abby pressed her face against the cool pane of the window and watched the puffy flakes float down gently from the gray heavens. Her mind drifted back to Lee, and the tears started to trickle down her cheeks once more.

Had he been lying to her all along? She so desperately wanted to believe that wasn't the case, but it was hard not to think differently. After all, by his own confession, he had supposedly used Celena as a pretext to gain Abby's attentions. Had he used Abby to gain Celena's? Some men would have used her vulnerability to their advantage. Had Lee done that very thing to her the weekend they had been marooned together?

Mara returned from the kitchen a few minutes later carrying a tray with the hot tea as Abby wiped ineffectually at her tears.

Her mother sat down on the sofa in front of the massive fireplace and patted the seat next to her. "Dry your tears and come over here and join me."

Abby did as she was told, and a few minutes later mother and daughter were making casual conversation as they sipped their cups of tea.

"You've changed your hair." Abby studied her mother's fashionable, upswept hairdo with a critical eye.

"Yes, it was getting so long I decided to wear it up for a change."

"What does Dad think about the new style?"

Mara smiled demurely. "I think your father missed me so much while I was gone I could have come home with a punk haircut and he wouldn't have objected."

Abby sighed wistfully and leaned back against the sofa. "You and Dad have such a special relationship."

"I can't help but think you'll find the same sort of happiness very soon, Abby. Have patience, little one, and never settle for anything less with a man."

"That's sure a switch," Abby said, laughing. "You telling me to have patience."

Mara laughed with her. Over the years it had been Abby coaxing her parents to be tolerant until she found the man she wanted to marry.

"Where is Dad?"

"He's out cutting wood with Fred Andersen this morning. You know how much he enjoys the fresh air and exercise when we come up here."

Abby stood up and strolled back over to the window. "I'm sure the roads are getting bad again," she commented as she watched the wet snow starting to gather on the shrubs and cedars surrounding the lodge. The scene painfully reminded her of the snowy weekend Lee had been with her, and the hurt began all over again.

"Did you have any difficulty making the drive last night?"

"No, I didn't run into any bad weather until I was almost here." Abby had been so emotionally distraught the evening before, she had barely taken note of the weather conditions.

"Mom, who do we know who drives a red Blazer?" she asked a few minutes later.

A late model four-wheel drive vehicle had pulled off the main road and was slowly making its way up the King's driveway.

Mara returned to her easel and sat down to study the painting before her. "I don't know, dear. Probably one of your father's friends." Mara shook her head thoughtfully and murmured to herself, "No, the colors in the trees just aren't right yet."

Abby turned to look at her questioningly. "What trees?"

"The trees in your father's Christmas present."

Her mother had a way of talking in circles at times that drove Abby up a wall, but over the years she had learned to read between the lines and make sense out of some of Mara's very vague answers.

"You're painting that canvas for Dad?"

"Yes, but I'm afraid I'm never going to finish it in time to give it to him for Christmas," she fretted.

Abby turned her attention back to the Blazer that had braked to a halt now. "You still have another few days . . ."

Her words faltered as she watched Lee get out of the driver's side. Her eyes widened as he walked around to the passenger side and opened the door to assist Matt and his cumbersome leg cast out of the truck.

Celena and another man followed moments later, and the four stood in the yard, looking expectantly toward the house.

". . . and I thought we'd warm up some of the stew we had last night for our lunch." Mara glanced at her daughter to see if she was listening. "Abby?"

"Mom, you'll never guess who just pulled into our drive," she murmured.

"Who, dear?"

"Lee, Matt, Celena, and—oh, my gosh . . . that's Gerald Metcalf!" she exclaimed in disbelief.

"All four of them?"

Abby bolted from the window and started in the direction of the steep stairway that led up to the loft bedrooms. "I do *not* want to talk to any of them," she hurriedly called over her shoulder.

"Abby King!" Mara's authoritative voice stopped her daughter dead in her tracks.

"Mother—"

"Don't 'mother' me," Mara ordered. "You march right back down here and face this thing head on. Wasn't it you sitting here not ten minutes ago mooning over that man?"

"But—"

"Immediately!" Mara walked over and retrieved Abby's coat from the peg it was hanging on near the door. "Now slip this on and go out there and get him."

"I can't 'go out there and get him,'" Abby protested as her mother helped her into the coat. "He probably thinks I'm crazy as it is!"

Mara turned her around and buttoned the jacket securely. "Don't forget to put on your hat. I don't want you getting sick."

"I already am," Abby grumbled, "of all of them. I really don't want to see them, Mother."

Minutes later the door to the cabin flew open, and Abby was physically forced out. "But, then again, I guess I will," she said weakly, pulling her jacket closer around her.

Lee glanced up and saw her standing on the porch. His face turned grim. "Do you think you could possibly spare a few minutes of your time?" he asked curtly.

Shuffling halfheartedly down the snowy walk, Abby approached him and paused.

Matt, Celena, and Gerald stood in the background and watched quietly as Lee spoke first.

"I'm glad to see you made it up here all right. That was a stupid thing to do, Abby. Running off in weather like this."

Abby's face clouded with anger. "What are you doing here?"

Lee crossed his arms and fixed his eyes on her stubbornly. "Remind me to tell you sometime how nice and peaceful my life was until you came into it."

"I won't be able to. I'm no longer speaking to you." She turned and started to walk away when he reached for her arm and dragged her back against him.

"Oh, yes you are. All four of us are going to have a long overdue talk." Abby froze as he drew her closer to his side and held her securely.

She glanced over at Matt, who was leaning against the fender of the Blazer, his face showing unmistakable signs of pain from being on his injured leg.

"And you're here to talk, too?"

Matt grinned weakly. "I thought it might be a good idea."

The snow had already dusted his dark head with a thin layer of white, and Abby noted his face was still very pale.

"Would you like me to help you to the house?" she relented gently. "There's a warm fire and I can fix you something hot to drink."

"No, thanks. It feels nice to be out in the fresh air again."

Abby's eyes came back to Lee in a silent challenge. "How did you find me?"

"Your father's secretary told me your family was up here for Christmas. I figured you'd be with them."

"I really wish you hadn't made the drive."

"I wanted to talk to you."

"We have nothing to talk about."

"Maybe you and I don't, but I think the four of us might find a mutual topic."

"I don't think that's necessary."

"I do."

Her eyes unwillingly drank in his virile good looks. The heavy coat he was wearing had a blue

181

lining that made his eyes look like glistening sapphires.

"I'm sure you don't need me to make your wedding plans," she returned curtly.

"Come off it, Abby! I can't believe you would honestly think that Celena and I were engaged," he protested. For a moment they both forgot there was anyone with them as their eyes stubbornly met one another's.

Abby's hastily constructed facade began to slowly crumble. "Lee . . . I don't know what to think . . . I prayed it wasn't true . . ."

"You know, this could make me damn mad if it wasn't for the fact I love you," he returned softly. "I thought I'd made it plain how I felt about you."

"You did, but—"

"Oh, Abby." Celena stepped forward and took her hand. "I'm sorry. I should have made myself clearer last night, but I was so excited . . . Gerald had just given me the ring, and I wanted you to be the first to know."

"Gerald?"

"Yes. We're going to be married, Abby!"

Abby let out a whoosh of disgust. "Well for heaven's sake, Celena! Why didn't you say you were engaged to Gerald?"

"You didn't give me time! How was I to know you were going to jump to such quick conclusions?"

"Jump to conclusions? When the elevator doors opened, you were standing there with Lee, jumping up and down waving an engagement ring in my face, and Lee was grinning like the cat who got the mouse . . . what else was I supposed to think? Especially since I was under the strong impression it was Lee's engagement ring you've been after the last six months, not Gerald's!" She cast an apologetic glance in Gerald's direction. "Sorry, but you wouldn't believe what I've been through with this woman!"

Celena hung her head sheepishly. "If you'd only give me an opportunity to explain, I can. I know it sounds crazy, Abby, but I really did think I was in love with Lee when we made all those plans. But when I started using Gerald to make Lee jealous . . . well, I found out what a really wonderful man Gerald can be, and I suddenly realized I was in love with him, not Lee."

"Well, I sure wish you would have let me in on the secret," Abby said reproachfully. All these weeks of unnecessary torture, and Celena was in love with Gerald all along!

Gerald smiled down at Abby in apology. "Look, I know what a terrible reputation I've had around town, but what people don't understand is that the reason I've played the field the way I have over the last few years is because I've just never found the right woman for me. That is, not until I met Celena. When she came into my life, I knew she was the one and I was never going to let her go." The happy couple smiled at each other affectionately. "I can personally guarantee that from now on Gerald Metcalf's reputation around town will be spotless."

"Celena . . . you should have let me know," Abby protested once more. She was hesitant to look in Lee's direction. She could sense his gaze probing for her reaction to this elating piece of news.

"I know. But you know what a scatterbrain I am." Celena excused herself lamely. "I knew Lee wasn't really interested in me from the very beginning of our relationship. And although I had suspected it many times, I honestly didn't know for sure that the two of you were interested in each other until I met Lee yesterday at the hospital. When he confessed the two of you were in love, I was elated." She looked at Abby fondly. "I really mean that, Abby. I think you and Lee would be perfect together."

"Well, I guess this is where I'm supposed to dutifully say I think you and Lee would make a perfect couple, too." Matt straightened his stance and held out his hand to Abby coaxingly. "Come here, carrot top."

Abby glanced at Lee, and he nodded as she walked over to stand next to Matt.

Gazing down at her in obvious affection, Matt sighed. "I can't say my whole heart is in on this yet, but after devoting most of last night to the subject, I have to admit that I think you and Lee would make a perfect couple."

Abby reached up and touched his face tenderly. "Oh, Matt, you don't know what it means to me to hear you say those words. And you've come all the way out here today . . . I don't know what to say."

"Just say you and that handsome, surly brute standing over there staring daggers at me still want my friendship. That'll be enough for me."

"Of course we still want your friendship," she scoffed, wiping the tears running down her cheek.

His face grew solemn once more. "I want you to know how sorry I am about giving you such a hard time lately. Lee and Celena came to my room right after you left last night, and we had a long talk. Lee made Celena and me see that we haven't been very good friends to you, Abby, and I want to apologize."

"I don't think any of us deserve a medal in that department," Abby replied.

"Well, I think I've been the most pigheaded of all, and I wanted you to know how sorry I am about the unhappiness I've caused you. You'll always be very special to me, Abby King."

"I know, and you'll always be very special to me, Matt Avery," she whispered.

"Can you forgive me for being such a nerd?"

"Sure. I love nerds," she said in a voice choked with tears.

Matt laughed halfheartedly. "Then you and Lee should be real happy together." Matt raised his head and winked mischievously at Lee. "Only teasing, MacNair."

Lee walked over and took possession of Abby once more, drawing her close to his side. "There're still a lot of things I'm willing to share with you, ole buddy, but not this particular woman."

Matt reached out and offered his hand in friendship. "I wish you nothing but the best, Lee, and I mean that."

Both men's eyes grew misty as their gazes locked in silent communication. As the snow continued to fall, they stood and shook hands.

"Thanks, Matt. You don't have to worry. I'll love her enough for both of us," Lee promised.

Matt clamped his other hand on top of Lee's and grasped it firmly. "I have no doubt about that. Name the first boy after me."

Matt reached for Celena and pulled her into the small circle. They stood hugging each other, their hearts overflowing with true friendship.

"You know, it seems to me as if Matt is the only one who this isn't working out for," Abby complained a few moments later as she wiped at her tears again. "Lee and I have each other; Celena and Gerald are going to be married. It just doesn't seem fair that Matt has no one."

Matt glanced at her sheepishly. "Well . . . there is this nurse at the hospital . . ."

All five burst out laughing as the tension of the moment was finally broken.

"Well, for heaven's sake," Abby scolded, "let's all go in the house before we freeze to death!"

"We'd like to, but I'm afraid Lee has to get me home," Matt apologized. "I don't want to overdo the first day out of the hospital, and we still have an hour's drive ahead of us, not to mention the fact that Sara's coming by to check on me."

"Sara?"

"Yeah, the nurse?"

Abby chuckled. "You sure don't waste any time, do you?"

Matt blushed. "I try not to."

"None of you are going to stay?" Abby's voice couldn't hide her disappointment as Lee proceeded to help Matt back into the Blazer.

"The roads are really getting bad," Celena explained, "and Gerald has to stop by his office today." She hugged Abby once more. "I still want you as my maid of honor," she whispered.

"I wouldn't miss it for a million dollars," Abby promised.

Abby trailed Lee around the side of the car as Celena and Gerald climbed into the backseat.

"Lee, this isn't your Blazer, is it?"

"No, I couldn't find a dogsled to rent, so I rented this. I knew I had to get up here soon, since I was sure you had misunderstood Celena's rash statement yesterday."

Abby smiled tenderly. "You knew I was upset?"

"Yeah. It must have been that crappy look you shot my way that let the cat out of the bag."

"I'm so glad you noticed." She sighed.

"Come here, turnip brain." Lee pulled her around and started to kiss her. They both stopped and looked up expectantly to see where Matt and Celena were.

"Do you mind?" Lee grinned at Matt.

Matt laughed, and both he and Celena discreetly turned their heads.

"Oh, Lee, I love you so very much," Abby murmured moments before his mouth claimed hers. Because they were not alone, they made it a short kiss, but it held a definite promise of many more to come.

"Do you want me to go back with you?" she offered shamelessly.

"No," he said casually, "I want you to stay up here."

"Oh?" Her face fell.

He smiled and tipped her face up to steal a quick kiss from her. "Because I plan on being back here in time to take my lady out tonight," he finished.

"You're coming back up here?" She couldn't keep the elation from swelling her voice.

"Just as soon as I get these nice people delivered safely back to their homes," he vowed. "Think your folks would mind giving their future son-in-law a room for the weekend?"

"I can give you my personal guarantee that they'll be absolutely delighted," she answered, grinning.

"Do you think they'll mind if I bring their daughter into that room to keep me company on a cold winter's night?"

"Yes." She was still grinning.

He shrugged and winked at her. "What the hell. I'm going to have her for the rest of my life, anyway. I can probably suffer through another few days until I can get her to the altar. Besides, it will make it all the more sweeter . . . if that's possible." His gaze caressed her tenderly.

"Why, Mr. MacNair"—Abby batted her eyelashes at him—"am I supposed to take that as a proposal of marriage?"

He leaned against the back of the car and crossed his arms smugly. "You can if you want to. Personally, I was thinking about renting one of those motor homes for the weekend and kipnapping you again. I thought we might ride out by the lake and get stranded for a week," he teased, letting his eyes run lazily over every square inch of her body. "After I had you eating out of my hand and drooling for any small crumb I might want to throw your way," he grinned wickedly, "that's when I thought I would actually pop the question . . . but I suppose your parents would nix that idea."

"Oh, yeah?" She cocked her brow and gave him a rebellious look. "And what happens if *I* refuse your caveman tactics?"

His eyes grew tender with longing. "Then I'd camp on your doorstep the rest of my life until you married me," he confessed huskily, "because I love you so damn much it hurts."

"Then I suppose there's no need to go to all the trouble of refusing," she whispered back, love overflowing in her eyes, "because I love you so very much, too."

They both ached to take each other in their arms and give credence to their words, but in respect to the three waiting in the car, they held back.

"I'll see you tonight, turnip brain."

"I'll be waiting." She pressed a kiss on her fingers and touched his lips softly. He caught her hand and held it for one brief moment before he smiled and let it go.

"Drive carefully."

"I will. Have I really told you how much I love you?"

She tipped her head and pretended to think. "Umm . . . you might have mentioned it."

"Well, if I didn't, I'm sure the subject will be brought up occasionally over the next fifty years."

Another stolen kiss passed between them before he climbed into the Blazer and started the engine. He gave her one of those devastatingly sexy winks as she stood back and waved good-bye.

It was hard for her to believe that Lee was all hers now, but he was. She smiled as she blew one last kiss to him and wrapped her coat tighter around her shivering frame.

*I might not have been able to put Humpty Dumpty together again, but then,* Abby thought with a cockiness her mother would have abhorred, *I never really wanted to in the first place.*

189

# PASSION'S FOLLY

*To Nancy Butcher.*
*It's always fun to work with you, and many*
*thanks for your support and encouragement.*

# CHAPTER ONE

T. J. Templeton was about to try and make the biggest sale of his life.

He had to sell himself, and he was more than a little nervous about it.

Reaching for the folder lying on his desk, he watched as his co-worker, Ellie Millstein, came back from the coffee machine and set her cup down on her desk, before he slowly began to saunter in her direction.

Moments later Ellie was looking up at him with her violet eyes widened in disbelief.

He had to be kidding, she thought.

But from the expectant look on his face, Ellie knew he wasn't.

"Go in on a boat with you?" she repeated.

"Yeah. Just look at it, Ellie!" A Polaroid snapshot suddenly appeared beneath her nose and she tried to focus her eyes on the picture. T.J. shoved aside a pile of books, propped one hip on the corner of her desk and began to systematically list the reasons why she should invest part of her

191

life's savings into the image projected on the paper before her.

"If we both live to be a hundred years old, we'll never find another deal like this one. Just look at the features! Luxury of the highest class yet we can practically steal the thing if we act fast enough."

Ellie's eyes tried to follow his rapidly jabbing finger, but it was jumping back and forth from the forward berth, to the convertible dinette, to the galley back to the mid-stateroom on the large pleasure boat so fast she couldn't keep up with it.

"But, T.J. . . . this boat would sell for—"

"Under ordinary circumstances? A mint," he acknowledged quickly, "but that's what I've been trying to tell you, Ellie. The fellow who owns it is in a real financial bind and he needs to get rid of it quick. I know for a fact that he's willing to take a substantial loss if he can move it in the next few days."

Her gaze lingered wistfully on the gorgeous cruiser, and she had to admit his enthusiasm was catching. For as long as she could remember it had been her dream to own such a vessel. But go in on one with a complete stranger?

No . . . T.J. was not a complete stranger, she retracted hesitantly.

They had worked together for the past year in the same real estate office, but as far as she could tell, he had never really known she'd existed.

True, they were as opposite in natures as peas and lemon pie, but, in all that time he not so much as offered her an impartial dinner date outside the realm of work.

At times she had tried to rationalize that the oversight was because he probably didn't like to mix business with pleasure, but that theory failed to hold water when she repeatedly saw him out with other female colleagues from the office, and they did not seem to be discussing "business matters."

Her mind quickly dismissed the annoying thought and tried to concentrate on what he was saying. He was still energetically extolling the virtues of the boat and urging her to take a closer look.

But what he was suggesting was ludicrous . . . or was it? About the only thing she *did* have in common with T. J. Templeton was their mutual love of pleasure crafts.

It wasn't unusual for their co-workers to walk in the lounge of Coastal Realty and find T.J. and Ellie, their attractive blond heads bent over a colorful brochure one or the other had picked up at a local boat show the night before, excitedly discussing their one mutual passion.

But whatever had possessed him to come up with the preposterous idea of buying a boat *together* was intriguing.

"I think we owe it to ourselves to at least take a look at it," he encouraged. "Who knows, it might not be such a bargain after all, but if it is, it's going to be a heck of a buy for some lucky person . . . or persons," he amended.

"I don't know, T.J. Where did you get this picture?"

"It was tacked on the board at the laundromat, along with the details of the boat, when I went to do my wash this morning. I called the number posted and talked to the guy myself. He and his wife are getting a divorce and he has to sell the boat this week."

"If it's such a bargain, then why don't you buy it yourself?" she reasoned.

T.J. sighed wistfully. "I'd love to, but I can't swing it alone. That's why I thought about you. I know how you'd love to own a boat like this one, and I thought maybe we could go in on it together and split the costs right down the middle." He leaned closer and she caught a faint whiff of his pleasant-smelling aftershave. "To be honest, I would never consider such an arrangement with anyone else, Ellie, but I knew you were reliable and trustworthy—and—and we would be able to keep this strictly on a business level . . . don't you agree?"

*And quiet, good-natured little ol' mousy Ellie won't try to read anything personal into it, isn't that what you're saying, T.J.?* she finished silently, feeling a surge of resentment building within her.

Ha. Why would I try to read anything personal into *the* most desired bachelor in the office asking me to go in partnership on a boat with him?

"—and if the boat had been just an ordinary boat, I would've forgotten all about it," he continued as the wary look on her face refused to go away. "But under the circumstances, I don't see how we can do anything less than at least consider the idea. We could use the boat on alternate weekends and then we'd both have what we've always wanted—but could never afford alone—at half the cost." He smiled persuasively. "Don't you agree?"

Ellie frowned at the staggering thought of insurance, interest rates, maintenance and docking fees for such a boat, not to mention the operating expenses.

She had to wonder if any of those small details had ever entered his mind. Still, her gaze lingered on the snapshot. It was a lovely boat and what he was saying did sound tempting. Commmon sense alone told her she would never be able to afford a boat like this on her own, and she admitted she was feeling a little flattered that T.J. had chosen her for such an unusual request—even if she didn't have the vaguest idea why.

"Look. It can't hurt to just look at it," he argued. "Do you have any appointments this afternoon?"

"No, not until four—"

"Great! That gives us plenty of time."

"Well, I don't know, T.J.—"

"It's worth checking out, don't you agree?"

"Well . . . it might be . . ."

Sliding off the desk before she could change her mind again, he started for his own cubicle. "We'll take my car and maybe pick up a sandwich on the way."

"But T.J. . . ." Ellie glanced up and sighed impatiently when she saw he had already disappeared behind the partition which housed his desk, and her gaze reluctantly turned back to the photograph.

Well, she supposed he was right.

It surely couldn't hurt just to take a look . . .

"Well, here it is, a real beauty, just like I said it was."

Ellie and T.J. paused before berth one thirty-two on the Ocean Tide Marina and waited as the owner of the boat, Mike Haran, fished in the pocket of his white tennis shorts for a key.

The afternoon was a hot one, not at all unusual for the southern tip of Florida this time of year, but a light breeze was blowing through the dock, making the unexpected outing a pleasant one.

T.J. had glanced at Ellie and grinned as they had approached the boat. It appeared to be all the advertisement had proclaimed—and more.

Extending a hand to her, Mike stepped on board the thirty-two-foot, twin-engine cruiser and motioned for T.J. to follow suit.

"Helen and I ordered the boat custom designed," Mike was saying as he began to unlock the door to the sleeping quarters. He glanced at T.J. apologetically. "My wife likes pink and blue, but I think you'll find it real attractive anyway."

Ellie had to stifle a laugh at the way the excited, expectant look suddenly fell off T.J.'s face. If ever a man was super masculine, it was T.J., and she could never imagine him in pink and blue surroundings.

But the disturbing news didn't seem to dampen his spirits for long, because from the moment he stepped into the boat, his gaze began to roam around the luxurious interior with unconcealed appreciation.

The boat was well equipped and more than pleasing to the eye, even if it was decorated a bit more femininely than most men would have cared for.

The forward berth, in shades of soft pink and powder blue, was spacious and airy. There were several throw pillows with pretty, symmetrical designs scattered about the bed to create a homey effect.

The small galley had all the essentials for cooking and entertaining with its tiny sink, icebox, and stove. Even the pink-and-white-checkered banquette was extremely eye-catching, right down to the bouquet of daisies gaily perched in the center of the oak table sitting in front of it.

Ellie was busy exploring the stand-up head, decorated in shades of navy and pink, with brightly striped towels and washcloths as accent. It wasn't hard to see a woman's touch everywhere she looked.

The mid-stateroom was decorated with the same loving care, and she suddenly found herself falling head over heels in love with the boat although common sense told her she was making a big mistake.

Number one, she and T.J. were too opposite in nature to ever make a go of such an arrangement. Unlike her, he was carefree, overly extravagant, and never gave a thought to where the next penny was coming from.

Number two, even though the boat was indeed a bargain, they were still talking about a great deal of money, and it was a well-known fact that Ellie Millstein did not spend money frivolously.

If anything, she was too tightfisted with a dollar, took life much more seriously than T.J., and zealously planned for the future.

"Real nice, isn't it?" Mike gazed around the interior longingly and Ellie thought he looked a little sad. He was a handsome man, close to her age, six foot tall with sandy blond hair and nice brown eyes.

In a way, his quiet, studious manner reminded her of an accountant she dated on occasion, Ferguson Waterman.

"Yes, yes it is," she said gently. "I'm sure you hate to give it up."

"Yeah," Mike conceded. "But I have to. I simply can't afford to make the payments another month. I'm either going to have to sell the boat this week and hope to salvage a little bit of the money Helen and I invested, or simply let it go back to the bank."

"I'm so sorry." She suddenly regretted giving in to T.J. and ever coming to look at the boat.

She found herself not only wanting it, but she could feel her tender heart wanting to help this poor man out of his painful dilemma, even though she *knew* it would be a mistake.

T.J. had said very little since they'd entered the cabin, but Ellie could tell he was quietly analyzing the situation. She thought he would have been more enthusiastic than she was, but instead, she was the one oohing and ahhing over the features as he coolly went about examining the boat's craftsmanship.

"Isn't it just marvelous!" she whispered under her breath as Mike allowed them a few moments alone after the boat had been thoroughly gone over with a fine-tooth comb.

"Oh, it's so-so," he agreed, then grinned as he saw the incredulous look steal across her face. "All right. It's great!" he conceded, then lowered his voice even more as he leaned closer. "Okay. So we both agree we love the boat?"

She shook her head hesitantly. "But do we have to decide on buying it this very minute?"

"No, but I'd sure hate to lose it."

"And I'd sure hate to make a mistake by acting too quickly."

T.J. looked disappointed, but he knew enough to stop while he was ahead. This was not an issue that could be forced, nor one that he knew Ellie would enter into lightly. "Okay. Then how about asking Mike to hold it for us a few days while we think about it? I'll give him a deposit so he'll know we're actually giving it serious thought."

She nodded her approval. "But make it perfectly clear he is to return every cent of the deposit if we decide not to buy the boat."

"Well, gee, Ellie. I don't know if the man will agree to an offer like that."

"If he's that desperate to sell, he should be willing to take a gamble," she said firmly.

"Okay, I'll see what I can do." T.J. hated to be such a skinflint, but since she was going to be controlling half of the purse strings, he supposed he'd have to be.

Mike accepted the offer without a blink, and said that he would be waiting to hear from them as soon as they reached a decision.

As T.J. dropped her by the office to pick up her car, he cautioned that they would probably never find another deal like this one, and for her to think it over very seriously.

And she did. For the next few days she agonized over the dilemma he had placed her in. Several times she had gone out to the marina alone and sat on the dock and just stared at the beautiful boat.

It was the loveliest boat she had ever seen. And to have the chance to share it with a man like T. J. Templeton—well, it was more than a dream come true.

But there was so much money involved . . .

T.J. didn't try to press her for an answer, but she caught him looking over her way more than once with a wistful look on his face.

There were a couple of sleepless nights, but on the morning of the third day, she knew what she was going to do. During the long hours before dawn she had come to the conclusion that buying the boat with T.J. would be frivolous, nonsensical, flighty, and utterly foolish, but she was going to do it anyway.

Picking up the phone beside her bed, she hurriedly dialed T.J.'s home phone number before she changed her mind.

When he answered in a sleepy voice a few moments later, she calmly stated, "Okay. I'll go in on the boat with you."

She could hear him yawning as he groggily tried to digest the good news. "Great. No reservations about buying it together?"

Well, actually there were. Her sane side was still sending out warning signals that screamed loud and clear that a partnership such as the one being contemplated would never work, while another small voice reminded her this was probably the nearest she would ever come to being in such close proximity to a man like T. J. Templeton.

"No, none at all," she fibbed.

She wasn't sure, but she could have sworn she heard him breathe an audible sigh of relief. But why not? She had just agreed to help buy the boat of his dreams. "All right, I'll give Mike a call and tell him to meet us at the boat around ten this morning and we'll make the final arrangements."

"Fine. I'll meet you at the office in an hour."

"I'll be there."

As they drove to the marina later that morning they discussed the enormous details of owning the boat together, but despite the slight feelings of apprehension, both found themselves growing increasingly excited about the prospect of the newly formed partnership.

"Okay, then I think we're in full agreement. We'll buy the boat and split the expenses right down the middle. Then we'll each use the boat on alternate weekends," T.J. summed up as he pulled the car in next to the marina and killed the engine.

"What about holidays?" Fourth of July was not that far off and she was already thinking about hosting a small party for some of her closest friends.

T.J. shrugged. "We'll flip a coin to see who uses it then. The main objective is to get the boat, then we'll figure out the details later."

"I agree." Her heart beat a little faster at the prospect of actually owning that gorgeous boat.

"Good. Now let me do all the talking," he warned. "Maybe we can get it even cheaper than we think."

Ellie nodded her agreement. It was a well-known fact that T.J. was a whiz when it came to making shrewd business transactions. Last year he was one of the top salesmen in the Million Dollar Club, and Ellie respected his uncanny ability to make money.

It was spending money that seemed to get him into trouble.

"But don't try to go too low. The poor man needs the money," she cautioned, remembering the worried look on Mike Haran's face the day before.

"So does this poor man."

While T.J. and Mike were discussing the details of the transaction, Ellie roamed through the galley of the boat again, mentally making notes on what she would change as soon as the boat was hers—theirs.

She still hated the thought of spending all that money, but she was able to salve her conscience by reminding herself that this experience could be worth much more than the value of a dollar. In a strange way, she had always admired T.J., and secretly longed to be more like him. Maybe now that they would own a boat together, she could be around him more and see just how a man of his caliber operated.

She smiled to herself. It should be extremely interesting.

Moments later T.J. stepped up on deck, a wide smile dominating his handsome features.

Ellie grinned at him expectantly. "It's ours?"

"It's ours."

She turned her face upwards and gave a huge sigh of relief.

At last! It may not be entirely hers, but at least she *had* a boat now.

# CHAPTER TWO

"I suppose you went ahead and bought the boat?" Janet Mason asked.

"Yes, and it's the most beautiful boat in the world," Ellie happily confided to her friend over lunch the following week. "We signed the final papers this morning."

"I can't wait to see it. When do we get the grand tour?"

"You and Mark will be my first guests," Ellie promised. Janet had been one of her very closest friends all during high school and college. They had even chosen to go into selling real estate about the same time. So there wasn't anyone with whom she would rather share her first weekend on the boat than Janet and her husband, Mark.

Janet picked up her tuna sandwich on rye and bit into it thoughtfully. "I must say, Mark and I were both surprised to hear that you had bought the boat on partnership."

The unspoken words, "with T. J. Templeton, no less" hung heavily in the air.

"Heavens, Janet. I could never have dreamed

of buying the boat by myself," Ellie defended lightly. "As it is, both T.J. and I are going to have to scrimp for a while."

"I know . . . I'm just surprised you went through with it."

Janet was sure she had detected more than a passing interest on Ellie's part when it came to T.J. and it worried her.

Ellie was up to something, but so far she hadn't been able to pry it out of her.

*All* women were crazy about T.J., and in all fairness, there wasn't a woman in the office who could not be found guilty of fantasizing over him at least once a week. And although Ellie had never openly shown anything but professional courtesy toward him, Janet had always had the feeling she had been looking him over with less than an indifferent eye.

"Well, of course, both T.J. and I would rather have been able to afford the boat on our own, but since that wasn't financially possible, we did the next best thing and bought it together."

"But aren't you afraid . . . that might cause problems?"

Anyone who knew Ellie Millstein and T. J. Templeton would testify they were as different as day and night.

T.J. was an easygoing, happy-go-lucky, endless bundle of energy who attracted members of the opposite sex like flies to molasses. He spent money as if it grew on trees, went out with fast women and lived his life as if there were no tomorrow. Ellie, on the other hand, quietly went about with as little fanfare as possible, dating only when an occasional man happened to pique her interest, and frugally watching her savings account grow each year.

Janet had always felt as if Ellie would grow old and die before Mr. Right would ever appear and it frustrated her to no end, but she didn't want her getting hurt, either. And in her opinion, that's what would invariably happen if she became involved with T.J. and this silly boat.

In Janet's opinion, men were deaf, dumb, and totally blind when it came to Ellie. She had so much to offer a man, and while she was certainly not unattractive, their fickle heads were invariably turned by someone like their flamboyant, voluptuous co-worker at Coastal Realty, Barbie Jenkins.

And it always seemed to her that T.J. always led the pack.

There wasn't a ghost of a chance that this strange arrangement would ever work out between T.J. and Ellie, and Janet knew it.

In fact, her and Mark's immediate thought upon learning of the unexpected alliance was that Ellie would end up being used by T.J., not only financially, but for her unfailing good-heartedness, and that disturbing thought had prompted her to bring up the subject of the boat today.

"Problems?" Ellie thought about the possibilities for a moment, recalling her own misgivings in the beginning.

She knew T.J.'s rather . . . unfettered nature, but that was the very thing about the man that fascinated her.

"Yes . . . Now come on, Ellie. You can level with me. He doesn't know some deep, dark secret about you that he's threatening to tell the world if you don't go in on the boat with him, does he?"

That was pretty far-fetched, Janet had to admit, but as far as she was concerned there had to be some logical reason for Ellie's uncharacteristic action.

"You mean, is T.J. blackmailing me?" Ellie chuckled and picked up her sandwich. "No, it wasn't anything like that. I'm telling you the truth. The boat was a good buy and we decided to share the expense, that's all."

Then an unexpected stab of guilt tugged at the strings of her conscience as she thought of what she had decided to do.

She knew she should be ashamed of herself . . . but she wasn't. An opportunity to be with a man like T.J. didn't come along that often—at least not for her—so she was going to grab it. Oh, she wasn't about to fall in love with him, or make any sort of demands on his time.

But she *was* going to study him.

Maybe with a little luck, she could learn to be more like him.

Actually they'd both be getting what they wanted—the boat—and she'd be absorbing his know-how and savvy. And they'd both be happy.

No, if Janet only knew, the real reason she had

succumbed to T.J.'s urgings about buying the boat had nothing to do with blackmail. Not in the least.

The poor guy was only going to be her guinea pig.

From the first day he had come to work for Coastal Realty, she had sat back and admired his unreserved zest for life, secretly wishing she could be more like him.

She knew she was too staid and reserved and she longed to be more electrifying . . . more stimulating . . . more T.J.ish.

So, in the end, that was what had really made her decide to take part of the money her Grandmother Morgan had left her and invest it in the boat.

No doubt it was one of the crazier things Ellie had ever done, but at thirty-four years old, she was beginning to realize that if she was ever going to find *the* man, then she was going to have to make some definite changes in her life-style.

To be honest, she was fed up with the men she had been dating. They were too much like her. Too inhibited, too restrained, too downright boorish.

Her dates usually consisted of dinner at a fast food restaurant and a bland game of Putt Putt or an even duller movie afterward.

Oh, she supposed she was attractive enough to attract a different sort of man—except her nose was a little larger than she would have liked—and she was probably bright enough . . . yes, to be honest, she had more than her share of intelligence . . . but she just wasn't dynamic enough for men like T. J. Templeton.

She would bet her last dollar *his* women didn't have to play Putt Putt for entertainment on a date.

So that's why she had decided to buy the boat. Perhaps by being in partnership with him, she could study and observe his actions, and by some miracle she could learn to project herself in the same energetic, totally fascinating way he did.

Maybe then, and only then, could she ever hope to catch the attention of such a compelling man as her unsuspecting mentor.

She could never hope to capture T.J. himself, and she wasn't sure she would even want to. He was nice, but every woman in the office was after him and she didn't want that sort of worry. But there were other men in the world as equally captivating as T.J., and if she could make a few simple changes, she was going to capture herself one!

Janet broke into her thoughts. "You're sure you haven't gone off the deep end?" She was still convinced Ellie didn't know what she had let herself in for.

"Believe me, I'm sure." Ellie grinned and leaned over to pat Janet's hand sympathetically. "Stop worrying about me," she cajoled happily. "Everything's going to work out just fine!"

"No it's not. You'll end up falling for the guy and getting your heart broken."

"Not a chance. I know what I'm doing, Jan."

"You will. Mark my words."

Ellie shook her head. "Do I look that dumb?"

"No, but T.J. looks that good."

"Stop worrying."

Janet finally relented and leaned forward and clasped her hand. "Be careful, Ellie. Have fun with the boat, but don't get emotionally involved. Okay?"

Ellie smiled and squeezed her hand affectionately. "Don't worry. I promise."


T. J. Templeton was in the best mood he had been in in ages. Not only had he made two impressive sales this week that would boost his savings account considerably, but he had convinced Ellie Millstein to buy the boat with him.

Maybe now he could get on with his plan.

Glancing up from the menu he had been studying, he smiled as his old time friend and newest client, Richard Demirillo Benson III slid into the seat opposite him, forty-five minutes past the time they were supposed to have met.

Ordinarily, it would have been T.J. running late, but for a change he had been on time today.

"Hi. Were you about ready to give up on me?"

"No. I figured you got tied up somewhere."

"I did. I was in court this morning longer than I had anticipated. Did you bring the contracts?"

"Yes, they're all ready for you and Penny to sign." T.J. pushed a stack of papers over the table and Dick stuck them in his briefcase.

"You realize I'm going to make you a rich man

off this one sale if you can get my asking price for that shopping center complex." Dick grinned.

"I'll get it, don't worry. If I can sell the McDaniel estate for what they were asking, I can surely sell your shopping center without coming down a penny."

"You sold the McDaniel estate?" T.J. thought he detected a note of surprise in his friend's voice.

"Well, I didn't get *exactly* what they wanted," he admitted. "But I'm going to try my darnedest to convince them they should take the offer I got . . . why?"

"Why I thought that old run-down piece of property would sit empty for years," Dick confessed.

"It could, but if the McDaniels refuse the offer then I'll just take the Evanses out to see the Murphy property and convince them it's a better buy than the McDaniel place," T.J. dismissed easily.

Dick shook his head with admiration. "Can you really do that?"

"Sure I can do that. I can talk ragweed into turning itself into roses if I really wanted to," T.J. boasted, still intoxicated with his phenomenal success with Ellie Millstein and the boat caper. He turned his attention back to the menu. "Wonder what's good today?"

"I don't know, but I'm starved."

"Not me . . . I'm sort of in the mood for something simple."

"Great. How about me fixing you up with my wife's sister Saturday night?"

"Not that simple. I was referring to food and there's no way I'm going to let you fix me up with another one of your relatives."

The last time Dick had fixed him up with a date it had turned out to be the longest evening of T.J.'s life. The girl had been so wild and uninhibited that *he* had been the one who ended up walking home. He was fed up with that kind of woman and he had decided to turn over a new leaf.

It seemed like uninhibited women were all he had been dating lately and he was more than ready for a change—a *big* change.

"Come on, T.J., do me a favor and take Cissy out this weekend," Dick pleaded. "Penny's been after me for weeks to set it up between you two—"

"Not a chance," T.J. interjected firmly. Even though Dick was a good friend as well as an important client, he had to put his foot down somewhere. "Besides, me and my partner signed the papers on our new boat this morning and we'll be taking possession this weekend."

"You honestly bought that boat with Ellie Millstein?" T.J. had done some strange things in his life, but Dick thought this one took the cake.

In a way, he could see his reasoning, but only vaguely. Going in on partnership with a woman could have its advantages. She could help make the payments, keep the boat nice and clean and well stocked and lend a homey touch.

Then, of course, T.J. would always be free to

bring his dates aboard and impress them with his new toy, and they wouldn't have to see how untidy and disorderly he could actually be . . . that would be nice . . . and if he didn't have a date Ellie would be around to comfort him . . . that would be nice. . . .

But still, buying the boat with Ellie Millstein?

It just didn't make any sense. Now, maybe with that sharp Barbie Jenkins he worked with or his wife's sister, Cissy . . . he could certainly understand that, but not with a woman like Ellie Millstein, for heaven's sake!

She was just too . . . *normal* for T.J.

"I don't know why everyone finds that so surprising," T.J. said calmly as he folded the menu and laid it on the table. He was getting a little tired of the stunned looks he had been receiving every time he announced that he and Ellie had bought a boat together.

He had to admit they did make a very unlikely pair in most people's eyes. But he had long ago come to the conclusion that maybe that's why he admired her the way he did.

She wasn't like most of the women he knew who wore outlandish hairdos and sweaters so tight they cut off the circulation, or had long, blood-red nails that struck cold terror in a man's heart.

Oh, she dressed as nice as anyone, but she did so with an understated elegance that T.J. appreciated.

She wore tiny little pearls in her ears instead of

the long, jangling earrings that were so popular nowadays, and her naturally blond hair wasn't filled with sticky mousse and gooky hair sprays, but was cut in a nice, stylish, shoulder-length style and always looked shiny and healthy.

She had clear, sparkling violet-colored eyes that always held a hint of seriousness to them, and he found himself every once in a while fantasizing about what a man could do to change that solemn expression.

Aside from their occasional impassioned discussions about boats, she never said much to him, just nodded pleasantly as they passed each other on the way to the coffee machine, but T.J. was discovering that he just liked to sit at his desk and look at her as she sat behind hers and worked. She had a beauty and elegance about her that was simply undefinable.

That's when "the plan" for the boat first began to form in his mind.

Since he knew their only shared interest up until now had been in boats and selling real estate, he began to look around for a bargain in a pleasure craft so that he'd be able to persuade her to buy one with him.

Because of the drastic differences in their lifestyles, he knew full well a lady as classy and well bred as Ellie was would never give him the time of day—not the way he was right now—so that's why he'd craftily decided to arrange a situation between them where he might observe her ways —study the art of refinement . . . of dignity

. . . or understated elegance, a commodity he felt himself strongly lacking in—without her ever suspecting what was going on.

Oh, he wasn't a bore or a slob. It wasn't that at all. But he had woken up one morning after a particularly rambunctious weekend with friends and discovered that here he was, thirty-six years old, going absolutely nowhere.

He hadn't necessarily planned it that way, it had just happened.

The women he dated were all nice, but definitely not marriage material. And before long he knew he would want to start thinking about settling down. Not right now . . . but maybe in a couple of years. . . .

Most of the women he knew had already had been through a couple of marriages, and settling down yet again was not high on their lists at the moment.

And even if one of them had been in the market, T.J. had yet to find the one he would have willingly given up his freedom for.

But if he could only be more like Ellie Millstein, it would be to his advantage when he did start shopping for a wife. That day was a long way off yet, but he supposed he did need to be at least thinking about it.

It occurred to him briefly that although the word "shy" would never be used in the same sentence with "T. J. Templeton," when he was around Ellie he found himself struck totally speechless the majority of time.

But he had always been a go-getter and a top-notch salesman and after considerable thought, he had formulated his plan with sly efficiency.

He would use her as a role model and it would be a pleasant and painless way to gradually develop a little more low-key personality.

Plus he'd have the boat of his dreams in the process.

By buying the boat with her and meticulously observing her actions he felt sure that within a few months he would know exactly how to be the sort of new man he wanted to be.

"It's just that you and Ellie Millstein are so . . . different," Dick was saying, and T.J.'s thoughts were forced back to the present.

T.J. glanced up at him and smiled. "I know. That's exactly what I'm counting on."

"Well, I don't know what you're up to, but you'd better be careful," Dick warned good-naturedly. "Or you'll find yourself tied down with more than a boat one of these days."

"Not a chance," T.J. assured him with a confident grin as he tried to make up his mind whether to order the tuna on rye or chicken fried steak with cream gravy. Ellie was a lovely woman and a perfect role model for what he had in mind, but that was as far as it would go, he thought absently.

He felt a sudden tug of uneasiness as he

glanced back to Dick who was downright smirking at him now.

Absolutely as far as it would go, he reiterated again firmly.

# CHAPTER THREE

"Hi, Ellie. Looks like we'll be able to get possession of the boat even sooner than we thought," T.J. announced over the interoffice phone later that afternoon.

"Really? That's nice to hear." It couldn't come soon enough for her.

Writing the check for her part of the investment this morning had been a traumatic experience. Her hand had trembled and she could feel a fine sheen of perspiration gather on her forehead and down her back as she thought about the horrendous amount of money she was spending. She was feeling much better this afternoon and was back to looking forward to her new adventure.

After all, it was only money, and if this partnership would bring about the changes she hoped it would, then the money would have been well spent.

"Yeah, I just talked to Mike and he's already been over and cleared out his personal belongings. He said as far as he's concerned, we can have the boat right now," T.J. told her.

"Right now! That is good news."

"Do you have any appointments this evening?"

Ellie quickly scanned her appointment pad. "No, nothing."

"Me either. How about meeting me at the marina around six? I'll run by a locksmith and have an extra key made so we'll both have one . . . oh, and Barbie made a sign for us." Ellie could hear the loud rustle of paper over the telephone.

"What does it say?"

"Look over here."

Ellie leaned back in her chair and peered around her partition, a tiny smile tugging at the corners of her mouth as she read the inscription on the large banner T.J. was holding up from across the room for her inspection.

It read, BON VOYAGE! WELCOME ABOARD, MATEY!

Somehow, she doubted if the banner had been intended for "us," but she thought it was nice for T.J. to include her as a recipient of Barbie's thoughtful gesture.

"That was really nice of Barbie."

"Yes, it was, wasn't it? That Barbie is an okay lady."

"Yes, I'm sure she is."

Those were not exactly the terms Ellie would have used in describing the infamous office gossip, but the men in the office tended to view Barbie Jenkins a little differently than the women did.

Perhaps it had something to do with her forty-inch bustline and the skintight sweaters she wore —year round.

"All right, then, I'll meet you around six. I'm on my way to show a couple of pieces of property and get the extra key made. If I'm a little late just hang around. I'll eventually get there," he promised.

"A little late" turned out to be two hours later than she had anticipated. She knew T.J.'s reputation for never being on time so she had deliberately lingered over her dinner and delayed leaving for the marina until right at six.

She knew she could have waited longer and still had plenty of time, but punctuality was a trait she prided herself on.

She was sitting on the end of the fishing pier feeding the ducks kernels of corn she had bought out of a machine on the boat dock when he finally arrived.

It took another ten minutes for him to gather various paraphernalia out of the trunk of his car and get himself organized enough to start up the ramp leading to the marina.

He was carrying a fistful of fishing poles, tackle boxes, a red cooler, a flashlight, a brown grocery sack stuffed full of clothes, and his BON VOYAGE, WELCOME ABOARD, MATEY banner.

He was wearing a life jacket, a dark pair of knit swimming trunks, a hat with assorted fly lures stuck all over it, and a pair of the most disreputable-looking sneakers she had ever laid eyes on.

She heard him coming a full five minutes before he finally reached the end of the pier where she was sitting.

Not only did he rattle when he walked, but he was busy calling out friendly greetings to the various people assembled on the dock, pausing here and there to spend a few moments chatting.

It was obvious the man didn't know the meaning of the word "stranger."

"Hi. I'm late."

No kidding. Lord! how she wished she could be so blasé about life. She couldn't wait. "Oh, that's all right. I was just sitting here enjoying the evening."

"Yeah, it's a nice one," he acknowledged as he tried to shift his load around to keep from dropping all of it.

He had been a little concerned about her reaction to his being late. The last thing he wanted to do was make her mad right off the bat. Being late was a bad habit he was going to have to work on.

As a rule, his tardiness put most of the women he knew in a real snit, but it hadn't seemed to faze her one way or the other. "Did you see that group of people standing over there next to that gold van?"

Ellie glanced in the direction he was pointing. "Yes."

"I stopped by and talked to them for a few minutes. They're our new neighbors. They just bought the boat next to ours, but they won't be able to use it much. Actually, they bought it more for their son and daughter-in-law to use since Harry and Velma—that's the people who bought it—aren't able to get away every weekend. Their daughter-in-law, Marcia—she's just had gall bladder surgery last week and since her husband, Tom, lost his job with the oil company he was working for they have a lot of free time on their hands.

"Harry and Velma thought the boat might be a good way to bring Tom out of his depression over losing the job, except Marcia's afraid he'll want to spend most of his time going to Greg's—that's their only son and Velma and Harry's grandchild —baseball games. If that happens, then the boat's going to be a complete waste of money. I think you'll really like them," he finished all in one breath.

Ellie looked at him vacantly. He had found *all* that out in the short time he had paused to speak to them? "Oh . . . yes . . . well, I'm sure I will. Here, let me help you," she offered, standing up and dusting off the seat of her jeans with one hand.

His eyes were immediately drawn to her shapely denim-covered derriere. Her jeans were not skintight like most women's, but they still did an inadequate job of concealing the lush, ripe curves T.J.'s experienced eye knew were hidden beneath.

Ellie's gaze unexpectedly lingered for a moment on his bare legs and she found herself thinking they didn't look a thing like she thought they would.

In a suit, he looked lean and trim, but in his swimming trunks he looked more sturdy—more solidly built. She quickly decided his legs were actually short. Short and muscular and covered with a thick layer of dark blond hair that made them undeniably—for lack of a better word—simply adorable.

"I would have been on time if I hadn't decided to run by the house to pick up a few things and change my clothes," he apologized again as he shifted a few of the articles over in her arms and they began walking toward the boat.

T.J. made certain that he followed just a few steps behind so that he could observe the way she walked. Straightening his usual, offbeat stance to a more regal pose, he marched along behind her, conscientiously taking in his first lesson on the proper way to walk.

"That's all right, really. Did you get the extra key made?"

T.J.'s steps faltered and his brows shot up with a disgruntled groan. "Damn! I knew I forgot something."

Yet another one of his shortcomings. Absentmindedness. And he was getting worse about it every day. One more thing he had to work on when he got the time. "Oh, well, I'll stop by Wal-Mart's on the way home and have one made and give it to you at the office tomorrow."

Before they could board the boat, T.J. insisted that they stop and let him introduce her to their new neighbors, Harry and Velma.

Harry and Velma were delighted to meet Ellie and insisted that they all have a "get-acquainted" drink. Consequently, it was well after ten o'clock before they were allowed to proceed to their own vessel.

For a while they just roamed the boat, reveling in the fact that it was theirs. T.J. offered to take it for a short spin out on the water, but the moon hadn't risen yet and Ellie was skeptical about venturing into unknown waters with so little light to guide the way.

They decided it would be wise to wait until the following evening before taking it out on its maiden voyage.

Together, they hung the BON VOYAGE, WELCOME ABOARD, MATEY banner, and felt as if now the boat were almost home.

"I have the figures on docking fees, insurance, sales tax, and so on. I think we should discuss these at length," Ellie suggested a little later.

They had helped themselves to the cans of cola that Mike Haran had thoughtfully left in the refrigerator, and were now sitting at the table relaxing.

The gentle swaying of the boat created an intimate, cozy atmosphere and Ellie could sense that T.J. was a little uneasy.

Oh, he didn't say anything, but she knew what he was thinking. He would have preferred to share this exciting time with some other woman. One more to his . . . taste.

In the soft glow of the lamp hanging over the

table, she could see him studying her from time to time, watching her every movement as if he were comparing her with the women he dated.

Well, he could compare all he wanted, she thought resentfully. True, she would come up short right now, but that would soon change.

"Yeah, I suppose we should discuss that." T.J. got up from the chair he was perched on and slid into the banquette next to her and watched as she withdrew a sheet of paper from her purse that had columns evenly distributed upon the page.

He let out a low whistle when he began to scan through some of the figures she had written down. "I think we're both going to have to increase our sales this month."

"It seems everything has gone up," Ellie confirmed. "The dock has raised its fee another twenty-five dollars a month, so that makes it close to twenty-three hundred dollars every six months to berth the boat and winter storage will be approximately eight hundred and sixteen dollars. Insurance is going to be around four thousand dollars a year, and transfer of title, the required boat stickers, and sales tax will run an additional . . ."

T.J. whistled again and slid down lower in the booth as her pencil added yet another column.

". . . and the new owner's manual says the gas tank will hold two hundred gallons of gas and gets approximately three miles per gallon . . . so let's see, gas is selling for a dollar seventy-five a gallon at the boat dock so that means every time we fill the tank it will cost us . . ." Both Ellie's and T.J.'s face began to turn pale as her pencil slowly revealed the sad fact. "Oh, dear . . . three hundred and—"

"Fifty dollars," T.J. finished glumly. He glanced at her and flashed a weak grin. "I hadn't thought about that."

"Me either . . . but the only sensible thing to do is conserve as much fuel as we can for a few weeks until we can get caught up on all these other bills."

"You mean we can't even use the boat until we get caught up on all those other bills?" He looked crushed.

"It won't be long. Maybe a month or two."

"But summer will be nearly over," he argued.

She lay her pencil down and looked at him patiently. "Do you have a better suggestion?"

He shrugged lamely. "No."

"Then I suggest we try to look on the bright side. We can always entertain on the boat. We just can't take it out on the water for a while." That would work out better, anyway, she thought. She had been wondering how she was going to have any time to study him if they took the boat on alternate weekends. This way she'd have plenty of opportunities.

He shook his head thoughtfully. "It's going to look pretty strange to our friends for us to have a boat and not be able to take it out of the dock."

"Maybe they won't notice. Velma said she and

Harry planned to entertain dockside most of the time," Ellie said. "We could do the same."

"Yeah, I suppose . . ."

"Oh, we might be able to take it out of the dock . . . occasionally," she relented. "We'll just agree to not go any farther than the mouth of the cove."

"Well . . ." The idea wasn't very exciting to him—to have the boat of his dreams, but couldn't afford to go anywhere with it—but she did have a point. They were going to be flat broke for a while.

The bank had required 20 percent of the purchase price down, and financed the rest of the loan for fifteen years at 14 percent interest. That made their payments $493 a month—a mere drop in the bucket when compared with all these other expenses.

So, it was easy to see that they would have to cut corners somewhere.

And the point of this whole partnership was not the boat in the first place. He felt he could always get his original investment out of it and even if he had to pinch pennies for a while, it would be worth it. "I have five closings at the end of the month. That should help."

"And I have three, so we should be able to swing the sales tax and the insurance with no problem. As far as the dock fee, the price of the boat included the first month free—thanks to Mike's generosity—so we're all right there until the last of July."

She folded the sheet of paper and stuck it back in her purse as T.J. slid out of the booth and went to explore the refrigerator.

"Hey, Mike left some bread and ham and mayonnaise. You want a sandwich?"

Ellie was repelled to think about eating someone else's food supply and she felt her stomach roll at his suggestion. The food might be perfectly edible and yet how was she to know where it had been or who or what had touched it. . . .

T.J. had unwrapped the ham and was sniffing it suspiciously. "I think it's still good. How about it? I make a mean ham sandwich."

Ordinarily, someone would have had to tie her up and ram the sandwich down her throat with a jackhammer, but she quickly reminded herself that the purpose of this whole, dreadfully expensive escapade was to be more like him, so that meant she had to swallow her previous qualms— no matter how repulsive that sandwich he was slapping together looked, and eat something.

"Well . . . maybe just a small one," she relented.

In a few moments T.J. had made several sandwiches, using only one piece of bread per sandwich, since the supply was running low. "This way we can eat more than one without feeling guilty," T.J. teased as he set the plate down in front of her.

She smiled back lamely and tried to decide how she would manage to get it down without disgracing herself.

The bread looked extremely unappetizing to someone who favored nice fresh bread as she did. It was ice cold after having been in the refrigerator for who knows how long and stiff as a board. She carefully examined it closer for signs of mold, and a small, relieved sigh escaped her when she found none.

T.J. was watching her closely to see how she went about eating. This lesson would be a valuable one. Although he never felt his manners were necessarily lacking, he was smart enough to know they could always stand improvement and there was no better time to start than now.

Ellie was still staring at her sandwich.

Now, how would *he* eat it, she asked herself. If she was serious about trying to change, then she would begin right now by copying his mannerisms.

But what would they be?

Other than the few times he had eaten next to her in the employees' lounge, she had never had the chance to observe his table manners. Her gaze quickly skipped back to him and she was shocked to see he was staring at her again.

They both grinned and dropped their gazes back down on the table. He seemed to be waiting for her to pick up her sandwich first.

Judging by the few times she had seen him eat, he had just picked his sandwich right up and started wolfing it down. No nice little tiny bites to savor the flavor, just get it in the hatch and wash it down with a cola!

Well, she supposed if that's what it took to be "exciting" then she might as well get used to it.

Taking a deep breath, she picked up the sandwich and began systematically gulping it down. Since she wasn't at all sure her stomach would hold out for the duration of the questionable fare, she knew she had to get it down fast.

T.J.'s eyes widened as he sat across from her and watched with amazement as her small teeth made their way through bread, ham, and mayonnaise with an appalling lack of grace.

In a matter of seconds, the meal had been consumed and she was fumbling blindly for her soft-drink can.

He wasn't sure, but he would not have been surprised to learn she had just set a new speed record for eating a ham sandwich.

"Well, now." She picked up her napkin and daintily wiped at the corners of her mouth. "I think there's one more thing we need to discuss concerning the boat."

"Oh?" T.J. was still stunned by what had just taken place, but he gracefully tried to cover his look of incredulity as he picked up his own sandwich and took a large bite.

In a way he felt relieved to know he had been eating properly all along . . . but it was still a bit disconcerting to see it displayed so . . . overwhelmingly.

The stale bread and suspect meat lay like an anchor in the pit of Ellie's stomach. "We need a new name for the boat," she finally managed to choke out in an uneven voice.

"You okay?" T.J. lifted a concerned brow as he noticed she seemed to be fighting for each breath.

"Fine . . . just fine." She took another sip of her drink and blinked to clear her watering eyes.

"A new name, huh?" T.J. thought for a moment as he picked up a second sandwich and absently offered it to her.

She shook her head frantically and he shrugged and began to eat it himself. "What's wrong with the one it has?"

Ellie looked at him in disbelief. *"Passion's Folly?* Well . . . uh . . . don't you think that it's a little inappropriate for our . . . uh . . . particular situation?"

The boat's colorful name, printed in big, bold letters across the transom had been worrying her ever since she had first seen it.

For Mike and Helen Haran, the name must have held significance, but Ellie wanted it changed as soon as possible.

"Maybe you're right," T.J. agreed. "But have we got the money to have the name repainted right now?"

"Oh dear, I hadn't thought about that."

"Well, I'll tell you what. Let's rename the boat now and then we can have it painted on the transom as soon as we get the extra money." It wasn't the ideal answer, but due to their financial strain of the moment it would have to do.

"I suppose that's all we can do. At least we

would be able to tell our friends we've changed the name."

"Right. So, what sounds good to you?"

"Oh, I don't know. What sounds good to you?"

"How about *The Poor House.*" He grinned. "You wanted something appropriate."

"Or *In Over Our Heads,*" Ellie bantered, relieved to find that she was beginning to feel less queasy.

*"The Dreamers."*

*"Out of Our Minds."*

"No, not *Out of Our Minds,*" T.J. scoffed. "I know it's a little expensive right now, but I'm sure once we get all the initial purchase costs behind us, we can breathe easier."

"Yes, I'm sure you're right," she relented. "How about *His and Hers?*"

"Or, *Yours and Mine?*" he improvised.

"Or, *Ours and the Bank's?*" They laughed.

"No, wait." Ellie held up her hand in a sudden, dazzling display of inspiration. "I've got it!"

"What?"

"How about *Templeton's Folly?*"

*"Templeton's Folly."* T.J. repeated the words several times and found that he liked the sound of it. *"Templeton's Folly.* Well, it sounds good to me, but don't you want your name on it? Like *Millstein and Templeton's Folly?*"

"Heavens, no! We'd have to buy a wider boat to name it that. No, *Templeton's Folly* is fine with me."

"Then that's what it will be." T.J. extended his hand and they solemnly shook on it. "Welcome aboard *Templeton's Folly,* Ms. Millstein."

"Delighted to be here, Mr. Templeton." She paused. "Now, about entertaining. Since we don't have the money to actually take the boat out on the water yet, why don't we just say that either one of us is free to bring guests aboard as long as we don't get in each other's way."

"That's agreeable to me." T.J. nodded. "But what happens if we should want to entertain . . . uh . . . privately."

"Then we simply let the other one know at least forty-eight hours in advance, and we agree to respect each other's privacy."

"Sounds fair to me." They shook again.

"Then I see no reason why this partnership shouldn't work out beautifully," she promised as she began to gather up her belongings in preparation to leave.

"Me either. I will probably be bringing clients aboard occasionally, but I'm sure you'll be doing the same thing."

"Yes, I'm sure I will." She picked up her purse and smiled at him. "I'm looking forward to sharing the boat with you, T.J."

*And even more forward to the chance to study you,* she added silently.

"I was just thinking the same thing," T.J. returned.

*And before summer's over, I'll be as elegant and classy as you are,* he thought happily.

"Well, I'll see you at the office, tomorrow."

"Yeah, tomorrow."

He watched her shapely backside disappearing up the stairway and he found himself still grinning long after she was gone.

This was going to be a piece of cake!

# CHAPTER FOUR

Somehow, things were just not working out the way they had planned.

Three weeks and a rash of unexpected expenses and *Templeton's Folly* was quickly becoming *Millstein's Headache.*

It seemed as if every time they turned around, some new expense cropped up. T.J. had thought the engine didn't sound "quite right" so that had brought about a complete motor tune-up.

After counting the life jackets, it was decided they needed at least four more to accommodate the number of guests they would be entertaining.

Then, of course, they had decided that it wouldn't hurt to have another fire extinguisher. And, although the boat was tastefully decorated, Ellie wanted to add a few touches of her own and that had ended up costing more than she had dreamed it would.

Instead of carrying groceries every week, they thought it might be nice to stock all the staples at one time and buy the perishables only when needed. That decision alone cost an additional two hundred dollars. And the list went on and on and on . . .

On top of it all, because of a sudden dip in interest rates, both she and T.J. had been so busy showing property to prospective buyers that she had barely seen him, much less been able to spend any time on the boat alone with him. Weekends had found them busy entertaining their own set of friends and it was as if suddenly the boat had turned into a popular resort hotel with T.J. and Ellie as the hosts.

The few times they had tried to talk privately had always been interrupted by someone looking for the head or in search of a cold drink.

There had been brief snatches of conversation during the "passing of checks" to each other in the office, but that was certainly not the ideal way to study his habits.

She wanted to see the jungle cat in his natural habitat . . . the eligible, carefree bachelor, without the business façade he wore in the office.

So far, the boat had only benefited their friends and lien holders.

It was certainly an expensive way to change one's life-style, she thought glumly as she tried to balance her checkbook at the end of a particularly harrowing day. And to think that, other than the one brief excursion out to the end of the cove the first week they had bought the boat, they hadn't even gotten to ride on the darn thing.

"Hi."

"Hi." She glanced up to encounter a pair of increasingly familiar blue eyes.

"Boy, have you been as busy as I have lately?" T.J. paused on his way to the copy machine and smiled at her.

She looked exceptionally pretty today. The plum color she was wearing made her eyes the shade of wild violets. She was wearing tiny matching earrings and a simple, thin gold chain that lay across the creamy skin around her neck.

He had looked for an excuse to stop and talk to her all day. It seemed he always felt he needed one to take up her time and he hadn't been able to come up with anything today. But as he had walked by her desk and caught the light, intoxicating scent of her floral perfume, he had finally gathered up enough nerve to stop for a few minutes.

"Yes, I've been snowed under."

"Hi, T.J." Peggy Miller walked by the desk and playfully rattled the papers she was carrying in his face, interrupting the conversation for a moment.

"Hi, Peg. How's it going?"

"Just fine." She moved on, but not without tossing him a flirtatious grin.

He promptly turned his attention back to Ellie. "Well, I guess we shouldn't complain about the brisk business. I don't know about you, but I can sure use the extra money."

"No complaint here. I can always use more money."

They smiled at each other and T.J. wished he had the nerve to tell her how nice she looked. With any other woman it would have been as easy as making another sale, but somehow he found his tongue tangled up in his mouth every time he was around her.

"Hi, T.J." Anita Bolinger was going out of her way to walk past Ellie's desk on her way to the employee lounge.

"Hi, Anita. How's it going?"

"Fine. Got time for a cup of coffee?"

"Not right now. Thanks anyway."

"Oh, hello, Ellie," Anita finally acknowledged Ellie's presence.

"Hello, Anita."

"Sure you don't have one teensy minute for coffee, T.J.?"

He grinned apologetically. "Sorry."

"Later, then." Anita smiled at him and continued on her way.

"Well, guess I'd better get busy. I'm writing up a contract for the Evanses on that Murphy property and they're going to wonder where I've disappeared to." T.J. turned to go, then glanced back over his shoulder at her. "You going to be out at the boat this weekend?"

"Yes. Janet and Mark thought they might drop by. I hope you don't mind?"

"Mind? No, not at all." Actually, he felt disappointed she already had plans. He had been hoping that she would be free this weekend so they could have a little time to enjoy the boat, alone.

Maybe charcoal some steaks and have a few relaxing drinks.

The few moments they had managed to snatch between guests had been pleasant and highly enjoyable. She was good company and he found himself wanting to spend more of his free time with her.

Dick's earlier warning about "being careful or he'd have something more than the boat to worry about" suddenly popped into his mind, but he quickly dismissed it. He wasn't falling in love with Ellie . . . he just enjoyed being around her.

And so far his plan to observe her ways was moving along too slowly.

But, he reminded himself, she was an attractive woman who had her share of male acquaintances, although he had never seen any one particular man hanging around her during the weekends.

Besides, Barbie had already halfway wrangled an invitation out of him to see the boat one day over the weekend and it would probably be Saturday. "Feel free to ask anyone you want. I wouldn't be surprised if some of my friends dropped by, too."

"Thanks, T.J. Then, I suppose I'll see you Saturday."

A sudden burst of confidence inspired him to grin at her and wink. "Yeah . . . you know, we really should slip away by ourselves some weekend and have dinner on the boat alone for a change."

She felt her pulse race at his words, then

quickly dismissed his invitation for what it was. Polite, flirtatious, T.J.ish conversation, nothing more.

"That would be nice." She smiled warmly and couldn't help herself from noticing how nice he looked this afternoon.

He always had that crisp, neat appearance about him she admired in a man. Even though he had been out showing property all day, he appeared as fresh—and smelled as good—as when he had first walked in the door that morning.

He always looked sporty, confident, successful, and energetic.

Her phone rang as her wistful gaze followed his broad shoulders until they disappeared around the corner.

"Ellie Millstein."

"Ellie? Fergie Waterman, here."

"Oh . . . Fergie. How are you?" Oh, no! Ferguson, alias Putt Putt Waterman, the man who refused to take no for an answer, and Ellie knew without asking that Fergie was going to try for a date with her again.

That's all she needed to top off a perfectly miserable day.

"Wondered if you were tied up this evening?"

"Oh, Fergie, I'm terribly sorry, but I am," she apologized guiltily.

It wasn't that Fergie wasn't a nice guy, he was just so . . . predictable. She always knew what he was going to say, going to wear and going to do.

He didn't have any more idea what to do for fun than she did, and that was exactly the kind of man she was trying to avoid right now.

Besides, she *had* promised herself to start sewing on the new jumpsuit she had been wanting to make for months now and tonight would be the perfect time to begin.

"Heard you bought yourself a new boat?"

"Well, yes . . . it's not completely mine. I'm in partnership with another person."

She hated to mention T.J.'s name for fear Fergie might read something suspicious into it. Already the rumor mill at the office was working overtime trying to figure out what was going on.

"What kind is it?" Ellie told him the brand and he was properly impressed.

Although Fergie was boring, he was far from bashful. "When are you going to take me out for a little spin in it?"

*The question is, when am I going to go out for a little spin,* Ellie thought wryly. "Well, we'll have to get around to that one of these days," she said lightly.

"I'm free all weekend."

"I'm not."

"Oh, come on, Ellie. Surely you could find time for an old friend sometime over the weekend."

"Oh, I don't know, Fergie . . ." She sincerely wished she weren't such a soft touch, but she knew that before the conversation ended she was probably going to agree to take him out to see the boat.

After all, he had always been nice to her and there was really no reason why she couldn't spare a few hours if it would make him happy.

She just wished he didn't have the personality of a rock.

"I'll bring my Scrabble board," he offered. "We might find time to fit in a few games."

Great. She would certainly try to make time for that, all right. "Yeah, that's a good idea, Fergie."

"How about Saturday night?"

She glanced at her appointment pad, praying that by some miracle she had overlooked an earlier engagement, but other than the question mark with Janet and Mark's name, the space under Saturday, the twenty-first of June, was still totally blank. "Yes, I think I can arrange my schedule to meet you. Janet and Mark Mason said they might drop by so we'll sort of make it a party."

"Sounds like fun."

Well, it wouldn't be, if it was anything like their other dates had been, but Mark and Fergie had always gotten along well together so she would let them keep each other company. "The boat is docked at Ocean Tide Marina, berth one thirty-two. I'll try to be there around seven."

"I can pick you up if you want me to."

"No, that won't be necessary, Fergie. I have a few errands I need to run first. But thanks anyway." Maybe with a little luck she could make it an early evening.

"Well, guess I'd better let you get back to work."

"Yeah, I guess I'd better."

"See you Saturday night around seven."

"Yes, I'll be looking forward to seeing you again, Fergie." She hoped her nose hadn't grown an inch longer.

When she hung up, she felt a sense of depression because she knew it was going to be another long, *dull* weekend.

"Oh, Elllleee!"

Flamboyant Barbie Jenkins teetered toward Ellie on a pair of spiked heels so high Ellie was sure she was going to fall off and break her neck anytime. She was waving a handful of paper in the air as she approached the desk. "You have tons of messages," Barbie announced petulantly as she handed the notes to her and parked herself on the side of the desk.

"I've been busy all day," Ellie excused, eagerly reaching for the messages in hopes there would be something in them that would prevent her going out Saturday night. "What are you doing taking messages?"

"Oh, Pamela is sick today so Ilga and I are manning the phones."

Ellie sighed and laid the messages aside. There was not the slightest hint of a reprieve in them.

It was no secret that Barbie was not exactly Ellie's favorite co-worker. She not only was the office busybody, but she had deliberately gone out of her way to inform the other people in the office that T.J. and Ellie's partnership in the boat was just that, immediately dashing all rumors that perhaps there was an office romance going on that had been previously undetected.

While Ellie had no desire for them to believe otherwise, it still rankled her to think that all her friends had the impression that T.J. would never view Ellie in a speculative way, which he wouldn't, but did Barbie have to go blabbing it all over the office?

"Have you seen T.J. today?" Barbie prompted.

"Yes, he was by a few moments ago. Why?"

"Oh, I was just wondering. I saw him, too." Barbie surveyed her incredibly long nails and frowned at a small chip in the bright red polish.

*Well goody for you,* Ellie thought irritably, wondering where this conversation was leading. Barbie did not waste her time making small talk with other women in the office. Only the men received such honors.

"He invited me out to the boat Saturday."

"He did?" That stung. She had been under the impression T.J. had no particular plans for the weekend. "How nice. I know you'll enjoy yourself."

So Barbie must have been one of the "friends" T.J. had been referring to earlier who might stop by the boat. Or at least one of them.

Well, that wasn't surprising. T.J. had an eye for pretty women and Barbie was pretty all right.

Ellie deliberately turned her attention to the messages once more, hoping Barbie would take the hint, which mercifully she did, and Ellie went back to balancing her checkbook.

But a few moments later she felt her gaze wandering over toward Barbie's desk. The dress she was wearing today was one of her usual get-ups.

It was a low cut, red jersey creation that clung in all the right places. Of course, her figure needed no apology and Ellie begrudgingly had to admit she did, indeed, look ravishing.

And no doubt when she arrived at the boat on Saturday, she would be dressed in something equally provocative and alluring, most likely shorts or a swimming suit. Ellie felt a tiny shudder race through her when she thought about just how skimpy those might prove to be.

Well, there wouldn't be a minuscule chance she would be able to compete for T.J.'s attention this weekend, but she could always watch Barbie in action and undoubtedly pick up a few pointers.

That way, at least the entire weekend wouldn't be wasted.

On her way home that evening, her thoughts were distracted by the attractive display of sportswear in the window of a small boutique that was adjacent to the realty office.

She paused for a moment to study the female mannequin, trying to visualize herself in the brief halter and short shorts.

Actually, it was more along the line of what Barbie would wear with its daring lines and highly suggestive neckline, but still the striking ensemble held her attention for an inordinately long time.

The upcoming weekend still wore on her mind heavily. She would be with Fergie, and T.J. would be with Barbie, and it would be just another painful reminder of how dull her life really was.

Fergie would be dressed in a conventional shirt, conservative shorts, white socks pulled up to the knees, and black wing-tip shoes.

She would be dressed much the same—minus the wing-tip shoes—and look as dull as dishwater.

On the other hand, if her guess was right, T.J. would be running around bare-chested, dressed only in a snappy pair of white surfing shorts that would fit his athletic body like a glove, and wearing a pair of white Nikes with no socks.

And Barbie would be dressed in something that was barely under the wire of decency.

Ellie's eyes focused once more on the bold yellow and orange outfit in the window and her chin suddenly lifted with grim determination.

Well, she might not be able to do anything about Fergie's clothes or Barbie's appalling lack of them, but she sure as the devil could do something about her own appearance!

Without a backward glance, she marched through the doorway of Merrilee's Boutique before she lost her nerve.

When she exited fifteen minutes later she had

her purchases in hand, and her bank balance had dropped by another sixty-five dollars.

But on Saturday T.J. Templeton was going to get his first glimpse of the new and more exciting Ellie Millstein!

The phone was ringing as she unlocked the door to her apartment and let herself in.

It was Janet Mason calling.

"Hi, sorry I wasn't able to catch you at the office before you left."

"Oh, that's all right. What's up?" Ellie set her packages down on the table and kicked off her shoes.

"It's about Saturday. Mark has to work all day and he just wants to come home and relax that evening, so I guess we won't be able to join you on the boat."

"I'm sorry. I was looking forward to your seeing it."

"I was, too, but maybe we can next weekend. It's probably better this way. I'm showing property that afternoon, plus I didn't have a baby-sitter lined up for Pud, so we would have all been miserable chasing him around all night."

"Pud" was actually Marcus Thorton Mason III, Mark and Janet's year-old infant son.

"Well, next weekend would be fine as far as I know," Ellie assured her.

"So, how're things going?"

"Just fine," Ellie said brightly.

"No problems with T.J. and the boat?"

"None at all."

"Good. Just see that you keep it that way."

Ellie chuckled as she had hung up the receiver before it suddenly occurred to her what Mark and Janet's absence would mean.

It would mean she was stuck with entertaining Fergie herself.

She sat down on the sofa and opened her package from Merrilee's Boutique and tried to bolster her sagging spirits by looking at her new purchases again.

What on earth would good ol' conservative Fergie say when she bounced in wearing this little number?

## CHAPTER FIVE

When Saturday finally arrived, Ellie was running low on confidence. She stood before the mirror late that afternoon and surveyed the new sportswear with a jaundiced eye.

The bright orange and yellow flowered fabric not only made her look completely ridiculous, she thought it made her look downright plump.

Why, of all days, did she have to be having a fat day?

She wasn't but three pounds over her normal weight, but today it looked like fifteen—all concentrated on her thighs and hips.

And the color. It was all wrong for her. The bright yellow made her complexion look as if she were just recovering from a long illness.

Turning sideways, she sucked in her cheeks and her stomach and let them out with a disgusted whoosh a few moments later.

Barbie would look like a sleek jungle animal and she would look like a sallow, overweight house cat.

If she was smart she'd march right in there and

put on her regular clothing, dull and uninteresting as it might be, and forget all about this sudden nonsense of trying to attract T.J.'s attention.

After all, it was undoubtedly a hopeless cause, and the purpose of buying the boat with him was to observe, not to try and catch him.

Besides, if he hadn't noticed her in the year they had worked together, what made her think he was suddenly going to miraculously notice her now?

But yet, if there was a chance in a million that he might see beyond the Barbies and Anitas of the office, then it might be worth the effort . . .

She found herself wincing at the thought of her friend Janet. She would be highly upset if she knew Ellie was thinking along this line, and would warn her again that T.J. was trouble.

But she wasn't falling in love with T.J. She was just doing what she set out to do . . . improve herself, and it was working.

She glanced in the mirror once more. If he couldn't tell she was alive by this outfit, then he not only was comatose, he was downright blind.

She gathered her beach bag and picnic hamper, then let herself out the door. Sitting in her garage was another example of what she was now beginning to view as the new, exciting Ellie Millstein.

On the spur of the moment, she had pulled her perfectly good four-door sedan into a new car dealership and traded it in for a deathtrap, otherwise known as a sports car.

It was bright red, grossly overpriced, and

looked almost exactly like the one T.J. was driving. Completely unrealistic for their line of business, but it certainly had not seemed to hurt his sales record, so she had decided to take the chance.

The salesman had patiently agreed to teach her to drive the five-speed stick shift, and she had taken the poor man on a jerky ride all over town before she finally got the hang of it.

Crawling into the driver's seat—because one did not get in a sports car any other way—she inserted the key in the ignition. When she started the high-performance engine, various bleeps and blips in colorful red lights appeared on the dashboard accompanied by a bell that sounded suspiciously like the one on planes giving prior warning just before they were about to become airborne.

Nervously, she fumbled for her seat belt and fastened it securely before she backed out of the drive.

Ripping the gear shift down into low, she grinned happily as she zoomed down the quiet residential street with a thunderous squeal of tires on hot pavement.

The plan was all coming together beautifully!

When she arrived at the boat, she immediately tried to locate T.J.'s vehicle so she could park next to it.

That way, he wouldn't miss seeing her new car.

But his car was nowhere to be seen and she decided he probably hadn't arrived yet. She knew he had worked today because she had run into the office earlier to leave her advertising for the daily newspaper and saw his car sitting out front.

Walking down the ramp to the marina she felt highly conspicuous in her new garb. She had always prided herself on being levelheaded and reasonable, and for a moment she felt a little uneasy when she thought about how she strongly resembled a Barbie clone now. But she quickly shrugged off the thought. This was her new look and she would eventually get used to it.

She put the corner of her purse in her mouth and tugged at the gaping neckline with her one free hand. She only hoped nothing fell out unexpectedly in front of the men.

When she stepped on the boat a few minutes later, she was surprised to see it was already teeming with activity. Barbie and Fergie were sitting with T.J., enjoying the beginnings of a beautiful sunset.

The lovely oranges and violets and golds reflected off the water in a breathtaking, dazzling array of color.

"Well, it's about time you got here." T.J. grinned as he reached out to take the picnic basket out of her hand.

His friendly gaze skipped over her lightly, but as suddenly as the grin had appeared, it slowly started to recede.

She blushed as she felt his eyes taking in her "new look"—then her face, to make sure she was who he thought she was—then back to her colorful ensemble.

"Hi," she said brightly, wishing that he would divert his attention somewhere other than her plunging neckline. "I didn't think you were here yet."

He was on time—a rare occurrence for T. J. Templeton.

"Yeah . . . I've been here awhile." His eyes were firmly fixed on the generous swell beneath the floral fabric and she began to edge away from him to say hello to Fergie.

She had always dreamed of a man looking at her this way. And she had not failed to see the way T.J.'s blue eyes had suddenly grown darker or the way his inquisitive gaze had slowed to run lazily over her—almost suggestively, ·actually. But now that he had, she felt strangely unnerved.

She was relieved to see him finally tear his eyes away from her and set the picnic basket down as she turned to greet Fergie. "Well, hello! Have you been here long?"

Fergie rose to his feet, his eyes fixed solidly on the dipping neckline too. "No, not . . . not long."

"How are you, Barbie?"

"Fine. How are you, Ellie?"

"Very well, thank you." Ellie felt her face turning a deep crimson as she finally noticed what Barbie was wearing. It was a very modest, simple sunsuit that bared little skin and fit loosely around her slender waist.

It was so demure it could have easily been worn at a church picnic!

Barbie's eyes lit up mischievously as she saw Ellie's blush deepen. "Gee. I love your outfit. The color is so . . . so right for you."

Shooting her a lame smile, Ellie murmured a pleasant thank you, and hurriedly turned her attention back to Fergie.

Thank goodness, good old reliable Fergie had not failed her. He was dressed every bit as conservatively as she had predicted, with his knee-length, camel-colored shorts and short-sleeved white dress shirt.

She smiled at him gratefully. "Can I get you anything, Fergie?"

"No thanks. I'm still nursing the wine cooler T.J. gave me earlier."

Her gaze wandered hesitantly over to T.J., who sat cocked up on the gunwale, still intently watching her.

Of course, he had held true to form, too. He was bare-chested, wearing a bathing suit in a shade of blue that made his eyes look even bluer, and a pair of white deck shoes.

It was all she could do to tear her gaze away from the sight of that broad chest covered in a heavy mat of dark blond fluff and center her attention elsewhere.

"Oh, then I see you've met my . . . uh . . . new partner?" Well, she had known Fergie would have to be told sooner or later whom she had chosen to buy the boat with, but she would have preferred to break the news to him more gently.

Fergie smiled at her coolly. "Yes, T.J. was just telling me about the partnership."

"Can I get you anything, Ellie?" T.J. asked as he casually slid off the railing.

"Thanks, I'll get it. I'll just run below and put a few things I brought in the refrigerator, and be back in a minute."

She escaped down the small set of steps leading to the galley, praying that perhaps she had left an extra change of clothing somewhere below.

But five minutes later, after searching through closets and cubbyholes, she sighed and realized she had not been so wise.

She was stuck for the evening in her disastrous choice of clothing and she would simply have to make the best of it.

But the evening turned out to be not nearly as bad as she had anticipated. T.J. and Barbie stayed aboard, and that made the evening go by more swiftly.

Around nine, Fergie suggested they play a friendly game of canasta, and although Ellie could sense T.J. wasn't exactly crazy about the idea, he proved to be a good sport.

He even insisted on popping corn to go with the drinks. Ellie watched with envy, and marveled that he could make a simple project like popping corn seem like such fun.

Around midnight, both Fergie and Barbie decided it was time for them to be leaving. T.J.

walked Barbie to her car while Fergie said his good night still aboard the boat.

"I've had a nice time, Ellie. Maybe we can all do this again some time real soon."

Ellie mentally prepared herself for the kiss she knew would be coming and tried to keep her mind off what Barbie and T.J. were probably doing.

What would it be like to have a man like T.J. take you in his arms and . . . She mentally dismissed the envious thought.

"That sounds like fun, Fergie."

"Ellie." Fergie's face turned solemn for a moment. "This partnership thing . . . well, the relationship between you and T.J. is purely business . . . isn't it?"

"Of course, Fergie."

He smiled, relief evident in his pleasant features. "Good. I was sure it would be, but the unexpected news took me by surprise."

"The partnership was just a way for both T.J. and me to have the boat," she explained.

"No need to defend yourself," Fergie assured her. "I know I have no cause to be questioning you. I was merely wondering."

"No need to worry. I'm not T.J.'s type." She laughed.

Just as Fergie bent to kiss her, T.J. stepped into the galley.

Ellie jumped away from Fergie guiltily as T.J. cleared his throat and murmured, "Excuse me. I didn't mean to interrupt."

256

"No, you weren't. I was just leaving." Fergie stepped back and gave her a brief peck on the mouth before he left. "I'll give you a call next week."

"Yes . . . that would be nice." She tugged self-consciously at her gaping neckline.

When Fergie had disappeared up the steps she began straightening up the small quarters as T.J. ran water in the sink to wash the dirty glasses.

She had to hand it to him. He had always been good about helping with the clean-ups after their guests had left.

"Nice night, wasn't it?" he said conversationally as he energetically squirted soap in the water.

"Yes it was. I enjoyed it."

"So did I."

The bubbles boiled up in a mountainous swirl as T.J. kept squirting. Such wastefulness set her nerves on end. Even soap did not come cheap nowadays and they had been out so much money on the boat . . . but she wasn't going to complain. T.J. was T.J. and that's what she admired about him.

But *still* . . . he was going to drown himself in bubbles if he didn't stop soon.

"Uh . . . T.J. . . . don't you think you have enough soap?"

He looked at the mound of swelling bubbles and shrugged. Snapping the lid closed, he placed it back under the sink and plunged four of the dirty glasses into the water.

He was going to break every one of them, she

fretted, and then they would be out more additional expense. She shut her eyes and vowed to refrain from expressing her opinion. After all, *she* was the one who needed to change, not him.

"Barbie seemed to be enjoying herself," she commented, as she fluffed throw pillows and replaced them on the banquette.

"Yeah, I think she was."

Ellie wiped off the table with a wet sponge and set the bouquet of silk flowers back in place.

"You and Waterman an item?"

She glanced up, surprised by his unusual question. This is the first time he had ever asked her anything about her personal life and it caused her pulse to flutter briefly. "Fergie and me?"

"Yeah."

"No . . . we're just good friends."

Good friends? The good-bye scene he had seen witnessed earlier hadn't looked that innocent to him, he thought peevishly and he suddenly found himself a little jealous of Fergie's position with Ellie.

It bothered him to think that Waterman was everything he wasn't. He was the suave, bookish type who wore tweed in the winter and smoked an ivory-bowled pipe . . . the refined, English gentleman . . .

Everything T.J. wasn't.

"And you and Barbie?"

"Me and Barbie?"

"Yes . . . are you two an item?" Ellie deliberately kept her voice light and noncommittal.

"Oh. No, I wouldn't say that. We see each other occasionally, that's all."

"Oh."

Ellie walked over to replace the butter in the refrigerator and she shook her head in exasperation when she opened the door and saw that once more it was almost empty.

For the last two weeks it had been virtually impossible for both T.J. and herself to keep the thing stocked.

Their friends had developed a bad habit of dropping by unexpectedly with just enough food and drinks to last an hour or two. Of course they would have so much fun that they always stayed until late in the evening, and their hosts would end up replenishing the refreshments.

"What's the matter?" He looked up from a pile of glasses he was washing and caught her irritated scowl.

"The refrigerator is almost empty again."

"Oh, yeah. I noticed that earlier."

"Didn't we just buy three cases of soft drinks?"

T.J. shrugged. "A couple of weekends ago."

She shut the door and went over to take stock of the pantry. She hated to sound like a shrew, especially in view of the fact she knew T.J. never worried about money the way she did, but these human garbage disposals they called friends were getting out of hand.

"Just look at that! Every chip, pretzel, and cookie in the whole place is wiped out again."

T.J. grinned, amused that she could get so bent

out of shape over something so unimportant. Money was to be spent, not hoarded.

"It's like trying to feed a herd of hungry locusts," she complained.

"It's not all that bad. Besides, I thought we both agreed that we like to entertain and I'm sure I certainly don't resent providing good hospitality when we have guests or clients come aboard. Do you?"

"No, but my checkbook is beginning to groan every time I open it lately."

"You're too tight," he accused, but she could tell he was trying to tease her out of her bad mood.

"And you're too loose."

His brow shot up playfully. "How would you know?"

"I guessed," she bantered, a grin tugging at the corners of her mouth. "But you're too loose with your money, too."

"Is that right. Well, maybe so, but I've noticed you've been putting out a lot of the greenbacks out lately, yourself."

"Only on necessities," she corrected.

He rinsed off the last glass and stuck it in the drainer. By the grace of God he had managed to wash each one of them without cracking a single one.

"Now correct me if I'm wrong, but isn't that a new outfit you're wearing tonight?"

Once more her face flooded with color. She had almost forgotten what she had on. "Well

. . . yes . . . but it was such a good price I could hardly pass it up."

T.J. wiped his hands on a paper towel while his eyes ran quizzically over the uncharacteristic attire. "It's a little different than what you usually wear . . . isn't it?"

"No!" Her face turned even redder as she busied herself picking up stray pieces of popcorn off the floor.

"No?" He grinned and made a big point of gaping and panting over her neckline.

"No. And even if it were, it's still very pretty . . . don't you think?"

The material and design was almost exactly like something that would be in Barbie Jenkins's wardrobe, and she would just bet he would have complimented *her* on her choice, not questioned it.

"Yes, I've always thought you had good taste," he agreed easily. "I just thought that particular outfit was a little . . . different than what I usually see you wearing."

Well, hallelujah! she thought triumphantly. This was the first indication that he might be starting to take notice. "Well, maybe it is a little," she conceded. "But I've decided I need a bit of a change."

"Well, be careful, and don't change too much," he cautioned with a sexy wink that turned her insides to mush. "I've always liked the way you look."

His remark caught her so off guard she found

261

herself becoming flustered, and she began to rattle on hurriedly. "Now about these supplies. I agree we should provide our friends with unlimited hospitality, but we're going to have to cut costs somewhere along the line."

"Okay," he said good-naturedly. "What do you want me to do?"

"First of all, I think the problem is, we're buying name-brand products and that's not only costing us more money, but the products are naturally going to disappear faster."

"Why?"

"Because they taste so much better. From now on, we're buying generic everything."

"Generic!"

Good God. Offer his friends generic pretzels? True, he needed to be more like her, but he wasn't at all sure he could tighten his purse strings to that extent.

Always before, if he wanted anything from the grocery store, he picked it up and threw it in his cart without ever giving price a thought.

"That's right. Most people will not be able to tell the difference, and it will save us a lot of money," she explained. "And, you can start clipping coupons. You won't believe how much we can save by doing that."

T.J.'s face was growing paler by the minute. "Clip coupons?"

His mind immediately conjured up all those economical women with their metal filing boxes who had held him up in the checkout lanes each week while they alphabetically counted out their little slips of paper.

"Sure. That way we can apply the savings toward other areas of the boat expenses," she explained.

"Well . . ." He wasn't at all happy about it, but he grudgingly had to admit that what she was saying made sense. "I suppose I could clip a few coupons . . ."

"Good." She gathered up her picnic hamper and prepared to leave. "I'll make out a list of what we need and give you half of it before next weekend."

"All right—are you going now?" He had been enjoying their brief time alone and he was hoping she would stay longer.

"Yes, I have an open house tomorrow. What about you?"

"No, not this week. What property are you showing?"

"That beachfront condominium I listed a couple of weeks ago."

"Oh, yeah. Nice house. It should move pretty fast."

"I'm certainly hoping so." She sighed. "I need the money."

"Hang on a minute and I'll walk to the car with you." T.J. gathered up his own belongings and followed up the steps behind her.

The night was beautiful, with a large, full moon casting its silvery beams over the rippling water. A soft breeze teased the air and there was still the faint smell of barbecue lingering pleasantly nearby.

As they began to stroll down the walkway, T.J. absently draped his arm around her waist. It was a natural gesture for him, but she thought surely he was going to hear her heart trying to pound its way out of her gaping neckline.

They chatted about small things and she could smell his aftershave and he could smell her perfume.

They both felt a sense of rightness, a sense of comfortable compatibility that they had a hard time recalling with anyone else.

"You know, it might be nice if we decided to have dinner on the boat some night this coming week," T.J. suggested and she felt her pulse jump again.

He had mentioned having dinner alone once before, but because of the crowd that was always on hand, they had never seemed to manage it. "Fourth of July's on Wednesday. We might even scrape up enough money to start the damn thing and take it out on the water," he suggested.

Was he actually asking her for a date? Maybe not. Before she made a fool out of herself, she'd better be sure. "That sounds nice. Who should we invite to share the great happening?"

"No one. Why don't we keep it small and celebrate the Fourth quietly . . . that is, if you don't have any other plans."

"No . . . no, I don't." Now he *would* have to

be deaf if he didn't hear the way her heart was thrumming.

"Good." He squeezed her shoulder. "Why don't I pick you up around seven? There's no sense in bringing both cars."

She agreed that would be the sensible thing to do as they stepped off the boat ramp and walked along the long rows of parked cars.

When she paused a few moments later in front of her car, T.J. kept on walking.

When he eventually noticed she wasn't beside him any longer, he turned around. She was standing beside a gorgeous red sports car, grinning at him.

"What's wrong?"

"Nothing. This is my car."

"Your car?" He laughed. "You drive a four-door Buick."

"Not anymore."

His eyes widened and he let out a low, appreciative whistle. "That's yours?" Striding over to her side, he began to examine the workmanship of the car. When he was finished she knew she had just scored several more points in his book of admiration. "You like it?"

"Like it? I love it," he confessed.

"Thanks. I just bought it this afternoon."

"What was wrong with your Buick?"

"Oh, nothing. I just thought I'd like a change. It's very similar to the model you drive, isn't it?"

For a moment he shuffled around uneasily. "Yeah . . . or what I used to drive."

"Have you traded cars?" That was hard to believe. She had just seen his car at the office this morning.

He grinned sheepishly. "Well . . . I was driving by the car lot I usually do business with this afternoon and they had a model that caught my eye. Before I knew it, I had traded my Corvette in."

She shook her head sadly. What this poor man needed was someone to manage his money or he was never going to have a thing, she thought. "Well, let's see what they stuck you with."

"Oh, it's nice," he said defensively as he led the way down the rows of parked cars. "I think I'm going to like it."

There wasn't quite the same tone of complete confidence that was usually evident in his voice. Ellie was fully expecting to be led to a Porsche or some other equally outrageous vehicle when he suddenly stopped beside a very plain model, a four-door sedan. "Well, what do you think?"

"About what?"

"My new car."

"Where is it?"

"Right here."

It was Ellie's eyes that widened in disbelief this time. "This is your car?" She looked at it blankly. He had to be kidding. It looked like the one she had just traded in!

"Yeah . . . what's wrong with it?"

Damn. The woman was beginning to be a real enigma to him. Here he was trying to be more conservative and levelheaded like she was and now all of a sudden she was out buying flowered outfits cut clear down to her navel and driving an IROC Camaro, practically turning her nose up at his new sedan.

He just didn't understand women at all.

"Nothing . . . it's just so . . . not you."

"Well, I like it."

Maybe he could bluff his way through and prove that he could be as sensible and as prudent as the next man, although he really didn't know why he should go to all the trouble.

He wasn't trying to make points with her.

"Yes . . . well . . . I'll trade you car payments," she conceded, growing ever more nauseous as she thought about the huge monthly payment she would be facing for the next thirty-six months.

"Yeah, that's the only . . . I mean one of the good things about the trade. My payment was cut in half. And, I'll be able to take more than one person at a time to look at property." He sighed wistfully as he looked at the bland four-door. "So I won't be having to borrow the company car anymore."

"Yeah." Ellie sighed, longing for her old four-door and lower payment back. "This will be much more convenient."

They were both suddenly very depressed.

"Well, I'll pick you up Wednesday night around seven."

"Yes, I'll be ready."

T.J. got in his car as Ellie walked back to hers. With a light flick of the wrist her car roared into life like a powerful jungle predator.

The four-door sedan's starter ground for several minutes before the diesel ignition backfired, then belched into life, spewing a revolting smell that strongly resembled a thousand rotten eggs back through the air conditioner vents.

T.J. fought the urge to gag as he smiled back at Ellie who had pulled out in front of him and gave a friendly wave.

*Damn,* he thought miserably.

There had to be an easier way to change his image.

## CHAPTER SIX

It was hard to keep her mind on work and off T.J. the following week. Every time she glanced over and saw him sitting at his desk, her stomach would do a little flipflop when she thought about his actually asking her for a date.

Was Janet's prediction about her falling in love with him coming true? She certainly hoped not, but she found herself looking forward to this date far more than she should have been.

Maybe Wednesday night would prove to her that he wasn't nearly as exciting and delectable as she thought he was. Then again, maybe it would prove to be the other way around . . .

She was beginning to wonder if buying the boat hadn't been a big mistake. True, she was gradually changing her image, but she wasn't sure it was all worth it.

She was broke most of the time and depressed the rest.

She could have had more privacy with T.J. on the public beach, and that wouldn't have cost her a penny.

And he was acting strange lately . . . not himself at all.

Imagine. Trading his beloved Corvette off for a plain four-door sedan.

It didn't make any sense at all.

When the Fourth of July finally came, she was dressed and waiting an hour before T.J. was due.

Of course he was an hour late, but he was properly apologetic even to the point of bringing her a bouquet of violets. To match her eyes, he had said, and she fell for the old ploy hook, line, and sinker.

It was the way he was dressed that puzzled her.

For a moment when she first opened the door, she thought Fergie had shown up unexpectedly.

But it was T.J.'s beaming face that grinned happily back at her. Although the knee-length walking shorts and white, short-sleeved dress shirt could have come straight from Fergie's closet.

Even the dark wing-tip shoes with white socks smacked of Ferguson Waterman, and she forced herself to not be too disappointed at yet another example of T.J.'s recent strange behavior.

After all, Fergie dressed nicely enough. It was just that she was used to T.J. looking like . . . T.J.

"Hi. Sorry about being so late. I got tied up with a client."

"That's all right."

He surveyed her attire and he felt a little let down himself.

She was wearing another one of those outfits that just wasn't her. It was flashy and colorful, and complete with a pair of huge gold dangling earrings.

"I know you must be getting hungry. I stopped by the meat market and picked up a couple of nice steaks, and the fixings for a salad. I thought we might cook our dinner while we sat and relaxed out on the water," he suggested.

It had been a long tiring day, and T.J. had found himself looking forward to this evening all week. And it didn't really matter how she was dressed. She was still the classiest woman he had ever met.

"That sounds nice." Ellie picked up her purse and beach bag and switched off all but one lamp in the apartment. "Would you mind helping me carry those?"

"Sure thing." T.J. scooped up an armload of the brown grocery sacks sitting next to the doorway while Ellie gathered up the rest. The door snapped locked behind them as they proceeded out to T.J.'s car.

"How do you like your new car?" she asked.

"Oh . . . it's okay. How do you like yours?"

"It's all right."

"How fast will it run?"

"I don't have any idea. Would you like to drive it?"

His eyes lit up hopefully. Driving that tank of

his around all week had been less than pleasant. "Would you mind?"

"No, not at all. Just leave your car here and you can pick it up later."

She was immensely relieved that he had offered to drive. She hated that little cracker box. All week long she had yearned to have her nice, big, safe car back.

"I'll get my things out of the trunk. It'll only take a minute."

Ten minutes later, T.J. was in his glory as they drove to the marina, zipping up and down the freeways like a bird let out of his cage. The powerful motor hummed along on all cylinders, its mighty engine sucking up gas like a deranged vacuum cleaner.

It was a soothing balm to his suppressed spirit of adventure.

"I got all of the things on my shopping list," he told her as they barreled around a semi, a motorcycle, and three church buses.

"Great . . ." Ellie was trying to keep from clutching the dash; her foot stomped an imaginary gas pedal as he squeezed back into a tight line of traffic. He was a good driver—just extremely fast. "I have mine, too."

True to Ellie's prediction, between the two of them they had managed to save over fifty dollars by buying the generic brands and clipping coupons. T.J. had been embarrassed, but he had managed to live through the humiliation.

When they arrived at the boat, both were feeling a sense of expectancy, knowing they were about to spend an evening they had looked forward to for a long time. They laughed and joked with each other as they unloaded the trunk and lugged the heavy sacks down to the boat.

Sporadic bursts of loud firecrackers being shot off in the distance, along with the pungent smells of sulfur and burning punk permeated the warm, muggy July air.

There was a festive mood among the vacationers and holiday revelers; they waved and called out in friendly greeting to T.J. and Ellie as they came down the narrow walkway leading to *Passion's Folly.*

They smiled back, having become acquainted with most of their fellow boat owners over the past few weeks. Ellie experienced a surge of pride when she thought about how they had been so easily accepted as a couple.

Almost everyone thought that she and T.J. had something going other than owning the boat together, and for some reason neither T.J. nor herself had ever bothered to discourage that image.

Over the weeks, they had been invited for drinks and cookouts that occurred regularly among the group who berthed their boats next to one another, and they just easily fit right in with the other couples.

Their new friends seemed to have a small city all their own and many times their boats never left their stalls on weekends, so T.J. and Ellie had ceased to feel bad about not being able to take the boat out.

But tonight they wanted to be alone. After promising to join some of the parties later that evening, T.J. hopped aboard the boat and unlocked the door to the galley.

While they put away the groceries, he began to tease her about the generic brands again, actually laughing out loud when she placed a package of the plain white paper–wrapped cigarettes on the table for future guests.

"You have *got* to be kidding! Generic cigarettes?" He burst out laughing again. "You expect me to offer my friends and clients generic cigarettes?"

She shrugged calmly. Obviously, the man didn't know the first thing about pinching pennies.

"Yes, what's wrong with that? They're no different than generic Jell-O."

She held up a black and white box and grinned back at him impishly. She liked it when he laughed out loud; it was the sort of laugh that made you feel good all over. But that's how T.J. made everyone feel. Alive and full of vitality, brimming over with enthusiasm for life.

When his laughter finally subsided, he moved closer to her and she felt her breathing quicken. The quarters were small and his standing so near gave her goosebumps.

"You're a crazy lady," he announced, reaching out to brush the tip of her nose with his finger.

A sudden, totally unexpected intimacy sprang up between them as she lifted her gaze shyly to meet his. "I hope you mean that in a nice way."

The blue of his eyes softened as he stepped closer, trapping her between the table and his large frame. His arms reached out and encircled her waist; her arms automatically circled his neck. "Of course I do. Let me show you."

And then before she knew what was happening, he was lowering his mouth to meet hers. He tasted every bit as good as she knew he would and she leaned into him to savor the moment more fully.

He tasted faintly of mint, and she felt that old familiar weakness when she was around him invading her once more.

"I'm going to confess something to you. I've been looking forward to spending this evening with you for a long time," he admitted when their lips parted a few moments later. He tenderly smoothed her hair with his hands.

"With me?" Somehow that was impossible to believe. Not when he could have so many other women who would undoubtedly be more to his taste.

He chuckled at the disbelief in her voice, then nipped seductively at her lower lip. "Yes, with you." Holding her even more closely, his mouth closed over hers in a long, probing kiss.

Sagging against him weakly, she returned the kiss wholeheartedly, refusing to try and analyze what had brought it on. She knew she shouldn't take it seriously, but there was no law as far as she knew that said she couldn't enjoy it.

"Yoohoo!" The sound of Barbie Jenkins's voice floated through the doorway as T.J. groaned and reluctantly broke the embrace. "Oh, hell. What is she doing here?"

"Is anyone home?"

Fergie Waterman's familiar baritone joined Barbie's as they began to peck on the side of the boat and make loud noises.

"Did you invite Waterman here?" T.J. sounded offended.

"No! Did you invite Barbie?"

The mere thought burned her. She had been under the distinct impression he had wanted them to be alone this evening. But if she had stopped to think she would have known that was unlikely.

T.J. was probably intent on celebrating the Fourth in a grand style, so, on second thought, he had composed his own guest list.

"No, I didn't invite her," he denied.

"Well, it's too late to worry about it now." Ellie sighed. "It seems we have company—again."

Fergie and Barbie were already on the deck when they came aft. Loaded down with picnic hampers and big, friendly smiles, it was apparent they were there for the duration of the evening.

But they had plenty of company.

By ten o'clock the boat and surrounding area around the stall were teeming with well-meaning friends who had just decided on the spur of the moment to "drop by and say hello."

For the rest of the evening, Ellie was down in the galley making sandwiches and trying to keep the sweat from rolling down in her eyes, while T.J. was running around filling glasses and trying to dodge Barbie.

The stereo was going full blast and several of the guests had brought sacks of fireworks that were now being shot off the bow of the boat.

Around eleven, Dick and Penny Benson came aboard with Penny's sister, Cissy Parkins.

Dick was determined to introduce T.J. to Cissy and he dogged his friend's steps until T.J. was forced to duck into the head, where he sat on the closed commode reading a magazine until people began banging on the door and demanding in belligerent voices to get in there.

And if T.J. and Ellie thought the generic beer and cigarettes would put a damper on anyone's good times, they shouldn't have gotten their hopes up.

There were potato chip and pretzel crumbs all over the floor, the ashtrays were overflowing, and Ellie even sat down in a glob of guacamole dip when she had collapsed for a few moments in the banquette.

"T.J.—hey, T.J.! Come over here a minute! I want you to meet my wife's sister, Cissy." Dick finally managed to corner T.J. around midnight. "Here, hold my plate for me, while I run and get us another drink. Say, I noticed you're running a little low." He fished in his pocket and withdrew two twenty-dollar bills. "Why don't you and Cissy take my car and run down to that all-night supermarket about a couple of miles down the road and pick up some more? We didn't think to bring any with us. This will be a good time for you two to get to know each other." Dick slapped T.J. on the back good-naturedly and went in search of more refreshments.

T.J. smiled lamely at the petite blonde giggling up at him. She was trouble. He could feel it in his bones and see it in her hungry-looking eyes.

"Hi, Cissy."

"Hi, T.J." She giggled again and crooked her arm into his. "I would just love to ride up to that little ol' supermarket with you."

"Uh . . . yeah, that would be nice, but I'm afraid I'm going to have to let one of my friends run you up there—Fergie! Hey, you busy?"

At the sound of his name, Fergie broke away from the Scrabble game he was deeply involved in with one of the other guests. "You call me, T.J.?"

"Yeah. You want to run Cissy up to the supermarket for more supplies?"

Fergie eyed the blonde suspiciously. "I don't know, T.J. We're in a pretty tight situation here."

"I'd sure appreciate it." He'd never know how much.

"Well . . ." Fergie cast a critical eye at the board, then back to his opponent. "I suppose we could take a break in the action."

Cissy was definitely disappointed and took no great pains to conceal it. "Oh, gee! T.J., can't you go?"

"Sorry." He handed her Dick's plate and the two twenty-dollar bills. "Maybe next time."

As T.J. hastened to make his exit, he bumped into a man trying to make his way off the boat with a paper plate piled high with food.

"Oh, sorry . . . Mike?" T.J. helped steady the former owner of the boat, his face clearly registering surprise at seeing him there.

"Hi, there. Nice party," Mike Haran greeted.

"Yeah . . . thanks."

Mike moved on as T.J. stood rooted to the spot, still trying to figure out what *he* was doing here.

By now there were so many people on the boat he could barely shove his way through the boisterous crowd. The meal he and Ellie were to share had long been forgotten, but his stomach told him he had missed dinner.

And so did his head.

He had a throbbing headache and his patience was beginning to wear thin with the party he had never intended to give. And he missed his date. He hadn't seen her but a couple of times this evening and he suddenly felt resentful.

Everyone was having a good time but him.

Ellie was washing dishes when she felt someone come up behind her and quickly untie her apron. It was T.J. "T.J. . . . what's the matter?" She raised her voice to be heard above the din.

"Ssshh!" He held one finger up to his lips and motioned for her to follow him, which she willingly did.

She was so tired she was about to drop, and she had been standing there feeling sorry for herself because of the way this evening had turned out to be such a disaster.

Hand in hand, they ducked out of the galley and up the steps, where they worked their way through the crowd, off the boat and down the walkway.

Outside, there was nothing but blissful, heavenly quiet.

The noise from the various parties going on faded into the background as T.J. led her out along the shoreline that was drenched in silvery moonlight.

When they came to a nice sandy patch of ground, T.J. spread the blanket he was carrying, and they both dropped down in exhaustion and drew long, deep sighs.

"That's a madhouse over there."

"You're telling me. I'll have dishpan hands for weeks." Ellie held up her hands and surveyed the evening's damage to her nails.

Lying back on the blanket, they watched the rockets lighting the starry sky with mutual contentment.

"You eat anything?" she asked.

"No, did you?"

"No."

"I happen to have a generic imitation Snicker bar in my front pocket. You want half?"

"I'd love it." She watched as he unwrapped the plain wrapper and split the bar into two.

They bit into the chocolate and nuts and both wrinkled their noses in disgust at the same time. The candy tasted as if it had been melted once and then reset; the nuts were tough and the caramel so sticky they couldn't get their teeth back out of it.

"Hiz izznot a Snisher bar," she accused, struggling to chew.

"I know. It's hat cheap garbage you shay will shave us money."

After they finally managed to swallow the candy, they settled back once more to stare at the beautiful starry night. A sultry breeze filtered about them, and Ellie felt at peace with the whole world.

Tonight had been disappointing, but there would be other nights. She felt reasonably sure of that. At the present time she had a few moments alone with him, and that's all that mattered to her.

"Now, this is more what I had in mind for the evening," he confessed. "I'm sorry it hasn't worked out that way."

"Oh, that's all right. Half of those monkeys are my friends, too."

"Am I going crazy or did I see Mike Haran walking around?"

"Yes, he was there. He sat in the galley and talked to me almost all evening."

"What in the world did he want?"

"Nothing in particular. I think he's lonesome, T.J. He told me he had just come down to the boat for old times' sake and saw we were throwing a party and joined in."

T.J. felt a tiny seed of resentment that Mike Haran had spent the evening with her and he hadn't. "He might as well have brought a date. Everyone else did."

"He says he isn't dating yet." Ellie yawned and stretched lazily. "But he's a nice guy and someone will come along one of these days—oh, you want to hear something funny?"

"Yeah, I'm strongly in need of a little humor at the moment."

"He says I remind him of his ex-wife. Isn't that strange?"

"Yeah, strange." T.J. was silent for a few moments as he struggled to overcome what amounted to nothing less than a shot of pure jealousy. Mike Haran was probably *her* type, too. Quiet and levelheaded, just like Fergie Waterman.

But he was probably also on the make, and she was buying his sob stories.

"I really feel sorry for him. I don't think that people realize that a divorce is as hard on a man as it is on a woman."

"What was their problem?"

"Oh, a lot of things I think. For one, he said he thought she had outgrown him."

"I suppose that happens."

"Yes." She glanced at him expectantly. "Do you think that can be prevented in a marriage?"

T.J. shrugged. "It won't happen in mine."

She smiled. "Now how can you predict a thing like that?"

"Because my wife will either come down to my level or I'll go up to hers," he said simply. "But, I don't want to talk about the Harans' problems right now." He rolled over on his stomach and grinned at her. "You wouldn't happen to have your suit on, would you?"

"Yes, I put it on under my clothing before I left the apartment, and haven't had a chance to take it off yet. Why?"

"It so happens I have mine on, too. Why don't we go for a swim?"

"Now?"

"Sure, why not?"

"But if they hear us, we'll undoubtedly have company," she argued, not wanting to share these few moments of bliss with anyone else.

"If they hear us, yes. But they won't. I seriously doubt with all that noise they're making they could hear the charge of the Light Brigade."

She couldn't argue with that, and in a matter of minutes they had shrugged off their clothes and let them drop to the blanket.

Ellie was happy to see T.J.'s magnificent body, which had been hidden by his conservative shorts and shirt all night, even if he was wearing a baggy

Hawaiian-print bathing suit instead of the nice, tight, suggestive knit one he had always worn.

T.J. looked at her in the moonlight and felt his pulse quicken.

Since buying the boat, he had seen her many times in a bathing suit, but the sight never failed to arouse him. She had a delicate build, slim and willowy—but enough soft curves to make it hard for him to take his eyes off her.

She couldn't help but notice his rapt attention. "Something wrong?"

"Nope. It all looks pretty right to me."

"Flattery will get you everywhere."

"Where's the red bathing suit?"

"At home. I bought a new one."

She didn't have to tell him that. The "new" one was a one piece, cut high on the thigh and laced up the sides, showing enough skin to make his blood pressure edge up another notch.

"What was wrong with the red one?"

"Nothing. I just wanted a new one."

He wasn't sure he liked the new look. It was more like something Barbie Jenkins would wear, not Ellie. The old one didn't show nearly as much creamy skin, and although it was fine for her to wear the new suit around him, he didn't think Fergie's heart could take the strain. And he teasingly said so.

"Fergie's stronger than you think," she informed him lightly.

"That holds no comfort for me."

She grinned. "Are we going to discuss Fergie

Waterman, whom I might point out is only a good friend, or are we going swimming?"

"Hell of a choice, but I pick swimming."

They ran out to the water and for the next hour relaxed and swam around the darkened shoreline. Every so often there would be a burst of laughter from the marina and they would grin at each other knowingly.

"You really know how to throw a party, Ms. Millstein," he complimented.

"Thank you, Mr. Templeton. Our guests do sound as if they're having a lovely time, don't they?"

"Just lovely. I can hear the melodic sound of crunching and the tabs being ripped off our generic beer cans all the way out here. But what the hell, it's only money."

"Aha! And I thought I was the one who was a tightwad." It was plain to see he would never let her live down the generic idea.

"You are."

"Well, I can say one thing. There's going to be a lot of horrendous headaches in the morning."

"Yeah, and not one generic Alka-Seltzer in the house." He cupped his forefinger and thumb together and squirted a stream of water in her eyes. "We may have to declare the boat a disaster area and let the government come in and clean up the mess after they leave."

"Good idea. I wonder if they even miss us?" She squirted him back.

"Nope. And I can't say I miss them overly much, either."

"Shame on you."

"Yes, shame on me." He dove in under the water and she suddenly felt herself being dragged under to join him.

Beneath the murky depths she reached out in panic for him, and he caught her to his broad chest, and then they were kissing.

Sweet, hungry kisses that made her forget all about her panic. Seconds later he brought them to the surface, his mouth never leaving hers. The kiss deepened even more as they stood up in the waist-deep water, and he molded her curves tightly against him, letting her feel the firm male response she so easily aroused.

This was the T.J. that excited her. This was the man whom she dreamed of, longed for, and desperately wished to be more like. His hands slid down her side and caressed her wet body, slowly awakening her own responses to his devastating presence.

It was strange how one person could make you forget decorum and propriety and all the reasonings of what should and shouldn't be, she thought in a hazy mist.

She knew she shouldn't be here in his arms, returning his kisses with a fervor that he could easily misinterpret.

True, he was everything she wanted, and yet she knew that to T.J. she was just another woman. And not even a particularly exciting one.

Once more she realized what a mistake she had made by buying the boat with him. Janet had been right. She couldn't keep her distance from him and that had to stop.

She began to pull reluctantly away from his embrace.

T.J. had sensed the moment the magic spell was broken and he wondered what had broken it. Their mouths slowly parted and he squeezed her affectionately. "It's getting late. You think we should start trying to break the party up?"

She gave him a shaky smile. "Yes. I think so."

He lowered his mouth to touch hers once more and she closed her eyes in silent agony. How much longer should she let this go on?

"I don't know about you, but it's been a nice Fourth for me, regardless of the change of plans," he whispered.

Dick had been right. He was growing more fond of her every day and it had to stop. He wasn't anywhere close to wanting to get seriously involved with just one woman . . . yet.

"I can honestly say it's been a holiday I'll never forget," she whispered back.

"Then we'll do it more often." Had he said that? He should be making some sort of excuse to avoid this sort of situation in the future! he thought frantically.

They kissed once more, suddenly clinging very tightly to one another. She felt so damn good in his arms it was easy to forget for a moment this was only a light flirtation.

"We'll see," she hedged, as their mouths finally parted again. She had some serious thinking to do about T. J. Templeton.

And she was going to start the moment she got home.

# CHAPTER SEVEN

"How did you celebrate the Fourth?"

"Oh, Mark invited a couple he works with over for a cookout. If we had known you were going to have a big party, we would have made arrangements to be there," Janet complained to Ellie over lunch in the employees' lounge of Coastal Realty the next day.

"As usual, we didn't know we were having a party."

"Oh, it's really getting bad out there, isn't it?"

Ellie nodded. "It's a real mess."

"Aw, gee, Ellie, I can tell by the look in your eyes you're getting in too deep with this guy," Janet accused.

"Let's not start that again." For the past week every conversation she and Janet had revolved around Janet's suspicion that Ellie was falling in love with T.J. At one point Ellie had given in and admitted she did find T.J. extremely attractive, but she was logical enough to realize nothing serious could ever come out of the attraction.

But that didn't satisfy Janet.

"Well, I know you don't like for me to say this, but—"

" 'You should have never gotten yourself in this predicament in the first place,' " Ellie quoted by heart.

"Well, it's the truth."

"I hate to admit it, but I'm beginning to think you were right."

Janet leaned over the lunch table, narrowing her eyes triumphantly. This was the first time Ellie had ever hinted at defeat. "I knew it! You've fallen for him, haven't you?"

"No I haven't."

"Yes, you have."

"No, I haven't, Janet. For heaven's sake. I just meant I think buying *Passion's Folly* might have been a big mistake."

"Why?"

"Why! Because, it's costing too much money, we haven't gotten to enjoy the boat because we're too busy entertaining other people, and it . . . it does throw me with T.J. too much."

"Didn't I tell you so?"

"Yes, old wise and wonderful one. I was a fool to buy the boat and try and change my personali —" Her voice trailed off as she realized she had finally let the cat out of the bag. Oh, good heavens. Now she would never hear the end of this.

"Ah ha! That's *exactly* what I told Mark you were doing. Ellie Millstein. How could you be so . . . so . . ."

"Stupid?"

"You are a perfectly lovely woman with your own special personality that does not need changing—or at least it didn't until you started messing around with it," Janet scolded.

"What wrong with my new personality? I think it's wonderful."

Janet groaned. "Have you taken a good look in the mirror lately? You don't even look like the same Ellie Millstein I used to know. Your clothes are different, and your hair—what is that awful stuff you've got in it this morning?"

"My hairdresser just put a little styling gel in it to give it more body," Ellie protested lamely.

"It's the same style Attila the Hun wore. What was wrong with the way you've been wearing it?"

Ellie shrugged. "Nothing. I just wanted a change."

"You're still doing it," Janet warned, but there was a softening in her voice that had not been there earlier.

"Doing what?"

"Trying to be the sort of woman who would attract T. J. Templeton."

"That's not true. I just wanted to change myself so that I could attract a man *like* T.J. Not T.J. himself."

"Well." Janet sighed and wadded up her napkin. "It may be my imagination, but it looks like both of you have changed since you've bought that boat together."

Janet had noticed that T.J. no longer drove his

Corvette, and while he was still a sharp dresser, he looked a lot more conservative these days.

And that car Ellie was driving! Totally out of character for her.

Ellie had noticed the change in T.J. too, and was puzzled by it.

Last night when he had kissed her, it had been the same dynamic T.J. she was so crazy about, but this morning he was back to acting strange again.

He had actually asked her if she would like to go play a game of Putt Putt after work. Absolutely not, she had told him. She didn't want to play Putt Putt! That's the kind of thing she had been trying to get away from, but in doing so, it seemed she had ended up falling out of the frying pan into the fire.

After soul-searching all night until the wee hours of the morning, she had come to the conclusion that she had better change their relationship back to what it was first intended to be. Business only. And she was going to forget about studying him, too. It was becoming too dangerous.

From now on, she would suggest that they have custody of the boat on alternate weekends, as originally planned.

With most of the immediate expenses out of the way, they could begin to take the boat out on the water for weekend excursions, and entertain their own sets of friends, thereby avoiding any more incidents such as the one that had occurred the night before.

With that weighty decision made, she had promptly called Mike Haran and invited him to spend the forthcoming Saturday aboard *Passion's Folly.*

It would be a treat for him to be back on his old boat, and Ellie needed someone she could be her old dull self with.

That afternoon T.J. stopped by her desk to chat for a moment. He had only stopped to be sociable but he suddenly found himself saying, "How about trying for that dinner again this Saturday night? We'll take the boat and anchor in some nice secluded cove and—"

"I'm sorry, T.J., I already have plans for Saturday night," she interrupted.

For a moment he looked surprised at her quick rejoinder, but hastily collected his thoughts again. "Oh. Are you working this weekend?"

"No, I'm not working. I thought if you didn't mind I would use the boat Saturday . . . but I'll have it back late that night," she promised. "You're welcome to use it all day Sunday if you'd like."

"Well, no, I don't mind . . . but you've never driven it—"

"There's no need to worry. Mike Haran will be with me."

"Mike Haran." T.J.'s face suddenly clouded at the mention of the former boat owner's name. "Why will he be with you?"

"Because I asked him to be," she admitted.

T.J.'s brow furrowed more deeply. "Are you and Haran dating each other now?"

"Well, no . . . at least we haven't been. I just thought that since he was so lonesome it would be nice for him to get away for a day. He seemed to have loved the boat so much. I just thought . . ." Her voice trailed off weakly as she saw the outright scowl begin to form on T.J.'s face.

She wasn't sure if he was unhappy because she had made plans concerning the boat without first consulting with him, or if he was worried about the precious gas they would be using.

"If you're worried about the gas, I'll make sure that we replace all we use," she assured him.

"I'm not worried about the gas. The motor isn't running right," he said with a touch of impatience in his voice.

"But we just paid to have it tuned up not long ago."

"It still has a funny sound in it."

"It does? Huh. I never noticed it. Well, maybe Mike will know what it—"

"I don't want him messing around with my boat," T.J. stated flatly.

*My* boat? Ellie lifted her brow at him coolly. Whatever happened to *our* boat, she thought. "T.J., are you asking me to cancel my plans this Saturday?" she challenged.

"No, I'm not asking you to cancel your plans, although I don't see what's so fascinating all of a sudden about Mike Haran."

294

"I didn't say he fascinated me. I only said I had invited him for a day on the boat."

"Great. But don't take the boat out until I get there to take a look at the engine."

"And pray tell, what time might that be?"

"I'll be there by eight."

She sighed. "That means nine thirty or ten, right?"

"It means, eight o'clock, Saturday morning!" This was the first time they had ever raised their voices to each other and they were beginning to attract attention in the office.

"All right," she said calmly. "I'm not deaf. We will wait until eight fifteen, but if you're not there by then, we'll go anyway."

She did not intend to spend her entire Saturday waiting on T.J. to show up. He could learn to be on time just like everybody else, or she would leave without him.

"Don't you dare take that boat until I get there," he warned.

She lifted her chin in defiance. "Eight o'clock, T.J. On the dot."

He shot her a sour look and started to stalk off, then whirled and pointed an accusing finger at her. "What have you done to your hair?"

"Nothing." She dispassionately turned her attention back to the papers on her desk.

"That is *not* the way you usually wear your hair."

"It will be from now on."

He made a disgruntled sound and marched on

to his cubicle, grumbling under his breath about she'd be joining a rock band next thing he knew.

Well, she thought, at least he noticed.

She had no idea why she was being so ugly to him this morning. But she just suddenly didn't like his whole attitude. Or else she was frightened of her ever-deepening feelings for him.

If she had to be honest, the latter was closer to the truth.

She sneezed and reached for a tissue.

And there was not one thing wrong with her hair!

When Ellie and Mike arrived at the boat a little before eight Saturday morning, T.J. was not only there, but he had half the boat's engine strewn all over the deck.

He smiled cordially as Ellie stepped aboard. "Hi there!"

"T.J.! What's with all these parts scattered around?" She was dismayed to see the condition of the motor. It would take half a day to get it back together properly. Half a day she could have been spending out on the water, enjoying her hard-earned investment.

Picking up a greasy rag to wipe his hands on, T.J. frowned thoughtfully. "Well, I'll tell you. I can't seem to locate the source of the trouble. Everything I take out seems to be working right."

"I wasn't aware you were a mechanic," she challenged.

"Oh, I'm not, but I've got the manual that

came with the boat and I'm being real careful to watch what I take out and where it goes so I can get it back in right." He grinned at her again. "Sorry to delay you."

"Oh good heavens." Ellie sank down on the seat of the helm, visions of another horrendously large repair bill facing them.

"I can't understand what the problem could be," Mike said as he finally stepped forward. "I kept this boat in tip-top condition while I owned it. Would you care if I take a look?"

T.J. voluntarily scooted out of the way as Mike began to tinker around in the motor. For the next hour, the two men consulted with each other on where the noise could be coming from.

T.J. tried to explain what the noise sounded like—sort of a kerthump, kerthump, ping ping—and Mike would only shake his head and say he just couldn't understand it.

He had *never* heard a kerthump, kerthump, ping ping in the motor before.

The morning slipped by and Ellie fixed lunch for the three of them. She was coming down with a summer cold and felt perfectly rotten.

The cold medicine had made her cranky and dried her sinuses to the point that she had developed a splitting headache. But despite her condition, that afternoon she swam and lay in the sun while T.J. leaned over Mike's shoulder and watched as he laboriously worked to put the motor back together again.

Around four o'clock they were still tinkering.

Ellie announced she was bored and not feeling well, so she was going to take a nap. She didn't know if they even heard her, since neither one glanced up or acknowledged she was on board.

Some date, she thought glumly.

When she awakened, the late-afternoon shadows lay across the bunk and one sleepy glance told her it was nearly seven o'clock. She listened to see if she could hear the occasional clang of tools, and Mike and T.J.'s muted voices, but all was quiet.

Rising from the bed, she started toward the head to splash cold water on her face and straighten her hair, when all of a sudden she was startled into taking a few steps backward. The door to the small bath had swung open and T.J. stepped out, totally nude.

Deliciously, delectably, mouth-wateringly, stark-raving nude!

For a moment they both just stared at each other in surprise, then to her dismay, a lazy grin began to form at the corners of his mouth as her round eyes traveled thoroughly over his glistening body, lingering disgracefully long in a most disturbing place before she noticed what she was doing.

She finally gasped, then quickly averted her gaze.

She heard his low, masculine chuckle as her face flooded with bright color. "Hi, sleepyhead. It's about time you woke up."

He began to briskly towel himself dry from the

shower he had just taken, not at all concerned about her catching him in such an embarrassing state. In fact, he seemed to be enjoying her misery!

"Feeling better?"

She cleared her throat and carefully kept her eyes averted. "I'm sorry . . . I had no idea you were in there."

Her mind refused to forget what she had just seen. It continued to tease and torment her with the image of T.J.'s bare, broad chest dappled with drops of water, running down in tiny rivulets to trickle off to . . . She snapped her eyes shut once more and tried to force the intriguing image out of her mind.

This is silly! she told herself sternly. She had seen him *close* to nude nearly every weekend since they had bought the boat together.

After all, what did a man's bathing suit hide but the bare essentials? But here she was, still reacting almost giddily to a man's naked body. Albeit a body which was the picture of masculine perfection.

His waist was narrow and trim, his tush was nothing short of adorable, and his legs were covered with the same soft blond hair that lay thick across his chest. And he was quite impressive . . . elsewhere, too . . .

But so what. He is just a man, Ellie. Underneath all that conservatism, men like Fergie Waterman were probably just as devastating, she rationalized. And if T.J. wasn't embarrassed by her catching him like this, then she wasn't either.

But after one more sneaky glance, she knew she might be being overly optimistic about Fergie in this particular case.

"Mike and I just got the motor back together," T.J. was saying as he finished drying off, then casually draped the towel around his waist and walked over to the mirror to comb his hair. "I had grease on me from head to toe."

"Is the motor running again?"

"Like a top."

Deciding it was safe to turn around now, she still carefully avoided his laughing blue eyes as she sauntered across the room and opened the refrigerator. "Where's Mike?"

"Up on deck. He's starting the charcoal."

"Oh? I suppose this means we're all having dinner together?"

It came as no surprise. Before she had dozed off, she had figured out that T.J. had deliberately torn that motor to smithereens just so she and Mike couldn't take the boat out for the day.

The thought had angered and annoyed her. He was acting like a spoiled child who didn't want to share his new toy, even though *she* was paying for half of that new toy and it was just as much hers as it was his.

Just before sleep overtook her, she had decided she wasn't going to let him get away with it.

"Yes—I hope you don't mind, but ol' Mike invited me to stay."

"Oh, he did."

"Yeah—you know. It's like you figured. He's lonesome and I thought well, what the hell. I could give up a few hours and stick around this evening and help you cheer him up."

T.J. casually dropped the towel and reached for his swimming trunks lying on the counter, completely ignoring the fact she was standing there watching him.

"Don't mind me, T.J.," Ellie said dryly as her eyes involuntarily ran over his bare backside.

He shrugged and flashed a devilish grin at her as he wiggled into the Hawaiian flower bathing suit again. She simply detested that suit and couldn't understand why he didn't wear that tight little knit job he wore around Barbie Jenkins. "I'm not modest if you're not."

"It doesn't look as if it would do me a whole lot of good if I were." She closed the refrigerator and stepped into the head to comb her hair. "So, ol' Mike invited you to join us for dinner."

"Yeah—hope you don't mind."

"Well, of course, you're welcome too, although you know it *is* my day to use the boat—privately."

"I know, but Mike seems to have his heart set on my staying."

"I'll bet."

"What?"

"Nothing."

T.J. stuck his head around the doorway. "Now, if I'm interfering, just say the word and

I'll tactfully disappear." He smiled at her guilefully, and she knew without a doubt her earlier suspicions about his ulterior motives had been correct.

She gave him a saccharine-sweet smile. "Heavens no, T.J. Why, the *three* of us have been together all day, why part now?"

"You're upset with me."

"No I'm not."

"Yes you are."

"No I'm not."

"Yes you are."

*"I am not upset with you!"*

"Oh, well, that's good to hear. How do you like your steak?"

"Alone."

"See, I told you. You're upset with me."

"You deliberately tore that motor apart so Mike and I could not take the boat out, didn't you?" she blurted.

He sighed with extreme patience and walked over to the refrigerator to get vegetables for a salad. "I knew that's what you were thinking and I have to tell you, I'm hurt."

"My foot."

"You're completely off base," he contended. "Not only did I not want you getting stuck somewhere out on the water, alone—"

"I would not have been alone. Mike would have been with me."

*I know,* he thought sourly. ". . . but it so happens, since it's my turn to use the boat tomorrow,

302

I wanted that motor running right. *You* may want to get stuck out there in the hot sun, but I sure don't."

"Oh, are you entertaining tomorrow?" She deliberately kept her voice light, although she was seething inside from his underhanded trick.

"Yeah—it is my turn to have the boat," he reminded her. "Dan, Penny, and Penny's sister, Cissy, are coming by." He glanced up as she stepped out of the bathroom. "Did you have a chance to meet Cissy the other night?"

"Why, yes, I believe I did. Wasn't she the one who had the bustline that matched her IQ?"

T.J. shook his head. "Ellie, I'm ashamed of you."

"That makes us even. I don't believe your cock and bull story about something being wrong with the motor."

T.J. shrugged. "If you want to make points with Mike, you'd better develop a nicer disposition. He dumped one woman because of that very thing."

"Dumped!"

"Well, you know what I mean. He said his wife griped at him at lot and it got on his nerves." T.J. glanced out the open door and frowned. "Looks like it's clouding up back in the north. I sure hope it doesn't rain tomorrow and spoil my day."

"Heaven forbid. I'm going up on deck with Mike."

"Sure thing. I'll bet he's getting lonesome

again." T.J. began to whistle as he sliced cucumbers in the salad.

"Oh . . . by the way, T.J., do you care if I put new shelf paper in the cabinets sometime this week?" She paused on the first step and smiled at him sweetly.

"No ma'am," he said jauntily as he hacked a tomato into tiny pieces. "You have my permission to perform that small, highly offensive chore."

"Gee, thanks."

"If you wait until the middle of the week, I might even be persuaded to lend a helping hand."

"Oh, thanks, but I don't know what day will be convenient for me. Just whenever I find the extra time."

"No problem."

"Right, no problem," she agreed, then turned and skipped happily up the stairway.

The evening turned out to be a pleasant one. Mike Haran was good company and entertained both Ellie and T.J. with stories of his days as a traveling salesman.

Around eleven they were sitting in the galley drinking coffee, when a terrible ruckus erupted up on deck.

T.J. looked at Mike and frowned. "What in the hell is that?"

"Probably some of those pesky animals that come aboard from time to time," Mike laughed.

"Animals!" Both T.J. and Ellie spoke at the same time.

"Sure, haven't you been bothered with them yet?"

"What sort of animals?" Ellie asked cautiously.

"Skunks and raccoons and whatever." Mike grinned.

The noise was ear-shattering by now as Mike and T.J. pushed out of their chairs and went to investigate the racket.

Ellie's hands stayed glued to T.J.'s back as they were going up the stairs. He turned around and grinned at her. "Are you making a pass at me?"

Her hold loosened immediately and she stepped back. "No, I'm not making a pass at you."

"I wouldn't mind," he whispered conspiratorially.

She gave him a frosty look and motioned for him to go on up the stairs before Mike overheard the conversation.

But Mike wouldn't have been able to eavesdrop if he'd wanted to. There was so much screeching and yelling taking place, Ellie couldn't hear herself think.

When she finally got the nerve to step up on deck, her eyes widened as she saw two fat raccoons rolling around on the deck, dueling over an open package of potato chips that had been left from dinner.

"What do we do now?" T.J. shouted above the increasing melee.

"Grab a mop and I'll grab a broom," Mike instructed. "We'll try to break it up."

T.J. glanced over at Ellie uneasily. "Is that safe . . . should I do that?"

"Can you think of a better suggestion?"

"Yeah, *you* do it."

"Not on your life."

"I'd rather you didn't put it that way." T.J. grimaced as he reached for the mop and reluctantly went to Mike's aid.

For the next few moments the battle raged hot and heavy. Mike and T.J. poked and prodded at the determined animals but they refused to give an inch.

When they were finally able to break them up, one started chasing T.J. around the deck. He ran over and jumped up on the railing beside Ellie and handed her the mop.

"What are you doing!" she screeched, scrambling to climb on the rail with him.

"Save me!" T.J. yelled playfully.

"You big coward." Ellie shot him a dirty look and took the mop and shooed the raccoon off the boat, while Mike drove the other one off.

When calm reigned once more, Ellie brought the two men something cold to drink. Mike and T.J. perched on the boat's railing to rest.

She placed the back of her hand on her forehead and sighed dramatically as she handed T.J.

his drink. "My hero. Shove the mop in my hand and run."

T.J. grinned at Mike, then glanced at Ellie and winked suggestively. "I was standing by with the big guns to intervene if the situation called for it. I just wanted to see how good you were with a mop."

Ellie suddenly reached out and nudged T.J. over the side of the boat with the handle of the mop. He hit the water with a loud splash and an indignant bellow of protest as Mike and Ellie broke into laughter.

She dusted her hands off, threw the mop in after him and peered over the side at him angelically. "Well, now you know how good I am," she teased.

He glowered back at her playfully as he flipped over on his back and started to float. "I'll get ya, Millstein."

*That's what you think, Templeton,* she thought merrily.

# CHAPTER EIGHT

Bright and early the following morning, Ellie unlocked the galley door and let herself into the interior of the boat.

By eight o'clock, every pot, pan, dish, and utensil aboard was piled out in the middle of the floor, and she was busily putting in new shelf paper.

When T.J. and his guests stepped into the tiny quarters, their arms loaded with groceries, coolers, and beach bags, she glanced up and smiled at him every bit as cordially as he had smiled at her the day before. "Hi there!"

T.J. looked stunned for a moment, then he casually set his armload down on the table and surveyed the cluttered mess around him. "What in the hell are you doing?"

She looked at him innocently. "Putting in new shelf paper. Why?"

"Now?"

"Sure, don't you remember? You said I had your permission to put it in any time I wanted to," she reminded.

"But I didn't think you meant today," he protested, as he smiled at his guests apologetically.

She sighed tolerantly. "Well, now if you're worrying about me interfering with your plans for the day, just let me set those fears to rest. You go right ahead and act like I'm not even here. I'll just do my work, quiet as a little mouse and you'll never know I'm on board." She turned to greet his guests with a pleasant smile. "Well, hello, Dan and Penny—and Cissy, isn't it?" Her smile was even more accommodating than moments earlier as she extended her hand to the sullen-looking blonde standing just behind T.J. "How nice to have you aboard. I know you're going to thoroughly enjoy your day."

T.J. tiptoed his way through the pots and pans, trying to get to the freezer with a sack of crushed ice, while Dan and Penny and Cissy cast uneasy glances at one another.

Ellie promptly turned her attention back to the cabinets while T.J. tried to make the best of the situation. It hadn't taken him long to realize he was being paid back for playing the same trick on her the day before.

The five people edged their way around each other in the crowded quarters, murmuring polite, "excuse me's," "pardon me's," and "oh, I'm sorry's" for a few minutes before T.J. finally suggested that they move up on deck for a little more breathing space.

Ellie wished them all a very pleasant day again

as she sat down on the berth and drew up her knees to let them pass.

T.J. was the last to leave, but not before he turned around and whispered over his shoulder. "This is dirty pool, Millstein."

"You should know, Templeton."

She noticed that he was back to wearing his tight-fitting knit bathing suit today. It irked her to realize that for Cissy he was the exciting, virile man Ellie drooled over, but when he was around his "business" partner, he wore boxer shorts, white socks or even worse, those horrible Hawaiian-print trunks!

Fifteen minutes later she heard the boat's engines roar into life, then a few minutes after that the boat began to move out of its berth.

Going over to the porthole, Ellie pressed her nose against the glass and watched as the boat cut a wide wake through the smooth aquamarine water and out of the marina.

Well, at least she was finally going to get to ride in the boat.

It promised to be a lovely day—so lovely that it was going to be hard to stay below and put new shelf paper in the cabinets, she thought wistfully. And it was also going to be even harder to watch T.J. on a date.

Funny, but in thinking back, the whole time they had owned the boat together she had never once seen him actually bring a woman aboard.

Oh, there were women coming and going all the time, but they were mostly friends that both she and T.J. worked with at the office, or prospective clients.

Her conscience began to nag at her. Actually, she picked a bad day to get even with him.

Dan and Penny Benson were important clients of T.J.'s, and she wouldn't blame him if he was more than a little upset with her. There was a multimillion-dollar shopping center involved, and if she tampered with that sale, she was quite sure he would never speak to her again.

The boat picked up speed and began to skim lightly across the water. She felt a thrill of exhilaration shoot through her.

No matter how expensive the boat had been— and now its use was even becoming a seed of contention between them—it had all been worth it to hear the power of the engines and see the shoreline slipping past her in a muted, exciting blur of colors.

She wondered if T.J. was feeling the same sense of triumph, and she suddenly wished she were up on deck to share this wonderful moment with him, not some stranger by the name of Cissy.

She sneezed and reached for a tissue. She should have stayed home in bed this morning and nursed her miserable cold, instead of trying to get even with T.J.

Sliding off the bunk, she returned to the cabinets and began to halfheartedly put shelf paper in the cabinets.

About thirty minutes after they had left the

marina, the engines finally stopped as T.J. pulled into a cove and anchored.

Ellie glanced up a few moments later to see Penny and Cissy coming down the stairway looking for a place to change into their swimming suits.

Pointing out the head to Cissy, she smiled and offered Penny a cup of coffee.

"No thanks. I've already had my quota for the day. Gee, this is really nice," Penny commented as she looked around the galley with renewed appreciation. "Dan has fallen in love with the boat and thinks we ought to have one just like it."

Ellie laughed. "Well, it has its good and bad points."

"Yes, I imagine so, but I bet you and T.J. have such a good time with it."

"Oh, yes. There hasn't been a dull moment yet."

The door to the head opened and Ellie had to look twice to make sure Cissy was indeed wearing a suit. The flesh-colored bikini was one of the most daring and skimpy pieces of nothingness she had ever seen.

Even her own sister was momentarily taken aback. "Oh, my . . . Cissy." Penny crossed her heart with her hands and looked properly mortified.

The well-built blonde smiled and twitched her well-defined fanny around sassily. "You like it? I got it on sale for half price."

You were still robbed, Ellie thought fleetingly.

There wasn't enough material in the suit to make a good-size handkerchief, let alone a decent bathing suit.

Her heart sank when she thought of what T.J.'s reaction was going to be to such provocative attire.

"Well." Penny laughed. "It is certainly going to make my one-piece look old-fashioned."

While Penny changed, Cissy preened and primped before the mirror. Ellie sat and watched her redo her eye makeup and gob a creamy, wet-looking rose-colored gel on her Cupid's-bow mouth.

Her skin was pale and delicate, and she had a cute, curvaceous figure that undoubtedly drove men wild.

The woman was dressed for big game and Ellie realized with a sinking heart there was a turkey up on deck just right for the plucking.

And there was not one single, solitary thing she could do about it.

If she overplayed her hand and took this episode farther than the relatively harmless little prank she had played on him, she would without a doubt seriously anger T.J.

Not only that, but she would also run the chance of offending one of his most influential customers. And that would be unthinkable.

And on top of it all, she wasn't even supposed to care what T.J. was doing. But she did. Miserably so.

Penny emerged a few moments later, dressed

in a modest suit that only intensified Cissy's scandalous lack of one. "I can't get over how darlingly this boat is decorated," she repeated. "Did you coordinate all of it, Ellie?"

"No, I'm afraid I can't take the credit. The boat's former owner's wife is responsible for most of it."

"Well, she did a lovely job," Penny praised once more. She glanced at Ellie and smiled sympathetically when she saw the downtrodden look on her flushed features. "When you finish up why don't you join us up on deck?"

"Thanks, but I'll be a while getting this all put back together."

Cissy had not seconded the invitation, nor did she seem interested in extending it. "I'm going to join T.J.," she announced unceremoniously as she picked up her bag and started up the stairway.

"I'll be along in a minute," Penny promised. "Don't forget to use your sunscreen." She glanced back at Ellie apologetically. "She burns so easily."

Ellie forced a pleasant smile back to her lips. "That's too bad."

There was a lot of exposed skin to worry about, she added silently.

Penny sat down at the table and chatted while Ellie continued her work. Once or twice Dan came down to check on her, and ended up drinking a cup of coffee and visiting with the ladies.

It was hard for Ellie to keep her mind on the

conversation at times. She could occasionally hear T.J. and Cissy talking and there were long gaps when she didn't hear anything. Those were the times she found it hard to concentrate.

The day crept by with miserable slowness. T.J. stuck his head in the galley about one and invited her to eat lunch with them, but she declined.

"Why not?"

"Because I'm busy!" She sounded a lot more snappish than she intended, but she couldn't help it. He was having a marvelous time while she was perfectly miserable. Her cold was getting worse, and she was seething with jealousy, not to mention feeling very neglected and unwanted.

It annoyed her even more that her revenge had not bothered his plans in the least.

"How long could it take to put a few pots and pans back in a tiny cabinet?" he reasoned.

"All day."

He grinned at her and shook his head. "You look terrible. Why don't you sack out for a while?"

Her face was flushed and her head sounded stuffed up worse than it had the day before. If she had to waste a whole day getting even with him, then she might as well be comfortable.

"I don't know . . . maybe I will later."

By two o'clock, she realized she was being foolish by deliberately dragging out a job that shouldn't have taken over thirty minutes. In a fit of pique, she threw the remaining pans back in the cabinet, took two more cold pills, and lay down on the berth.

But she couldn't rest. Now she could hear the small party swimming off the bow of the boat more clearly. She turned over so her back would be to the wall and tried to ignore the sounds of splashing water and Cissy's asinine, constant giggling.

If he had one ounce of decency about him, he would be chastising her for her ridiculous bathing suit! she thought irritably. He should be scolding her for her shocking immodesty . . . But then her mind went back to yesterday when he had stood before her naked and proud as a peacock.

Well, cancel the immodesty, but he should still never condone such a display of all that rich . . . creamy . . . skin . . . But along more realistic lines, she knew he wouldn't criticize Cissy's suit.

He would be too busy ogling it.

The next thing she was aware of was the boat gently bumping the sides of the marina as it came back into its berth. A quick glance at her watch and she found out she had slept the entire afternoon again, and it was now close to six o'clock.

Trying to shake off the grogginess brought on by the cold medicine, she slipped out of the berth and went into the head to freshen up before leaving.

When she appeared on deck a little later, T.J. was the only one still aboard. He was sprawled out in the captain's chair snoozing, his feet propped up on the railing, the large straw hat he was wearing pulled down over his face.

He looked tan, totally relaxed, and incredibly handsome.

Ellie took a deep breath and began to tiptoe around him. She had toyed with the idea of waking him to say good-bye, but then thought better of it.

Although he had remained pleasant with her today, she still sensed an undercurrent of hostility because of her childish actions.

"Well, are you finally through?"

She froze at the sound of his voice. "Uh . . . yes . . . all finished," she said brightly.

Darn. She had hoped to leave before he noticed.

Pushing back the hat at a rakish angle, he looked at his watch. "Not bad, Millstein. It only took you ten and a half hours to put clean paper in three little drawers."

His eyes traveled lazily over her slender, bare legs. She was wearing another one of those short outfits that didn't suit her at all, but she still looked damn good to him.

"Well, I didn't hurry," she admitted. "I knew I had all day."

She was a bit uneasy about the way he was looking at her. T.J. had so many looks—some bold, some curious, some indifferent—but this one was unusual. Almost like he was mad at her and enthralled with her all at the same time.

"I'm sure it looks better."

"Yes, much."

"You leaving?"

"Yes, I'd better get home."

"Well." He yawned and stretched idly. "It's been a nice day."

"So I heard." *All afternoon long,* she thought miserably.

"That Dan and Penny're real nice."

"Yes, they certainly are."

"And Cissy, too. She's not bad once you get to know her." A devilish grin tugged at the corners of his mouth as he squinted up into the late-afternoon sun.

"She certainly leaves little to the imagination," Ellie agreed, her mind once more taunting her with the scandalous bathing suit T.J.'s guest had almost had on.

She started to step out on the dock when he suddenly stood and caught her arm. "Ho, hold on a minute."

She paused and glanced up at him expectantly. "Why?"

He stepped closer and she felt her gaze going straight to his bare, broad chest as his voice dipped into a sexy baritone. "Before you leave, there's something I've been wanting to do to you all day."

Ellie's pulse tripped faster. Was it possible he was going to kiss her again? Even after the way she had tricked him?

"Oh?" She grinned with happy anticipation. "What's that?"

She would gladly accept his kiss, because after all, wasn't that all she had thought about this afternoon? How handsome he was and how good he tasted and smelled, and how green with envy she was that Cissy was spending the day with him and not her.

It had occurred to her this afternoon that despite her vows to the contrary, she *had* fallen in love with this crazy, lovable, impossible man.

It wasn't an easy thing to admit, but a fact nevertheless.

But *after* the kiss, she would tell him what she thought about his revolting choice of women, and how she didn't appreciate the fact he would let a woman run around half nude on *their* boat, right in front of her and—

T.J. interrupted her thoughts as he stepped closer and reached down to scoop her up in his arms.

"Oh, T.J., I thought you would be mad at me," she blurted out with a relieved sigh.

He smiled. "I am."

She smiled back, then the smile slowly began to recede into a frown as his words sank in. "You are?"

"Yes, I am. That was a rotten trick you played on me today, wasn't it?"

It was and she was big enough to admit it. "Yes, but no more rotten than the one you played on me yesterday."

"True, but I think yours was more rotten since

my guests were clients and your guest was just a friend."

"I wouldn't say that. Mike mentioned something to me about putting his house up for sale and he said he wanted me to be the listing agent if he did . . ." Her voice trailed off lamely and she sighed again as she saw her arguments were falling on deaf ears. "Oh, dear. You're not going to kiss me, are you?"

"I might later, but no, I'm not going to kiss you right now."

"What are you going to do—oh, no! T.J.! I have a cold! Don't you dare throw me in that water!"

She started kicking and shrieking at the top of her lungs as he calmly hauled her over to the railing and proceeded to dump her over the side. But her hold around his neck was more firm than he realized and he suddenly toppled over the railing with her as she continued to try to writhe out of his grasp.

They hit the water amid both of their loud, protesting screams and a huge, resounding splash.

Their inquisitive neighbors ran to peer out portholes and around bows to see what all the noise was about, and chuckled when they saw T.J. and Ellie having a water fight beside their boat.

"You beast," she accused good-naturedly, and screamed again as he grabbed her soggy sneaker and pulled her under the water.

"That pays you back for dunking me last night." He laughed.

"I thought it was for today," she sputtered, choking on half the ocean she had just swallowed.

"Oh, no. *This* is for today," he explained, and promptly dunked her again.

They splashed and cavorted for the next half hour, reluctant to climb back in the boat.

"This is the most relaxed I've been all day," T.J. confessed as he floated past her on his back. "I feel great!"

"Oh, really? You and Cissy looked mighty relaxed to me," she grumbled.

Satisfied with the undertone of jealousy in her voice, he grinned and flipped water in her face again. "I'll make you a deal. Dinner. I'll fix the sauce if you'll cook the spaghetti."

"Now?"

"Yes, now. You haven't got a date, have you?"

"No . . . but—"

"Then I'm asking you for one," he said lightly. "Notice, Ms. Millstein. We are completely alone for a change. No friends running in and out, no clients to entertain, no relatives to eat our generic stock of food—no one but you and me." He glanced over at her and winked. "Let's eat dinner and then play doctor and nurse."

"Who gets to be what?" she bantered, used to his outrageous suggestions by now.

"We'll flip a coin."

The offer was too good to pass up. They had

been trying a long time to get in just this situation, so even if her cold was making her feel as if her head were as big as a balloon, and her eyes were red and weepy, she wasn't about to refuse his invitation.

T.J. climbed aboard first, then extended a helping hand to her. He wrapped a fleecy towel around her shivering body and belatedly realized that maybe he shouldn't have been so impulsive.

Although the water was warm and the temperatures in the eighties, she was beginning to sneeze again. He briskly set about helping her to dry off.

"Hey, are you all right?" There was a note of genuine concern in his voice now as she sneezed a couple more times and hugged the towel closer around her.

"Yes, it's just this miserable cold I've come down with."

"Hold on a minute. I know exactly what we need." He disappeared into the interior of the boat and came back a few moments later carrying two navy blue windbreakers. "Here, we can wear these," he said as he helped her on with the smaller one.

"Where did they come from?"

"They must have been Mike's and his wife's. I found them hanging in the back of the closet." He put on the second jacket and turned around so she could read the bold white lettering written across the back.

"Oh, good grief." The name of the boat, *Pas-*

*sion's Folly,* was scrawled neatly across the dark polyester fabric.

"I knew you would love it." He grinned as he leaned over to give her a quick peck on the mouth.

They both laughed as he wrapped his arm around her waist and gave her an affectionate squeeze, then went in search of dry clothing.

While she dressed and put on fresh makeup, she could hear T.J. whistling around the galley as he prepared the spaghetti sauce.

She felt giddy and lightheaded, just thinking about spending the evening with him . . . alone.

When she emerged a short time later his lazy perusal of her scanty shorts and halter top assured her that the evening might turn out to be very special.

"Whatever happened to the nice, conservative Ellie Millstein I used to know?" he murmured, as he threw a pinch of oregano in the fragrant sauce bubbling on the stove.

"Oh, she's much more exciting now," Ellie informed him.

"Impossible. The Ellie Millstein I knew was always exciting . . . and different from other women. That's what I liked about her."

"Not exciting enough, and too different."

"For what?"

"To attract . . . exciting men," she reasoned, as she filled a large pan with water and set it on the stove.

He looked at her, lifting his brows in disbelief.

"You honestly don't think you're an exciting woman?"

She blushed. "No, but I'm working on it." She decided to change the subject. "Are you going to change?" She noticed he was still wearing the windbreaker and his swim suit.

"Yeah, what do you want me to be now?" he bantered.

"I meant, are you going to get out of that wet swim suit?" In a way she hated for him to take it off. Of course he had put on the blue knit suit for Cissy, but that didn't stop her from enjoying it.

"In a few minutes." He lay the wooden spoon he had been holding down on the cabinet and turned to open a bottle of red wine, to let it breathe before dinner.

With that task completed, he turned to take her in his arms as naturally as if he had been doing it all his life.

"T.J., you'll catch my cold," she protested as his mouth slowly lowered to take hers.

"I consider that a small price to pay considering the pleasure I'll be getting out of it," he murmured.

Their mouths touched and his tongue toyed with her bottom lip. She sagged weakly against his solid frame.

For the next few minutes they stood necking in the small galley like teenagers. Both had a strong sense they were approaching a turning point in their relationship. The ever-growing physical at-

324

traction between them was becoming harder to ignore.

And Ellie wasn't at all sure she wanted to ignore it any longer. She knew by heart all the reasons why it would be foolish to let herself become caught up in this tempting web of sensuality that he was so adeptly creating.

Her relationship with him should be strictly business, she reminded herself, yet she found herself wrapping her arms around his neck and pressing even closer to his bare chest. His kisses became more aggressive and his hands more exploringly bold.

At the sound of the water boiling over on the stove, T.J. reached back and turned off the burner, his mouth never leaving hers.

"T.J. . . . the spaghetti . . ." she murmured against the pressure of his mouth.

"I've suddenly lost my appetite," he confessed as he pushed aside her hair and nibbled seductively along her earlobe. "How about you?"

"I think Frank and Geraldine Pinehurst are watching us," she cautioned.

T.J. glanced out the doorway and swore under his breath as he saw the curtain jerk back in place on the boat docked next to theirs.

"Old busybodies. Let's shut the door."

"Let's eat," she suggested sensibly. "I think it will be safer."

He looked down at her, his blue gaze growing amused. "Okay. But I'm not through with you yet. Keep that in mind."

She smiled and kissed the corners of his mouth as he drew her up closer against the hard surface of his body. She could feel the imprint of his maleness pressing against her middle as his mouth captured hers once more for a long, disturbing moment. "What about our 'business only' arrangement?" she asked when she was finally able to speak again.

"What about it?" he challenged, nipping gently at her earlobe. "There's no law that says business can't be fun, is there?"

"None that I know of." His mouth found hers again and she gradually blocked out all other protestations.

But she was sure that by tomorrow, she would belatedly remember one or two.

While he changed into dry clothing, she finished cooking the spaghetti and set the small table. She looked at her watch to see if it was anywhere near time to take another cold pill and was disappointed to see that it wasn't.

By the time T.J. reappeared, she had thrown caution to the wind and taken two more anyway.

If tonight was going to be the night she had always fantasized about, she wasn't going to be blowing her nose at highly intimate moments.

The galley was warm and cozy. She lit a candle and set it on the table while T.J. poured wine into the glasses.

"Not much for me," she cautioned. "I'm taking medicine."

"Then you shouldn't have any."

"A tiny drop won't hurt."

They turned the lights out and ate by candle-light, sipping the wine slowly and exchanging idle conversation. Several times their gazes would meet and hold, and Ellie found it increasingly hard to concentrate on what he was saying.

He was going to make love to her tonight . . . and she was going to let him. It was written in their eyes and the tone of their voices when they spoke.

She could feel the tip of her tongue instinctively tracing her bottom lip as she thought about the way his mouth felt on hers and how good he always smelled . . . and looked . . . and acted . . .

At one point, she was mortified to hear herself babbling nervously away about some mundane thing in an effort to conceal her growing sexual frustrations.

She could not recall ever feeling such aching desire for a man, yet being torn by such conflicting emotions at the same time.

A serious relationship between two such opposites could never work. She was sure of that now . . . and she felt foolish. Totally foolish.

If nothing else, buying the boat together had shown her that no matter how much she wanted to change, in her heart she would still be the same old dull Ellie Millstein.

Clothes and new sports cars and all the other fancy trappings of life could never change that.

And in many ways, she was beginning to realize that maybe that wasn't so bad. Men like Mike Haran and Fergie Waterman were good, solid men who would make wonderful, supportive husbands for a woman like herself—even if they didn't attempt to set the world on fire.

And men like T.J., who were so vibrantly, utterly alive, would need the Barbie Jenkinses and Cissy Parkinses of the world to ensure their happiness.

After much soul-searching, she had finally come to accept the fact that she and T.J. might not be meant for each other.

But tonight *was* hers, and she would enjoy it to the fullest before she put all her silliness aside and went back to being her old self.

Whoever Ellie Millstein was, and no matter what her shortcomings, it had to be better than the garish creature she had been pretending to be lately.

Her plate was virtually untouched half an hour later as she held her wineglass out for more. T.J. frowned and shook his head. "You've already had more than you need."

"But I want more," she complained. The wine made her feel warm and relaxed and gave her the false sense of courage she needed to get her through the night.

She wanted him to make love to her. She might never again have the chance to hold him in her arms, or be with a man like T.J. . . .

"But you can't have more," he said. He picked

up her hand and kissed it. "Now be a good girl and eat your dinner."

"My spaghetti's cold." She felt cranky and irritable all of a sudden.

And sleepy. Incredibly sleepy.

"All right, then why don't you come over here and sit on my lap," he invited.

She smiled expectantly. "All right."

And he smiled back, anticipating the pleasures to come.

"But first, I think I'll just lay my head down here for just a teeny minute." She yawned and her head began to droop downward.

T.J. sat up straighter and peered over at her anxiously. "Ellie?"

"In a minute, Teej." She needed to think of something subtle and provocative to say, to let him know she was willing to fulfill the promise that had been in her eyes all evening . . . if she just wasn't so drowsy . . .

She heard her voice coming from a long way off. "You can make love to me in a minute . . . I'm so sleepy . . ." Her voice trailed off with a snooze; vaguely, she realized that she had knocked over the bottle of wine, and that it was streaming in his lap.

And what had she just said! "You can make love to me in a minute." Good heavens, surely she hadn't said *that* . . .

T.J. jumped out of his chair and started mopping at the liquid cascading off the table. In his haste, he knocked several plates and glasses to the floor, as he jerked the tablecloth off to try and stem the flow of water and wine seeping through the cracks.

Then the candle rolled to the floor, and he jumped over to stomp the flame out before it ignited the small throw rug in front of the sink.

When the situation was finally under control, he walked around to her side of the table, where he knelt and gently picked her face up out of her plate and began to wipe the strings of spaghetti off her flushed cheeks.

She was out like a light.

He chuckled and lifted her up in his arms and looked down at her tenderly.

And Ellie Millstein thought she wasn't exciting enough?

## CHAPTER NINE

The gentle rocking back and forth of the boat made a soothing, comfortable cradle as Ellie snuggled closer to T.J.'s warmth.

Sometime during the evening he had carried her to the bunk and laid her down. She could hazily remember him holding her in his arms while they both dozed, exchanging periodic kisses and soft murmurs of contentment.

It was not light yet, although she could hear the first sounds of birds as they awoke to the new day. She cautiously opened her eyes. A shaft of blinding pain knifed between her eyes and she quickly clamped them shut again.

For a moment she berated herself for being so foolish. She should have never drunk the wine while she was taking medicine. She groaned aloud and opened her eyes once more; they encountered a set of incredibly sexy blue ones looking back at her.

She smiled lamely at him. "Good morning."

"Good morning. How you feeling?"

"Horrible." They were lying together in the

small bunk, pressed tightly against one another. Although they were still dressed, it was only in shorts and T-shirts, and the feel of his bare legs against hers caused a familiar warm weakness to invade her.

"Want me to get you an asprin?"

"No thanks. Maybe it'll go away in a few minutes."

"Want me to kiss it and make it go away?" he offered as his mouth moved to her earlobe, then down the side of her neck, sending shivers of delight racing up and down her spine.

"Teej . . ." she pleaded weakly as his lips finally found hers. The kiss was long and slow, sending tingling sensations throughout her body as he hooked his leg around hers and brought their bodies closer together.

Ellie sighed and leaned further into his hard contours. Her arms circled his neck as she returned his kiss with full measure.

When their lips finally parted, he covered every inch of her face with his probing mouth. "Ellie . . . my sweet, sweet Ellie."

His hands began to boldly explore her exquisite beauty. She felt so soft, so feminine, so perfect to him.

"T.J. . . ." She wanted to tell him to stop but she had suddenly gone so weak with desire she found it impossible to do anything but return his fevered kisses.

"Ellie, I want to make love to you," he whispered in a hesitant voice that sounded almost as if he expected her to refuse.

He lifted his head and his eyes met hers. They gazed at each other in the morning's first light and she smiled. "I can't think of anything I would like more."

"I've wanted to for such a very long time," he confessed. His mouth took hers again slowly and the world begin to tip and spin in a sensuous, erotic swirl.

He had never meant to fall in love with her, but he had. There was no longer any doubt in his mind, and he was tired of fighting his feelings. All he wanted now was to love her—for the rest of his life if she would permit it.

He knew he should be telling her all of these new and exciting revelations, but he was so caught up in the beauty of the present he found himself speechless once again.

The moments passed and their passion continued to grow and build. Ellie thought she had to be dreaming. T.J. was making love to her . . . wonderful, exciting T.J. . . .

She felt no shyness with him. It was all so very natural.

His breath caught in his throat as she slid off the bunk and began to slowly undress for him.

He watched silently, admiration and love glowing in the depths of his eyes as each piece of clothing fell away. She kept her eyes on him unashamedly.

When she was through, he stood and took her

in his arms. His low groan of appreciation was the only assurance she needed that he found her pleasing and all that he had hoped for.

Moments later his clothes joined hers on the floor, and he lay her back in the bunk tenderly.

"I know there's a lot of things I should be saying right now," he confided in a voice that had suddenly gone husky with desire. The depth of sincerity in his eyes touched her. "And I promise I'll say them all to you . . . a hundred times over, but right now, I just want to hold you and touch you . . . do you mind?"

"No." She reached out and touched his face with the tips of her fingers, marveling anew at his warm and masculine features.

She could feel the trembling, the urgency in his body as he lowered himself over her and buried his face in her hair. When he finally raised his face again to meet hers, she looked at him and smiled, and he came to her.

With all sanity shattered, he began to make love to her, muffling her cries of ecstasy with his own. She buried her face in the hard line of his shoulder and held on as she felt herself being lifted away from time and reality. They soared together into the clouds of unbelievable sensations until they could stand no more and a sweet, velvet mist completely suddenly engulfed their passion.

Long after they had reached their stormy pinnacle, they clung to each other tightly, kissing, murmuring their feelings of joy as they drifted gently back to earth.

Later, T.J. reached down and pulled the light blanket up over them to protect them from the early-morning chill as they fell asleep in each other's arms.

When they awakened, the sun was up. They could smell the tempting aroma of coffee and someone frying bacon from one of the other boats.

"What time is it?" Ellie murmured as T.J. proceeded to lazily kiss her awake.

"Close to eight, I think."

"Umm . . . what about work?" She sighed and nuzzled against his mouth.

"Let's play hooky today."

"Can you?"

"I can do anything."

"I don't know about that, but I do know of one thing you're pretty good at," she teased.

"Oh, yeah. I'm pretty good, huh?"

She shrugged. "Well, fair."

"Fair?" He leaned on his elbow and wrapped a lock of her hair around his finger.

"Well, maybe more than fair," she retracted. "Fair to middling." If she knew him, his ego did not need boosting in that area.

"Middling's no better than fair," he reminded in a sexy voice, pulling her over by the strand of hair to give her another long kiss. When their lips finally parted, he eased her on top of his bare chest and cupped her cheeks with his hands. "Only fair?" He arched his brows pleadingly.

She buried her fingers in the springy mass of golden hair and winked at him. "Maybe you'll score higher next time."

"If I don't, I can assure you I'll keep at it until I get it right." He brought her mouth back down to meet his, and for the next hour, he very conscientiously did his homework.


While she showered and dressed, T.J. ran down to the local convenience store and called the office to let them know that neither he nor Ellie would be in today.

The day was not as pleasant as the previous one. An overcast sky threatened rain and the temperatures were in the low seventies.

He picked up rolls and coffee and was on his way back to the boat when he encountered Mike Haran.

"Well, hello, Mike. What brings you out here this morning?"

"Hello, T.J. I was hoping I might catch you." Mike glanced around expectantly. "Is Ellie with you?"

"Yes!" T.J. straightened his stance defensively. If Haran had any ideas about her, he might as well let him know right now: Ellie Millstein was T. J. Templeton's.

"Where is she?"

"On the boat."

Mike sighed with relief. "Good. Have you got

336

a minute to run over to the restaurant and have a cup of coffee with me? I need to talk to you, alone."

T.J. glanced in the direction of his boat. "Can't it wait?"

"I'd rather it didn't." By the look on Mike's face, T.J. could tell it was important—at least to him.

"All right. I can spare fifteen minutes."

The two men walked across the parking lot and stepped back on the floating restaurant adjacent to the marina.

When they were seated at a table next to the window, Mike looked out the window at the mother duck and her babies swimming along beside the building. "Helen and I used to come over here every Sunday morning and eat breakfast," he began. "Those were some of the happiest times of my life, T.J."

T.J. was watching the ducks, too, but pictures of Ellie were floating through his mind. A loving and giving Ellie in his arms, a silly Ellie with her face in a plate of spaghetti, a puzzling Ellie who dressed funny, a sporty Ellie driving a fast car she couldn't handle, a jealous Ellie who took all day to put paper in three tiny shelves so she could be there to keep an eye on him and a piece of senseless fluff named Cissy Parkins.

Once more it occurred to him that he was deeply in love with every one of those Ellies, and if she were ever taken away from him, he wouldn't be able to bear it.

"You miss your wife, don't you, Mike?"

"Yes." Mike's voice broke and he caught himself. It wasn't manly to cry in front of another man. "I still love her very much."

"Any hope of reconciliation?"

For the first time there was a small ray of hope in Mike's eyes. "There might be."

T.J. was surprised. "Great."

"Helen and I have been seeing each other lately. The other night she suggested we go for counseling . . . something we should have thought of in the beginning." The waitress brought their coffee and set it down in front of them. "You see, Helen just sort of outgrew me," Mike admitted as he opened a packet of sugar and sprinkled it in his cup. "We got married when we were real young. She was always the kind who liked bright lights and discos, while I preferred candlelight and a stereo. I'm not blaming her, understand, but I think she wanted a more exciting kind of guy . . . someone like you, T.J."

"Like me?" T.J. chuckled. "I don't know where you get that idea. I'm not exciting."

"Well, maybe not to me you aren't," Mike clarified with a grin. "But you know women. Ellie mentioned to me that she thinks you're the most exciting man she's ever met. That's what women like, you know. A man who'll get out and do things . . . someone who lives life to its fullest, a sharp dresser, up on all the world events."

T.J. glanced up, embarrassed by his statement,

yet intrigued at the same time. "Ellie thinks I'm like that . . . I mean . . . she doesn't think I'm a reckless fool?"

Mike shook his head thoughtfully. "No, I got the impression she was in love with you."

"You did?" T.J. grinned broadly. Then his grin quickly disappeared as he realized Mike didn't really know Ellie that well. "Well, she isn't."

What Mike didn't know was that Ellie Millstein usually preferred men like himself or Fergie Waterman.

But T.J. wasn't about to tell him that. If things didn't work out for Mike and his ex-wife, then he didn't want him hanging around Ellie again.

"Well, of course she didn't say she was, but I just sort of got the feeling there was more than the boat bringing you two together . . . which brings me to the purpose of this conversation. If Helen and I do go back together, I'd like to buy the boat back. Would you and Ellie even consider such a proposal?"

"Buy the boat back?" T.J. thought about it for a moment.

"I know we could always buy another one, but *Passion's Folly* holds a special sentimental value for us. I'll even pay you a small profit if you would agree to sell it back to us."

"Aren't you jumping the gun a little bit?"

"You mean because Helen and I aren't reconciled yet?" Mike smiled hopefully. "Well, maybe, but I'm hoping to entice her with the bait that we can get it back if we do get back together."

T.J. shook his head in amusement. The boat didn't actually mean that much to him. It had only become a huge financial strain, instead of the great pleasure he had first anticipated.

Besides, there wasn't anything that couldn't be replaced, in his opinion, and he enjoyed the thrill of new adventures. If he sold the boat, he would get something else to interest him.

But he wasn't sure how Ellie would view the offer.

"I'll talk to her about it," he promised. When the time was right—preferably when another large, unexpected bill rolled in—he would mention Mike's offer.

By then, she would probably be willing to *give* the boat back to the Harans.

"Good." Mike stood up and shook his hand. "I'll give you a call sometime next week and find out what she said."

"Oh, by the way. You and Helen left a couple of windbreakers on the boat," T.J. said. "Stop by the office sometime and you can pick them up."

"No, just leave them on the boat. You may need them sometime and . . ." He smiled. "I may be getting the boat back one of these days."

By the time T.J. returned, Ellie had started to grow worried about him. "Where have you been?"

"Getting doughnuts and coffee." He set the wilted sack down on the cabinet and took her into his arms. He gave her a long, hungry kiss.

Mike's problems had made him realize what a lucky man he was to have such a woman.

Now all he had to figure out was how to keep her.

"You've been gone over an hour," she chided, surprised at his exuberant greeting. She hadn't really been all that worried. After all, when a person like T.J. says he'll be back in ten minutes, one could start looking for him sometime later that day.

"Did you miss me?"

"Never."

"Only fair, huh?" He was back to worrying again.

"Only fair," she contended, and once more he was forced to hit the homework again.

They spent the day lolling around on the boat, totally content with each other's company. Late that afternoon, they took the boat down the coast and moored it out in a cove.

Even though it was a bit chilly, they swam and then put on Mike and Helen's *Passion's Folly* windbreakers and walked along the beach, arm in arm.

Late in the afternoon, they stopped to eat in a seaside restaurant called "The Grass Shack."

They talked about their families and how many brothers and sisters each one had, and how they thought the President of the United States was doing.

They wondered if the interest rates would dip

any lower in the coming months, and how it would affect the housing industry.

It was mundane, everyday talk, and yet they couldn't keep their hands or eyes off each other. All during the meal they would sneak quick, hungry kisses when they thought the other dinner guests were not looking.

Stuffed with lobster and fresh crab, they walked back along the beach. A pale golden sun was sitting over the sparkling water.

Neither one could ever recall having had such a wonderful day, and they hated to see it end.

"This has been so nice," Ellie sighed.

He playfully grabbed her head in the crook of his arm. "Only fair, huh?"

She grinned up at him. "All right, Mr. Super Colossal Ego. You were p-e-r-f-e-c-t."

He leaned down and ran the tip of his tongue suggestively around her ear. "I k-n-o-w." He kissed her hot and passionately to prove his point and she punched him in the side.

"Ouch."

"Male chauvinist."

"As long as you didn't add 'pig.' "

"I wouldn't do that. I might think it, but I wouldn't say it," she teased.

T.J.'s steps slowed and he turned her around to face him. Taking her chin in his hand his eyes grew solemn as he looked deep within her eyes. "Okay, Ms. E.R.A. Millstein. Why in the hell have you completely changed your looks lately?"

Her eyes dropped away from his guiltily. "I haven't . . . no more than you have."

"You haven't? Now, come on. Whatever happened to those nice understated dresses you used to wear?"

"What happened to those wild suits *you* used to wear?" she countered.

"And that car you're driving. That's not you at all."

"*My* car! Well, speaking of cars, what about that four-door thing you're driving?"

Again, he ignored her question. "And your hair. Now what kind of style do you call that?"

"Stylish. And while we're on the subject, you're wearing yours ten times shorter than you used to." She could have sworn he had been to Fergie's barber.

"I went to Fergie Waterman's barber this time."

She knew it!

His hand went up to smooth his shorn locks uneasily. "Don't you like it?"

"Not really. I liked it better the other way."

"Well, I liked yours better before you started putting all that junk on it."

"Junk! It's mousse! Plain old mousse, for heaven's sake. Everyone uses it."

"You didn't used to," he accused.

"Did you notice Cissy's hair?"

"How could I have missed it?"

"Well, it had mousse on it."

"It looked as if a *moose* had done something else in it," he grumbled.

They began walking again, each one thinking about what the other had said.

*Could it be possible he really liked the way I looked before, and I've gone to all this trouble and misery for nothing?* she thought.

*The way she was acting, you would think she liked men to dress the way I did, and drive wild cars,* he steamed silently.

They marched down the beach in silence a few more minutes before she stopped and looked him straight in the eye.

"And your bathing suit."

"What about it?"

"Why is it that around *me,* you choose to wear that floppy, red-flowered Hawaiian thing, and for Cissy and Barbie you wear that indecent, scanty little scrap of material that leaves no doubt as to your gender."

"Because I *thought* you preferred the Hawaiian one," he defended in a hurt voice.

"Now where in the world did you get an idea like that!"

"Fergie Waterman wears—"

"Fergie! Leave Fergie Waterman out of this! Fergie is a nice person, but he certainly doesn't personify the man of my dreams!" She was so frustrated she could scream.

"Well, who in the hell *does?*" He frowned. "You're confusing me, Ellie. The men you date seem to be conservative and low-key, yet when I try to be like one of them you get all bent out of shape. I just don't know what your idea of Mr. Right is anymore."

"*You* are!" she blurted before she could stop herself.

A slow grin tugged at the corners of his mouth. "Me?"

"Yes . . . you," she admitted lamely.

"But I thought I was too spirited, too . . . too unrefined for a classy lady like you."

That caught her attention. "Classy? You think I'm . . . I'm classy?"

The man was full of surprises.

He reached over and put his hand on the back of her head and pulled her face forward until her nose was almost touching his. "You want to know something? Since we're doing all this confessing, I think you should be aware that up until this morning you had me scared half to death."

"Why?"

"Because you happen to symbolize everything I've always admired and wanted in a woman, Ellie, and I've always been a little in awe of you."

"Me?" She knew her voice sounded positively squeaky now, but she couldn't help it.

"Yes, you," he squeaked back playfully.

"You don't find me dull and uninteresting?"

"Dull! No, I find you beautiful and intriguing," he confessed as he smoothed a lock of her hair back from her face, then tenderly touched his mouth to hers. "Not to mention mature and levelheaded. You don't play silly games to attract men's attention like those other women in the office do, and you have a mind of your own. I can't tell you how much I appreciate that in a woman."

She swallowed as a lump grew in her throat. What would he think if he ever found out the real reason she had brought the boat, and the childish thinking behind her attempted personality change?

He would find out she was just like all the other women trying to trap a man! Well, maybe if she was lucky, he would never find out.

"Then women like Barbie and Cissy aren't necessarily your type."

He looked properly offended. "Did you honestly think they were?"

"Well, yes . . ."

He winked. "No, you're my type and always will be. Look, I'm not sure what's been going on, but I think we've both been stepping out of character lately, and it's just not working. Why don't we agree to go back to being our old selves?" He put his arm around her shoulders and they began walking again.

He was good and tired of trying to be someone he wasn't. The idea to change had been a bad one and maybe with a little luck she would never find out what he had been up to.

"I think you're right," she confessed, immensely relieved that this silly farce would not have to go on a moment longer. The first thing she was going to when she got home was wash the gook out of her hair and get into some decent clothes!

"Good. And . . . uh . . . listen. While we're on the subject, how would you feel about switching cars? My four-door is brand new and since I know you're not particularly crazy about your IROC, how about trading with me?"

He still couldn't understand why she traded her car in for a sports model.

"Oh, T.J. I'd *love* to," she said gratefully. At least she wouldn't be terrified of driving to the grocery store and she would be back to a car big enough to accommodate more than one client. "How about first thing tomorrow morning?"

"Sounds good to me. I'll call the bank and have them draw up the papers."

They both drew tremendous sighs of relief.

"This has been an absolutely perfect day," she told him as they walked hand in hand into the sunset.

"Yes it has, but this is only the start of many, many more," he promised.

They paused again and he took her into his arms and kissed her, a stimulating, exciting, typically T.J.ish kiss that made her tingle all the way down to her toes.

"Oh, by the way, I saw Mike Haran this morning and he wants to buy the boat back."

He dropped the unexpected bombshell as if he were telling her the time of day.

"He wants to buy . . . our boat?"

"Yeah, can you imagine? Even wants to pay us

a profit. He thinks he and his wife are about to get back together and he wants to buy it back for old times' sake."

"And you would sell it?"

Try as she may she couldn't help the overwhelming sense of hurt and betrayal she was suddenly feeling. Had this special, wonderful day meant nothing to him but a casual coming together of two people who were in a partnership with a boat together?

Did the relationship they had gradually developed over the past few weeks—or the sweet intimacy that had taken place between them this morning—hold such little value in his heart?

All of what she deemed precious and worthwhile had come about because they owned the boat together. He would never have noticed her otherwise. The partnership with T.J. had enabled a dream to come true for her and now he was talking about dissolving that partnership as if it meant absolutely nothing to him. The boat had come to symbolize her lifeline to him and now he was talking about severing it.

The reality of his true feelings cut deeply.

"Are you kidding? Of course I'd sell it." He grinned, and then the grin began to falter somewhat when he noticed she wasn't as happy about the unexpected stroke of luck as he was. "Wouldn't you?" he finished lamely.

"Of course." She began walking in a fast clip down the beach as T.J. hurried to keep up. "Well, look, if you don't want to sell it we can always say no—"

"That would be silly," she cut in. "Obviously, you want to sell the boat, so we'll sell it."

"But I thought you'd be happy about the news, Ellie. The boat is costing us a small fortune and we never get to use it ourselves, and gas is too expensive—"

He couldn't understand why she had suddenly grown so cool. Was she upset over the fact that Mike Haran was trying to reconcile with his ex-wife?

A streak of white-hot jealousy shot through him. She'd better not be!

"I said, I agree, T.J. We'll sell the boat!" she said curtly.

"Okay!" he snapped back, still steamed that she would care what Mike Haran did. He ceased trying to keep up with her, but instead stood and watched helplessly as she started running toward the boat.

"Okay," he said again lamely, most of the anger draining out of him now. "We'll sell the boat."

# CHAPTER TEN

"If you say I told you so one more time I swear I'm going to scream." Ellie and Janet waited until the light turned green before they started back across the street to the realty office.

All during lunch Janet had talked about how both she and Mark had just *knew* something terrible like this would happen.

The entire, miserable hour, she had reminded Ellie that she had always thought that buying a boat with T. J. Templeton was comparable to building a straw house on top of the San Andreas Fault—not that he wasn't a nice guy, but he just wasn't very predictable—and if she would have listened to her best friend she wouldn't be in this mess—and on and on and on . . .

Ellie had heard the same rhetoric all week long and it was beginning to grow old.

True, she had had a good, long cry after T.J. had told her he was in favor of selling the boat, and true, she had foolishly gone right ahead and fallen head over heels in love with him, knowing

perfectly well that this very thing could happen.
But she wasn't angry with him.

She had gone into this business venture the
same way she had stepped into the brief, intimate
relationship with him. With her eyes wide open.

But now that he had tired of his latest adventure, then she was certainly mature and adult
enough to step gracefully out of the picture.

Stinging tears suddenly flooded her eyes.

Even if she was in love with the big heel.

"And Mark and I never even got to see the
boat," Janet lamented.

"It isn't sold yet," Ellie said absently.

"But it will be."

"Your optimism is inspiring."

T.J. was just coming out of the conference
room as Ellie came in the front door of the office.

He glanced up, and when he saw her he hurriedly excused himself from the clients he was
with and started in her direction.

She kept walking in the direction of her desk,
hoping he would be distracted before he reached
her, but luck wasn't with her. She had been evading him all week and had been surprisingly successful in dodging the phone calls and messages
he had left on her desk.

She wasn't trying to punish him, and she knew
she wouldn't be able to avoid him forever, but it
was necessary for her to begin pulling away from
the sticky situation she now found herself in.

After they sold the boat, she planned to transfer out of this office into a branch of Coastal Realty that was on the other side of town and then she wouldn't be forced to see him every day.

That would be entirely too painful.

"Ellie, hey, wait a minute." T.J. grabbed her hastily retreating form and pulled her into an empty cubicle where they could speak privately. "Where in the hell have you been all week?" he demanded.

She shrugged. "Busy."

"Busy?" He looked at her expectantly, waiting for a more detailed explanation. Surely she had been more than just busy.

"Yes, busy." She stepped around him and started out of the cubicle when he promptly pulled her back in again.

"Wait a minute." Propping one arm up on the partition so she couldn't get around him, he cornered her and forced her eyes to meet his. "What's going on?"

"Nothing, T.J. Now let me pass. I have an appointment." She dropped her gaze away from his probing one and quickly ducked under his arm.

A few moments later she was sticking her purse in her desk and trying to avoid the icy blue glare that was shooting across the room in her direction.

Perhaps she hadn't been subtle enough, she thought worriedly . . . maybe she had been *too* subtle . . . maybe she should be nicer and he would see what a marvelous woman she really was . . . kind, gentle, slow to anger . . . no that wouldn't work, either. The best course was the one she was taking.

She would simply ignore him until he realized she wasn't just another woman who could be toyed with and cast aside like old shoes.

If he wanted to sell the boat back to Mike, then so be it. She had lived without it and T. J. Templeton long before this fiasco ever began.

No. She sniffed and cast a hurt look in his direction. If he actually meant all those wonderful things he had whispered in her ear the morning he had made love to her, then he would apologize for even thinking about selling their boat.

Why, it was like . . . almost like their baby! Like doting parents they had tenderly cared for it, nursed it, proudly showed it off to friends and clients, and suffered the agonies of repair bills and docking fees and gas bills just as steadfastly as if it had been braces and college tuition.

And he wanted to sell it? She sniffed again. Fine with her.

T.J. was sitting at his desk, trying to figure out why she was so angry. He was more than aware of the sharp glances she kept sending in his direction, and the hurt countenance on her face, but for the life of him he couldn't figure out what he had done wrong.

When they had parted Monday night, she had seemed quiet, but he had only thought that her cold was still bothering her.

But when she had failed to answer any of his

calls or return any of his messages the next few days, he knew he was in real trouble.

He just didn't know why.

The rest of the week a state of cold war went into effect. When they passed each other in the corridors, Ellie would just keep on walking.

Finally, he stopped trying to be cordial, and became just as cool and aloof as she was.

When they sat in meetings together—sometimes even right next to each other—they never said anything more profound to each other than, "Can I borrow your pencil, please" or "Hand me the sugar, please," and their misery continued to grow with each passing day.

The following two weekends, she stayed away from the boat. They were the longest weekends in history.

T.J., on the other hand, decided she must be seeing Mike Haran, and it irked him no end.

By Monday morning of the third week, she was forced to cross the front line to confront him about a business matter.

Striding over to his desk where he sat making paper airplanes out of computer print readouts, she paused and took a deep breath. "I need to talk to you."

He glanced up, then turned and made a big point of looking over his shoulder to see if she was talking to someone else. He finally turned back to face her. "Me?"

"Yes, you."

"I was under the impression we weren't speaking these days."

"This is business."

"Oh. Sorry."

"Mike Haran called this morning. He's been trying to reach you for days and you haven't returned his calls."

T.J. picked up one of the paper planes and sailed it across the room. "I've been busy."

"Doing what?"

"Manufacturing planes."

"Well, I hate to interrupt, but he wants to know if you still want to sell the boat."

He glanced up. "Did he and Helen reconcile?"

"Yes."

A tremendous feeling of relief washed over him. "I'm sorry. That must have been disappointing to you."

"Why would it be disappointing to me?"

"Haven't you been seeing him lately?"

Her eyes narrowed angrily. "I have not."

"Oh." Was she lying?

"Well, what do you want to do about the boat?"

Another paper plane zipped by her head. "Is he still willing to pay a profit?"

"That's what he implied."

"Well, since you don't seem to be using it much anymore, let's go for it." His unspoken accusation that *she* hadn't been around for the past two weekends went ignored.

"If that's what you want." She had still harbored a faint ray of hope that he had changed his mind, but obviously he hadn't. She turned on her heel and started to walk away when an airplane hit her on the top of the head.

She whirled back and gave him a dirty look.

"Do *you* want to sell the boat, Ms. Millstein?" he asked patiently.

"If you do."

"That's not what I asked."

"I don't think it matters what I want."

He watched as she flounced back to her desk and turned her back to him.

A few minutes later another paper airplane came zooming in and landed neatly on her desk.

She was about to pick it up and throw it in the wastecan when she saw the note T.J. had written in red ink across it. "Are you sure you haven't been seeing Haran lately?"

Impatiently ripping off a sheet of paper from a legal pad, she quickly fashioned her own airplane and wrote across it, "I certainly have not! He's been trying to reconcile with his wife. What sort of a person do you think I am?"

Standing up, she soared it in the direction of his desk. It landed beside his chair.

He calmly reached over and retrieved it, read the message, then wrote another one on a new plane and had it airborne in a few minutes.

Giving him a sour look, she plucked the perfectly aimed missile off her desk and read, "Then is it selling the damn boat that has you so upset?"

By now their co-workers were watching the

planes taking off and landing with increasing regularity.

Once more she made a paper missile and scribbled a quick, efficient reply. She stood up and hurled it in his direction, but her plane never reached its landing point.

The agent sitting next to T.J. calmly plucked the paper plane out of his coffee cup and handed it over to him.

"Yes! How astute of you." As T.J. read the note, his face registered no emotion. He wadded it up and threw it in his trash can, and then immediately reached for his phone.

Later that afternoon, a man from the florist walked in the office with a huge bouquet of red roses and sat them on Ellie's desk.

"For me?"

"Yes, ma'am, if your name plate's right and you're Ellie Millstein."

"I am." She plucked the note out of the greenery, thinking that perhaps Mike had sent the flowers in appreciation of getting the boat back. He had been overjoyed when she had called him this afternoon and told him the boat was his again.

But the note read instead: "I think we've had a breakdown in communication. Meet me at the boat tonight at eight and we'll talk. Love you, T.J."

Love you, T.J. She clasped the note against her breast and hugged it tightly. It didn't mean a thing, and yet those two simple words brought fresh tears to her eyes.

It was nearing eight when she pulled her car into the marina and stopped. She realized how very much she had missed coming out here lately.

She stopped to feed the mother duck and her eight babies part of the bread she had brought from home, then sauntered down to the ramp.

Since T.J. was never on time she figured she would visit with some of the neighbors before she went to the boat.

Harry and Velma would be leaving to visit Velma's mother in Iowa soon, and probably wouldn't be back at the boat until next season.

Ellie had to laugh when she recalled how reticent she used to be with strangers. T.J. had certainly brought her out of that.

Now she knew as much about the people who owned the surrounding boats and their families as he did.

She sighed. Yes, he had changed her in many ways, but tonight she looked like the old Ellie Millstein. Conservative skirt and white peasant blouse, shiny clean hair in a modest style, and tiny pearl earrings.

She didn't feel exciting and glamorous as she had there for a while, but just plain comfortable and totally at peace with herself.

It was a nice feeling.

"Hi, Ellie." Meredith Lawton waved as Ellie passed her boat. "Haven't seen you in a while. Hope you haven't been sick?"

"No, just real busy." Ellie smiled.

"Saw T.J. a few minutes ago."

"Oh?" Ellie glanced toward *Passion's Folly*. "Is he here already?"

"Yes, he came in about thirty minutes ago," Meredith said.

Ellie smiled again. "Then I suppose I shouldn't keep him waiting."

She quickened her steps down the walkway and in a few minutes she stepped aboard the boat.

T.J. was just coming up the steps. They both paused and looked at each other for a moment.

"Thank you for the flowers," she finally managed.

Seeing him again, all her pent-up anger and resentment of the past few weeks suddenly evaporated into thin air.

She loved him, no matter what.

"You're welcome." He held out his hand and she took it.

"And I'm sorry I've been so impossible lately," she added. If she had to eat humble pie, she might as well make a pig of herself.

"Oh, babe. I've missed you," he said softly.

"I've missed you, too. I've been unreasonable."

She looked so beautiful tonight it took his breath away. All he wanted to do was get this unpleasant time behind them.

"Come here."

Without another thought she stepped into his arms and they were kissing, passionate, hungry kisses, their hands eagerly reacquainting themselves with the feel of one another.

Lifting her into his arms, he turned and carried her into the interior of the boat and kicked the door shut with his foot.

"They're at it again, Frank." Geraldine Pinehurst's nasal voice was filled with awe as she peeked out from behind her curtain and clucked her tongue.

"Let 'em alone." Her retired husband yawned, and stretched out on the sofa in his houseboat, ready for his nap. "They're young and full of energy."

She let the curtain reluctantly drop back in place. "Do you suppose we were ever like that?"

"Of course."

Geraldine shook her head. "I can't remember you *ever* being like that."

He stared at the ceiling for a moment thoughtfully, then a smile began to appear on his face—tiny at first, then quickly broadening into a devilish leer. "Come here, woman."

She glanced at him expectantly. "Frank?"

He nodded happily.

"Oh, Frank!"


There was one thing Ellie had not been wrong about. Being made love to by T. J. Templeton was more than exciting. It was a revelation.

And being in love with him was even more stimulating. Even if it might still prove to be hopeless.

T.J. had taken her to the bunk and hurriedly began to remove her clothes.

"T.J. . . . don't you think we need to talk first?" she murmured between snatches of ravenous kisses.

"If you knew how much I wanted you," he said gruffly as his trembling fingers undid the last of the tiny buttons on her blouse. After peeling the sheer fabric off her shoulder, he began to sample the creamy perfection of her bare shoulder with his mouth.

She closed her eyes and reveled in his touch, incredibly proud that she could elicit such a searing urgency in him. Her hands tangled in the thickness of his hair as his mouth searched and found hers in a kiss that threatened all sanity.

His hands worked to loosen the clasp on her silky bra and it soon fell away in a whisper. His breath caught, and he moaned her name again into the sweetness of her mouth.

His clothes followed hers. Their mouths touched and their tongues teased, and the feel of their bare skin pressed against each other's sent their passion soaring to dangerous levels long before they wanted it to go there.

Ellie's fingers explored the planes and hollows of his back, then moved down to mold his masculine strength more tightly to her feminine contours. He moaned softly as her mouth opened to accept his tongue.

"You feel so good, babe . . . so good. I love

you, Ellie," he murmured between smoldering kisses. "I should have told you that long ago."

"Oh, Teej, I love you, too." But her words were quickly snatched away by his mouth roughly taking hers again.

They fell across the bunk and the world became magical again, sweeping them up in a white-hot fury, urging them on until they were rushing headlong to meet an ultimate, all-consuming goal.

They both gave of themselves openly and freely, any barriers they had previously built against each other scattering like dry leaves in the wind.

Without a doubt, Ellie Millstein would forever belong to T. J. Templeton, and he made sure she was aware of that.

He sighed with pure contentment.

"I never knew it could be this good," he whispered in her ear.

"I did," she said smugly and pulled his mouth back to meet hers in a kiss that went on and on and on . . .

It was growing very late when their passion was finally assuaged enough to want to talk.

There was a bright, full moon overhead as T.J. pulled on his jeans and leaned over in the bunk to kiss her once more.

"Why don't you fix us some coffee? I'm going to pull the boat out in a cove and anchor it for the night."

"Are you suggesting I stay on the boat with you tonight?" she asked playfully.

"No, I'm *telling* you." He winked and stole another kiss before he went up on deck.

She had made sandwiches and a pot of coffee by the time he came back down twenty minutes later. The boat lay anchored off the shoreline, in a secluded cove.

Taking her into his arms once more, he kissed her for a full five minutes before he finally released her again. "Now, I think we have a lot of talking to do."

She sighed, and they sat down at the small table and began to eat their dinner.

"Why were you mad at me for wanting to sell the boat?"

"It's a long story, T.J."

"We have the rest of our lives."

Her gaze lowered to the table as she fidgeted with the crust on her bread. "You won't laugh at me?"

"Probably. You do some funny things at times," he admitted.

"This wasn't funny. It was stupid and childish . . . and costly—extremely costly."

"It couldn't be that bad. And by the way, you look exceptionally beautiful tonight . . . more like my old Ellie." He leaned over and stole another kiss from her.

She blushed at his compliment and absently reached up to smooth her hair. "Thank you. But what I've done is bad."

She knew the moment she told him what had ultimately convinced her to buy the boat, he was going to laugh right in her face and tell her to go home and grow up . . . no, he wouldn't do that, but she would reveal herself to be every bit as silly as the other women in the office who were always chasing him.

He leaned back and reached for the coffeepot to refill their cups. "If you're talking about the real reason you went in on the boat with me, forget it. I'm guilty of the same thing," he said casually.

"What?"

"I bought the boat for the same reason you did."

"Oh, no, T.J. I bought the boat because—"

"You thought you were not exciting enough, so you got this harebrained idea that I was, so you picked me as your mentor," he supplied. "Why, I don't know, but you did. You thought that by 'studying' me you could turn yourself into some sort of fun-loving free spirit, and life would be one big bed of roses."

She looked at him, her mouth dropping open. "How did you know that?"

"I started putting two and two together. The way you suddenly changed your life-style and the way I suddenly changed mine. Well, it all started to make sense to me. We were both trying to be something or someone we weren't. But to make sure, I went to Janet Mason and she confirmed my hunch."

"She *told* you? She told you what a fool I was?"

"No, she told me what a fool she thought *I* was." He grinned. "So don't be embarrassed. There's two idiots in the world, and you're looking at the other one."

"If you think you're going to sit there and tell me you bought the boat because you wanted to be more like *me,* forget it, T.J. You're only trying to make me feel better. I would never in a million years believe it."

He shrugged. "Well, it's the truth."

"You bought the boat to become more like me? Boring, unexciting me?"

He shrugged again. "I think you're pretty classy. I've told you that before. And I wish you would stop saying you're boring. You're all I can handle, believe me."

"But you're so . . . so . . ."

"Normal," he finished again. "Just an average, normal man who happens to enjoy living. I'm not that exciting, sweetheart. I just like to go and do and see what the world has to offer. Lots of men are like that."

"No, they're not," she revealed glumly.

He frowned. "You're trying to tell me the truth about Mike, aren't you? You haven't been seeing him these past couple of weeks."

"Good heavens, no. I've never seen Mike socially."

T.J. breathed an audible sigh of relief and leaned forward to reach for her hand. "You realize what we've been doing, don't you? I was attracted to you for the very unique and special qualities that you were trying to change, and apparently you were attracted to me for the same reasons. All along I've been trying to make myself a Fergie Waterman or a Mike Haran and you've been trying to make yourself a . . . a . . ." He couldn't think of a good example.

"Barbie Jenkins."

"Barbie Jenkins! Good Lord." He shook his head in disbelief. "Is *that* who you were trying to be?"

She nodded.

"Why?"

"Because I thought that's the kind of women *you* liked."

T.J. shook his head with amusement this time. "Come here."

She slid out of the booth and came over to sit on his lap. They kissed again for a very long time. "Now, will you please tell me why you were so upset about selling the boat?" he prompted when their lips finally parted.

"Because I love you and I was afraid if we sold the boat you might not . . . we might not . . ."

"Be together?"

She nodded again.

"I offered to sell the boat, Ellie, not you."

"I know, but nothing seems to hold any sentimental value to you," she accused. "The happiest time of my life has been spent here on this boat.

Why, if it weren't for the boat, we would have never found each other—"

"Wrong."

"Wrong?"

"Wrong. I would have found you, Ellie." He smiled at her tenderly. "It just wouldn't have cost me as much money. And as far as the boat goes, I have never attached sentimental value to anything that could be bought with money. Particularly something that's keeping me financially drained like this boat has. But that doesn't mean I don't love and cherish you. I wouldn't trade you for all the tea in China. And if selling the boat makes you that unhappy, then we'll turn around and buy another one," he promised.

She frowned. Now that he put it that way, she realized she didn't want another one. "No way. Once Mike and Helen take over this money pit again, I'm through with boats for a while."

He laughed and hugged her tighter. "Okay, we'll invest our money in stocks and bonds, or at least some of it."

*"Our* money?"

"Yes, our money—oh, you are going to marry me, aren't you?"

She laughed happily. "Certainly, I just wasn't aware that you knew it."

"Well, I hadn't planned on it," he confessed. "My original thoughts were to try and clean up my act a little, but I'm hooked, I'll admit it."

They kissed once more and he patted her fanny affectionately when their lips parted. "About those investments I mentioned? I figure the profit we make off the boat can be used as a down payment on this new investment I've been thinking about making."

She slid off his lap and began to clear away the dishes. "What is it this time, T.J.?"

"A helicopter."

The dish in her hand nearly tumbled to the floor. "A helicopter!"

"Yeah, just think of it, Ellie! A copter of our very own. Why we could fly all over the United States if we wanted to—"

"T.J.," she interrupted, turning to stare at him as if he had just lost his mind. "Do you know *how* to fly a helicopter?"

"No . . ." His face grew thoughtful for a moment, then it brightened once more. "But I always wanted to learn."

Well, she thought as she affectionately wrapped her arms around his neck and smothered an amused giggle.

She had always wanted an exciting man.